2/15

FIREBREAK

ALSO BY TRICIA FIELDS

The Territory

Scratchgravel Road

Wrecked

FIREBREAK

TRICIA FIELDS

MINOTAUR BOOKS

A Thomas Dunne Book
New York

A THOMAS DUNNE BOOK FOR MINOTAUR BOOKS.
An imprint of St. Martin's Publishing Group.

FIREBREAK. Copyright © 2015 by Tricia Fields. All rights reserved. Printed in the United States of America. For information, address St. Martin's Press, 175 Fifth Avenue, New York, N.Y. 10010.

www.thomasdunnebooks.com
www.minotaurbooks.com

The Library of Congress Cataloging-in-Publication Data is available upon request.

ISBN 978-1-250-05505-7 (hardcover)
ISBN 978-1-4668-5810-7 (e-book)

Minotaur books may be purchased for educational, business, or promotional use. For information on bulk purchases, please contact the Macmillan Corporate and Premium Sales Department at 1-800-221-7945, extension 5442, or write to specialmarkets@macmillan.com.

First Edition: March 2015

10 9 8 7 6 5 4 3 2 1

With much love to Mom and Dad for giving me the courage to persist through all the first drafts along the way

ACKNOWLEDGMENTS

While reading news accounts of the fires that raged through West Texas in 2011, I was awed at the job the firefighters faced. I spoke with Marfa Volunteer Fire Department chief Gary Mitsche, who said most of his employees are volunteers with families and homes and paying jobs that are put on hold while they risk their lives for the community that desperately depends on them. The information that Gary provided was invaluable. I learned about a dangerous line of work that I only have the courage to write about from afar. If my fictional storytelling got some of the details wrong, those errors are strictly mine in the making. In no way did I want to sensationalize the job these men and women do, but I hoped in some small way to show the bravery of the people who put themselves in harm's way so that we don't have to. Thank you for the hard work that you do.

Thanks also to Todd, Molly, and Emily, and to Linnet, Merry, and Mella for your continued support and encouragement. And to Peter Joseph and Melanie Fried and all of the talented people at Thomas Dunne Books for making Josie Gray a lasting force. Thanks to Dominick Abel, the finest literary agent there is. And, finally, to my best friend, Jenna Turner, whose representation in the pages of this book illuminates her badassness, but not the lifetime friend whom I value so much.

FIREBREAK

ONE

The wind from the east pounded the watchtower and sliced across the guy wires, moaning like a violin. Josie felt the building shudder, but her attention was drawn to the north, fixated on a swirl of gray billowing upward and then disappearing against the overcast sky. The paint-splattered transistor radio propped on the window ledge beside her crackled through another lightning strike. The announcer for the Marfa public-radio station warned of forty-mile-per-hour wind gusts and dry lightning that would spark the parched grasslands like a match to paper.

The wooden rafters that held the observation room fifty feet above the ground groaned and creaked from the battering winds. Josie grabbed the binoculars off the bookshelf under the lookout window and stepped out onto the balcony and into the gusts. Pressing her back against the side of the tower, she scanned the land for smoke as sand and debris stung her bare arms and face.

Through the binoculars she located the river, and worked her way across the Mexican border to Piedra Labrada, a town similar in size and population to her own town of Artemis, Texas. The wind was blowing so hard it was difficult to tell if she was seeing dust or smoke.

All over Arroyo County, spotters scanned the roiling sky, trying to stay ahead of the wildfires that raged across Texas in the worst fire season the state had ever seen.

Then she saw the unmistakable curling tendrils in the sky. She took the binoculars down and squinted into the layered shades of gray, sifting through the clouds and smoke and the desert sand beneath them, until she was able to reestablish the location. She estimated the smoke was about ten miles west of the watchtower. She went back inside the lookout to examine the maps and identify the nearest road for the spotters on the ground.

The watchtower was used jointly by Border Patrol and local police. Standing on the U.S. side of the Rio Grande, a half mile from downtown Piedra Labrada, the vantage point gave her a clear view to the access road that followed the Rio and led to four blocks of factories and bars in Piedra. On the U.S. side of the border, scrub brush and mesquite dotted the landscape, as well as brittle clumps of grass that allowed the wind to rapidly spread the fire. Canyons along the Rio Grande added to the problem, causing unpredictable gusts of wind that could carry the fire embers like a rock skimming across water.

Downtown Artemis was located ten miles northeast of the watchtower and was Josie's principal concern. The town had been spared intense wildfires over the past several years, but the result was they had fuel ready to burn. The commissioners' court had just extended the burn ban for an additional ninety-day period; now the combination of drought, high winds, low humidity, and dry lightning had everyone in the county watching out their back doors for the first sign of smoke.

Josie knew the thunderclouds she'd seen were deceiving. With no humidity the rain evaporated before it could ever reach the earth. With no rain to extinguish the spot fires caused by the lightning, a single strike could turn into a fire blazing across thousands of acres in a day.

She glanced at her watch. It was three o'clock in the afternoon, and the radar showed cloud cover across northern Mexico and into south Texas for at least the next eight hours. It would be a long night of watching and worrying.

A map rack made of old pallet wood sat underneath the make-shift table at the center of the watchtower. Josie bent down and sorted through the stack of laminated maps and pulled out one with marked roads into Piedra Labrada. She knew every road in Artemis, and most along the northern edge of Piedra, but with land and property at stake she had to be certain.

Josie smoothed the map out on the table and oriented it toward the west in the direction of the smoke. Running her finger along the Rio, she identified the major roads heading into Mexico and dialed Doug Free's number. Doug was the Artemis fire chief and a thirty-year veteran of the volunteer fire department. He was a friendly man, quick with a handshake and a smile, and dead serious about his job.

When the wind picked up that morning and the forecast called for dry thunderstorms, the fire department, the sheriff's department, and Josie's own Artemis Police Department were put on notice. When the humidity reached such low levels, car crashes, trucks dragging chains, and even tire blowouts were enough to create a spark that could ignite a grass fire. Doug wanted to ensure that every available person was on the lookout for fire until the extreme danger passed.

"This is Doug," he answered.

"It's Josie. You have a minute?"

"You bet. What's up?"

"I'm on the watchtower. I've confirmed smoke on Del Comercio in Mexico, just across the Rio Grande, about eleven miles west of the watchtower."

"Any idea on the size?"

"The wind's blowing so hard it's difficult to estimate. I'd say the fire is contained at this point. It took me ten minutes to know for sure I was looking at smoke and not dust."

"I'm at the sheriff's department. Hang on. I'll get dispatch to call it in."

Josie couldn't see her house on Schenck Road, located about eight miles from the watchtower, but she was uneasy. The gusts were hard to predict. Not only was her own house a worry, but she also was concerned about her neighbor Dell's cattle ranch.

Several minutes later Doug came back on the line. "There's a spotter in Piedra headed that way. What's the river look like down there?"

Josie walked to the window and examined the banks of the river. "It's a good four feet below normal. The water's maybe fifteen to twenty feet across in that area. If the fire gets too close a strong gust will carry it over." She paused, scanning both sides of the Rio for several miles north of the smoke. "There aren't many trees along the Mexican side of the river, but the salt cedar's thick on our side."

"It'll catch, as dry as it is."

"You have somebody connecting with Mexican authorities?" she asked.

"Dispatcher already called the fire officials. Will you be up there through the night?"

"Marta Cruz just came on duty and is headed this way. She'll be stationed here through midnight. I'll come out then if things still look bad." Josie turned toward the north, in the direction of the fire that had already consumed thousands of acres. "What's the status of the Harrison Ridge fire?"

"Unstable. The heat's causing unpredictable wind conditions. It's probably fifty miles northeast of Artemis and headed south. That open grassland around the mudflats worries me."

"You'll keep me posted?"

"Will do. Be safe."

———•———

Josie walked slowly around the perimeter of the observation room, scanning the two sister cities on either side of the Rio Grande and the vast unpopulated Chihuahuan Desert that spread out before her.

With populations that hovered around twenty-five hundred people, both Artemis and Piedra Labrada faced many of the same difficulties as other border towns across the Southwest: unemployment, scarce resources, underfunded state mandates, understaffed local fire and police departments. What both cities shared was a hardscrabble spirit and determination that came from making a good life in such isolated, unforgiving conditions.

Josie faced the northern expanse and leaned against the ledge: no houses or signs of human habitation for miles. She imagined herself working as a fire spotter at one of the remaining national park lookouts, spending several months stationed in a tower not much bigger than the one she was currently standing in, with a five-mile hike from the outpost to the tower and a donkey to ferry in supplies—isolation at its finest.

Josie heard Marta Cruz's PD boots clomping up the zigzag wooden steps below her, and then watched her appear on the outside deck that wrapped the tower.

She pushed open the door and entered, her expression betraying her fear. "Hi, Josie. How's it going?" she asked.

"I called in smoke in Piedra Labrada. If it crosses the river we've got major problems. We could have fire approaching from both the north and the south. For now, it's a watch-and-wait."

"Someone alerted Mexico?"

Josie nodded. "Doug's working with spotters in Piedra."

Marta pulled her water bottle off her gun belt and drank. She had a sturdy presence, short and squat, and a resolve like no one else Josie knew. Marta's high-school-age daughter gave her fits, but Marta never gave up hope, never gave up her demands for respect and reliance on the rules. Josie admired her, as both a single mother and a police officer. She approached both with the same commitment and determination.

Josie pointed toward the west window and they both looked out, searching for the gray smoke Josie had seen just a few minutes before. Marta drew in a sharp breath and pointed; slow spirals reached straight up into the charcoal sky, now calmed by a break in the gusty wind.

"The spotter in Piedra Labrada is headed that way. Keep an eye on it. Anything new, call it in to Doug." Josie glanced at her watch. "There's a crew of smoke jumpers flying into Marfa, scheduled to arrive at four. They're flying in for training exercises in Big Bend."

"I hope they'll give us a hand. Are you going to the airport?" Marta asked.

"An old friend of mine from high school is on the crew. That's where I'm headed."

Marta smiled. "Small world."

Josie nodded. "It'll be good to see him again. Then I'll be at the briefing at the firehouse at six. I'll fill you in."

TWO

Josie leaned against the concrete barrier facing the airstrip, smiling as Pete Beckett caught her up on life since leaving rural Indiana after high school to discover the world. Pete was now a grown-up version of the rebel she'd once spent every weekend with: he, Josie, and two other kids had crammed into the front seat of his Ford F-250 with a rusted-out floorboard and a four-wheel drive that took them through more cornfields and creek beds than she could count.

He was taller than she remembered, more bulked up around the shoulders, wearing a white button-down shirt tucked into faded Levi's. Pete had the leathery-textured skin of a man who worked under the desert sun. Deep wrinkles framed his eyes, and silky brown hair hung over his collar in the back, giving him the same offhand measure of cool that Josie had always loved. When she escaped from home at the age of twenty, she had lost touch with the three friends who had saved her from the chaotic world her mom had created after her father's death. It had been fifteen years since she'd talked to Pete, and she realized how much she'd missed him.

"I couldn't take college and a forty-year desk job," he said. "I painted water towers for a year, moved from town to town, but I couldn't shake that need for a rush."

"The air force wasn't rush enough?"

"It should have been. I joined in '96. Two years later I was in Iraq when Clinton signed the order to bomb. It was a thrill ride." He grinned at the memory like he was remembering an old girlfriend.

"Why'd you leave?"

He shrugged and didn't speak for some time. Josie was certain the answer was long and complicated. His gaze followed the airstrip out into the desert flatland until it hit a jagged outcropping, part of the Chinati Mountains.

"I got tired of the hierarchy. The rules. The kiss-ass." He turned back to Josie. "I'm not much of a rule follower."

She laughed at his lopsided grin. "Or an ass kisser."

"That either."

"So you left the air force and became a smoke jumper?"

"Best decision of my life."

Josie pointed toward the north. "We're hearing this is the worst year yet. We had a fire pass through Presidio County that destroyed quite a few homes. People are worried Arroyo County's due."

"Last count there's thirty-nine major fires burning in twelve states. In 2012, over nine million acres burned in the U.S. A record. At this rate, we'll top that unless we get a break from the heat wave and some rain." He nodded his head toward the airfield. "Look at that brown grass out there. Nothing but fuel."

"Floods two years ago, then steady rain. It was beautiful for a while. Green grass across the desert. Then this year, no rain. Not a drop for nine months."

"That's life. Rain then drought."

Josie tilted her head toward the north. "What's the latest with the Harrison Ridge fire?"

"The wind's blowing southeast through the center of Arroyo County. If the wind whips up and throws sparks into that grass?" He shrugged. The result was obvious.

"Will your crew be at the briefing tonight at the firehouse?"

"We'll be there. The rest of the guys are inside, gathering gear up."

Josie put her arms out to give him a hug. "I'll get out of here and let you get to work. It's good to see you again."

"Hang on a minute." Pete crossed his arms over his chest and looked at Josie hard. "I heard about your boyfriend. They arrest the bastards that kidnapped him?"

Josie took a step back at the abrupt question. "How do you arrest a Mexican cartel?"

"No kidding?" He shook his head, his expression incredulous. "He got kidnapped by the cartel? I figured that was rumor."

She felt the familiar dread over the topic she had discussed ad nauseam since it took place. She said nothing in response, but Pete had never understood verbal cues or body language. If he had a curiosity he pursued it, oblivious to a person's discomfort—sometimes endearing, other times infuriating.

"Why'd they kidnap him? He have a lot of money?"

She blew out air in frustration. "No. It was a money-laundering scheme gone bad." She shrugged and stared at him. Four months after the incident she was still reluctant to discuss the horrific position she had been placed in as a police officer whose lover was being held captive.

"I thought the stories were just rumors gone crazy. The cartel get their money back?"

She shook her head. "That was the one satisfaction in the whole mess. The feds got the money. The county's supposed to get a cut, but we haven't heard anything yet."

"How long ago?"

"Four months."

"How's he doing?"

Josie looked away.

"Sure, I get it. He's going through hell," Pete said.

She said nothing.

Pete took a step toward her. She felt his eyes on her, but she continued staring at the ground. Dillon was seeing a therapist, but he was not doing well.

"Let's all go out one night while I'm here. Might do him good to get out and talk to new people," he said, but Josie stopped him.

"He left me, Pete. He moved out about two months ago. He closed his business and moved back with his family in St. Louis."

"You still talking to him?"

"I tried for the first month. I still thought he might come back. Then one day he said talking to me was too hard, the memories of what happened too awful for him to stay connected to Artemis, or to me."

"You think about moving away too?" he asked.

She shook her head, feeling the familiar resolve. "This is my home. When we left high school, I never looked back. This is the first place that ever felt right to me. I can't imagine living anywhere else."

"You gotta be messed up after all this. You seeing a shrink?"

Josie grinned. "What's with the interrogation? You haven't changed a bit."

His eyes fixed on her and his expression didn't waver. "Seriously. Are you seeing a shrink?"

"I talked to somebody a few times. The guilt over what happened is pretty bad. The kidnapping, the murder, none of it would have happened if it wasn't for me."

"Murder? Are you serious?"

Josie sighed, frustrated. This wasn't the conversation she had imagined having with her old friend. "I don't want to rehash this, Pete. It's all too hard to get into again. You understand?"

"The shrink doing you any good?"

Josie sighed. "I'm not sure how a therapist can fix me. I know the guilt is misplaced, but it's still there. My involvement wasn't intentional, but it's a fact. And I can't get it out of my head."

Pete crossed his arms again and leaned back to get a better look at her. "I saw more shrinks during high school than you could count. You remember."

She nodded. She did remember. Pete could do no right in his parents' eyes. He had spent many nights sleeping on a cot in her garage after his own parents would kick him out for not obeying their rules. Then they'd come to collect him, to drag him off to another therapy session.

"Mom and Dad thought I was psycho because I wanted to skydive and drag race and raise hell. Everybody wanted to figure me out. Fix me. Drug me. They put me on diets. No meat, no sugar, no whatever. No alcohol. I was on so many drugs for a while I couldn't function. It was crazy. Everybody wanted me to crawl around inside my own head twenty-four/seven. Thinking about everything but what I wanted. Talking about it. They tried to get me to live like somebody I wasn't."

Josie said, "I don't think that's my issue."

"You don't get it. You gotta get out of your head." He paused, and she could tell some inner dialogue was taking place in his mind, swirling at speeds other people could never keep up with. He reached out and squeezed her arm, the grip tight, not friendly. "We'll get together before I leave. I got your cure."

Josie laughed in spite of his serious expression. "I don't think I need a cure."

Pete's eyes widened and she remembered the old intensity of their days in high school. If Pete wanted something, the rest of them went along for the ride because there was no stopping him. "Josie, don't act like I don't know anything. I can help you. Hell, I could have helped Dillon if he was still here."

A man dressed in a khaki jumpsuit opened the door and yelled, "Get in here and suit up, Pete. We're headed out."

Josie smiled. "We'll talk again before you head back to Montana. Be careful up there."

He nodded his head slowly and gave her a half grin. "I know the look. You're thinking, He's crazier than ever."

She laughed. "That's not true. I never thought you were crazy. Maybe a little manic, but never crazy."

Pete looked back over his shoulder; the man who'd come to get him had disappeared. "Then trust me. I got my own method for getting your head clean." He stood and wrapped her in a rough hug, then pulled away and jogged toward the door. When he reached it he turned and winked. "Look at me, Josie. I'm living proof."

THREE

The Artemis firehouse was located a block west of the police department. The town was laid out in a grid formation aligned with the Rio Grande, just six miles to the south, and the Chinati Mountain range, about twenty miles to the north. Artemis struggled to keep the storefronts around the town square occupied and the businesses if not thriving, at least maintaining. Several large ranching operations brought most of the commerce into town. Artemis was primarily populated by those who wanted little to do with the outside world; they desired privacy and the freedom to run their lives as they saw fit with as little government interference as possible. Living off the grid wasn't just unplugging from the electric company: it was an isolated way of life that Josie respected and often aspired to.

The streets around the firehouse were already packed with a mix of firefighters' pickup trucks, sheriffs' cars, and police jeeps. Josie parked in her designated place at the PD and walked to the firehouse, sticking to the side of the street where the shade trees provided a measure of relief from the sun. The bank sign down the street read 103 degrees, and the heat showed no sign of breaking. Temperatures in the hundreds down in the river valley were typical for early July, but

Josie held out hope for an early monsoon season, especially with the fire risk so high.

Josie walked through the empty engine bay and figured the fire truck was probably already positioned up north near the mudflats and the prairie grasses. An open door at the back of the bay led to a training room for the volunteer fire department. She found every seat taken, and most of the standing area in the room occupied as well. Dozens of voices mixed together as worried officers and firefighters prepared for the worst.

Officer Otto Podowski stood at the other end of the room, smoothing down the white flyaway hair that never seemed to stay put on his balding head. He had been her boss when she'd first been hired by the police department, nearly fifteen years ago. When he decided to give up the extra stress that came with running the department he'd encouraged her to put in for the chief's position. Otto was a first-rate cop and one of her closest friends.

He offered a friendly smile as she approached, although his demeanor was sober. "What's the word?" he asked.

"Marta's at the watchtower. I saw smoke in Piedra Labrada just before she came on duty. I called it in to Doug. We're hoping it doesn't jump the river," Josie said.

"I hope Mexico's got somebody working it. We're stretched pretty thin."

"We've got some extra help coming in today. I just left the Marfa airport," she said. "I met up with an old friend of mine from high school that's with a smoke jumper crew out of Montana."

He leaned back slightly at the news. "No kidding?"

She smiled. "I hadn't seen him since school. I'd heard he was jumping but I never imagined we'd meet again like this."

The noise level of fifty people all talking among themselves died down as they noticed Fire Chief Doug Free walk to the front of the room. It didn't take long for him to get their attention. People were desperate for news. Not only were the group of first responders worried about their town and their neighbors, but they were also concerned for their own homes and families.

Finally Doug began. "Thank you all for coming. You know we're low-tech here. No air-conditioning and no microphone, so bear with me. This should take about twenty minutes with the law enforcement, then I need the firemen to stick around another twenty for direction. I'll get you back out on the front lines as soon as possible." He pulled a blue bandanna out of his back jeans pocket and wiped the sweat off of his forehead. He had brown hair that he wore combed back to one side and he had dark-brown eyes filled with an intensity that was evident even from across the room. He was a trim man with an athletic build. Josie noticed that all the firefighters in the room were in good physical shape. In the field they carried fifty-pound water sacks, additional equipment, heavy fire suits, and they had to be able to walk for miles at a time.

"As you know, yesterday I requested a voluntary evacuation for the southern part of Arroyo County," he went on. "The northern half of the county has already evacuated. But things just got worse about ten minutes ago. We're looking at a mandatory evacuation. The Harrison Ridge fire is headed toward us from up north. It's slowed down somewhat as the wind gusts have died down. Hopefully as evening falls we'll lose the wind and be able to stay on top of it. The bad news is we've got a fire that started late afternoon in Piedra Labrada. My spotter just called and said the fire's jumped the river in two places. I just sent Joey, Jake, and Luke over there about twenty minutes ago. The wind has me worried. We've got wind gusts coming up out of the canyons down by the river blowing northeast. And the Harrison Ridge fire is continuing to spread south. Both fires could potentially strike Artemis."

A new EMS driver that Josie had never met spoke up. "What's the difference between a voluntary and a mandatory evacuation?"

Doug smiled. "In reality, nothing. We had reached the point where people weren't taking the calls for evacuation seriously, so we added the mandatory evacuation level to let folks know the danger is imminent and immediate. We can't actually force someone off their property." He paused, as if deciding if he should say more, and then turned to face the whiteboard behind him.

Someone had already drawn a crude map of Arroyo County, shaped like a piece of pie with the tip pointing north. A square represented Artemis on the south end of the county, taking up about half the crust. Six miles separated downtown Artemis from the river and the border with Mexico. The other two towns shown on the map were smaller circles up north, and they represented the towns of Hepburn and Riseman. A wide strip of red was shaded over the central part of Arroyo County, and it covered both Hepburn and Riseman. The amount of red provided a disturbing visual.

Doug ran his hand down the middle part of the county, from the tip of the pie, directly toward Artemis. The red stopped just above the town.

"Over the past two days the fire has destroyed both towns, burning homes and property. At this point we still don't know exact numbers, but the devastation is immense for them." Doug tapped his finger on the clear area between the red band and Artemis below it. "I'd say we have about fifty miles between the mudflats at the north end of Artemis and the fire's path." He paused and turned to the group of officers and firefighters, all grim-faced and obviously distraught over the news. They were concerned about the limited resources available to fight a fire of this magnitude.

Gabriel Vasquez, who Josie knew was one of Doug's best volunteers, asked, "Can you estimate how long before it gets here?"

"The high temperatures and the storm clouds are giving us really unpredictable conditions. I'm not ready to put an ETA on it. As evening approaches, I would predict the wind will die down, but we have to prepare for the worst."

"Which is?" Vasquez said.

Doug turned back to the whiteboard and drew arrows on either side of the red vertical strip representing the Harrison Ridge fire. The arrows angled in toward the red area. "We have to assume this fire will follow the same trajectory, which is a straight path south toward the mudflats north of town." He pointed to the outskirts of town, on the northern edge. "We'll flank the fire on either side of it and try to squeeze it out before it gets here."

One of the younger sheriff's deputies, Dave Phillips, called out, "Why not get in front of it? We draw a line in the sand and put a line of fire trucks across it. We put everything we got out there, slurry drops, water trucks, water packs. We just hit it head-on."

Doug again wiped his forehead with the bandanna and put a hand up. "You have to realize, we're not talking about a forest fire that burns sections for hours at a time. We're talking about grass fires that can spread at lightning speed. The fire comes at you so fast you don't have time to get out of its way. And, don't think a grass fire can't kill you. They burn hot and fast, and with the wind gusts we've seen? You don't want to put yourself out in front of it."

The room was silent. Josie thought about Doug's description and wondered how a team of firefighters could discern the front end of a fire at night and with no aerial view, just the knowledge passed along by the firefighters themselves and the spotters throughout the county. It was a frightening thought.

"We've got a positive going for us tonight. A hotshot crew out of Montana is here in Artemis. They're smoke jumpers who were flying in to train at Big Bend National Park this weekend. They've agreed to help us until we get this under control. It'll put more feet on the ground." Doug motioned his head toward the back of the room and Josie noticed that Pete and several other men in khaki jumpsuits had entered the room. Several people began clapping and then the room filled with applause. The men standing in the doorway grinned at the reception and waved it off.

Doug spent the next ten minutes discussing the plan of action and making it clear that he didn't want the law enforcement officers fighting the fire; he wanted them supporting the firefighters with evacuation efforts.

"If I can use one of you on the line I'll ask you personally." He pointed toward the men and women sitting at the desks in front of him. "Most of these volunteers have been with me for several years now. It takes two years to really begin understanding fire suppression. The variables are endless, from the fuel on the ground to wind speed and direction, humidity, firebreaks, number of men and the tools being used. Homes and ranches and barns all burn different. All these things affect how we approach a fire. It's not just a matter of pointing a fire hose at it. Without proper training you could put yourself and everyone else in grave danger."

Doug pointed at Josie. "Chief Gray and her department are in charge of evacuations in and around Artemis." Josie nodded once, acknowledging what she already knew. Doug gestured across the room at Roy Martínez, a burly, retired marine. "Sheriff Martínez is in charge of the evacuation at the jail. Gray and Martínez already have a working evacuation plan. They'll be contacting their volunteer groups to aid in the evacuation. Just make sure you're ready for your call tonight."

After the law enforcement officers were dismissed, Josie and Otto walked to the police department to discuss plans for the night. The department was located directly across the street from the main entrance of the Arroyo County Courthouse. The PD was connected to the City Office on one side, where Mayor Steve Moss worked, and Tiny's Gun Club on the other. The PD had two large plate-glass windows facing the courthouse square, with a glass door in the middle. *Artemis Police Department* was painted in gold across the window to the left of the door, with their motto, *To Serve and Protect*, painted on the other. She and Otto walked into the building and both sighed at the cool of the air-conditioning and the familiar stale smell of the office. Dispatcher Lou Hagerty rolled her desk chair back from her computer when she saw them.

Lou had recently gone on a health kick, giving up snack food, coffee, and soft drinks. She had lost thirty pounds, which had left her white dispatcher shirt and navy pants hanging loosely on her thin body. Josie was certain that Lou could pull on the pants and shirt without unbuttoning or unzipping anything. Her pants were cinched around her waist with a belt that Lou had proudly drilled a new hole in to accommodate her smaller size. Josie had suggested several times that Lou needed to order a new set of clothes, but Lou hadn't taken the hint.

Despite this change in diet, Marlboro Lights still poked out of the side of Lou's purse, which sat on her desktop, waiting for the break when she could leave the building and smoke two. Lou had made it very clear she had no intention of quitting cigarettes; she said they were keeping her healthy while she got through the first year of breaking the snack food habit.

"I just heard about the second fire," Lou said. "You ready to start evacuations? I've already had several calls."

"When people call, tell them we'll be announcing all road closings and evacuation routes on Marfa Public Radio. Otto and I are pulling together the mandatory evacuation plans now. They'll be announced first on MPR, and then we'll start the phone trees. We could be moving people as early as tonight. My suggestion is head for the evacuation centers in Marfa or Presidio as a precaution."

FOUR

Otto followed Josie up the stairs and waited behind her as she unlocked the door to the office. She flipped on the lights and heard the familiar buzz of the fluorescent bulbs. The room was split into three workspaces, for Josie, Otto, and Marta, furnished with matching metal desks and filing cabinets, with a large conference table in the front. Josie's attention was drawn beyond Otto and Marta's desks to the large windows that made up the back wall. The view was grim; the sky was dark and she was no longer able to tell if she was seeing the overcast sky or smoke from the Harrison Ridge fire.

She found the Artemis evacuation plan in her filing cabinet. She ignored the county map. The fire had already spread through the upper two-thirds of the county and the residents there had been evacuated days ago to Presidio County. Doug had said it would be several days before residents of the two towns up north would be allowed to return home.

Otto grabbed them each a water bottle out of the dorm-sized refrigerator located at the back of the office. He handed one to Josie and said, "It's been almost six years since we faced an evacuation like this. I got a call from the director of EMS. She says they're ready with shelters set up at the schools in Presidio."

"I talked to Helen too. She says they have meals ready on standby to cover three days, and bedding for three hundred. I sure hope it doesn't come to that."

Josie sat down beside Otto at the conference table and opened a photocopy of the local map they had drawn up several years ago. It was split into three regions encompassing the town of Artemis and the ranches closest to the town. Circling the top part of the map with her finger, she said, "I'll take the region up north by the mudflats. That'll be the area hit first."

Next, she pointed to the middle of the map. "Obviously this is the most populated because it includes downtown. You'll take this area. You've got your list of volunteers?"

Otto nodded. "I'll start calling as soon as we're done here. I have six people designated, all business owners who offered to make their own phone calls."

"Good. Marta's in charge of the most remote areas on the east and west sides of Artemis. She'll have the hardest time reaching people."

"She'll also have the largest number of people who refuse to evacuate."

Josie ignored the comment. It was a frustration, but one they had little control over. "Let's get our volunteers called now and put them on alert. I want them ready to make their calls immediately when we get orders from Doug."

"You got it," he said.

"I'm going to run home and check in with Dell. Then I'll start making calls."

The fifteen-minute drive from downtown Artemis took Josie along one of the few paved roads outside of the city limits: Farm Road 170, a rolling, curving road that washed out each year when the monsoon rains started, but now allowed for clear and easy driving. Josie passed by the Spanish daggers with their six-foot-high stalks topped with creamy white blooms just now drying, and she tried to imagine the landscape as nothing but scorched earth. She turned off onto Schenck Road and crested a hill that provided the perfect view of her small adobe home at the base of the Chinati Mountain range. At sunset, the house seemed to absorb the colors of the sky, often appearing pink. That evening, with the setting sun blocked by clouds, the house took on the gray cast of the mountains behind it. The house had a deep front porch held aloft by hand-hewn pecan timbers that her neighbor and closest friend, Dell Seapus, had helped her install. The front of the house faced the Chihuahuan Desert, which stretched beyond the Rio and deep into Mexico. The lane ran back behind her house and a quarter mile farther up to Dell's ranch.

Josie pulled onto the lane and drove on past her house to check in with Dell. He had been worried about his cattle and the possible evacuation if the fire came their way. She got out of her jeep and he opened the front door of the cabin so her bloodhound, Chester, could bound outside to greet her. While Josie was away at work, Chester spent his days following Dell around the ranch, lying in the shade and watching him tend to chores.

Dell was a seventy-something-year-old bachelor who claimed to like animals more than people. He'd never been married, having sworn off women as a pain in the ass many years ago. Josie was his one exception. She had gotten to know Dell during a monthlong investigation involving the theft of his prized Appaloosas. When Josie brought the horses back unharmed, he had deeded her ten acres in front of his property and helped her build her home.

Dell skipped the small talk. "What's the latest on the Harrison Ridge fire?"

"It's not good news. It's headed directly toward the mudflats. Another fire jumped the Rio and it's burning along the riverbank just south of us."

Dell frowned. "Fire coming at Artemis from both directions?"

"That's the fear. We're facing mandatory evacuations tonight."

"Damn it. How about us?"

"Unless the wind direction changes, I hope we're far enough to the west that we'll be okay. Marta is in charge of the evacuation on this side of town."

"I got the cattle moved over to the Saddle Market this afternoon. At least they're safe."

"You'll keep Chester with you tonight?"

"You bet," he said. Dell rubbed his hand over the stubble on his cheeks. His silvery hair was matted around his head from the band on his cowboy hat. He was shirtless. His bare chest was the color of tanned leather, and his blue jeans looked as if they might disintegrate through one more trip in the washer.

"What does that mean for you?" he asked. "For the department?"

"I came home to call the volunteers and put them on alert."

"What can I do?"

"I'd like you to ride with me if we evacuate the mudflats. I need to keep Marta and Otto open to cover other areas of the county in case Doug needs them."

"You're talking about the homes out where the Blessings live?"

"That's it. There's less than a dozen houses in the direct line of fire, but we'll go door-to-door if it comes to that. My guess is the order will come tonight."

Dell nodded. "I'll be ready. Who gives the order?"

"Doug Free will call me."

"You need supper?"

She raised a hand to brush the question off. "I'm not hungry. I need to start calling volunteers."

"I'll bring some brisket down."

Josie took Chester home, got him a bone, and watched him settle on his rug, oblivious to the drama around him. She was sitting at the table under the kitchen window with her papers spread out before her when Dell walked in carrying a roasting pan covered in tinfoil. While she made calls he dug through her kitchen drawers and opened a can of baked beans, which he doctored up with mustard and brown sugar and heated on the stovetop with the brisket.

"How many people you have to call?" he asked, setting plates down on the table. He had changed into a newer pair of jeans, a Western shirt, cowboy boots, and his hat.

"There's roughly two hundred families in my region. I have ten volunteers to call. Then they'll make their phone calls to the people who signed up for the phone list. Otto's working downtown. His crew will go door-to-door to reach more people. Marta has the ranches farthest from town."

Josie knew there were people who had refused to take part in the phone tree. All she could do was hope they paid attention to the radio. The county emergency team had worked hard to put a solid communication plan into place for disasters. It was time to put it to the test.

Shortly after she'd reached her last volunteer, Josie received a phone call from Doug.

"Josie. We've got lightning strikes again and the wind isn't letting up. I just called MPR and told them to announce the evacuation routes. You get your volunteers going. I'm ordering mandatory evacuation for the area inside the city limits, and the northern and eastern regions. You ready to jump on it?"

"Absolutely. I'll call Otto and Marta, and I'll text my group. They're waiting for the signal."

"The smoke jumper crew has been on a line just north of downtown, about ten miles south of the mudflats. They're working with about thirty firefighters to clear debris and expand Lonesome Road to make a hundred-foot firebreak that's clear of fuel."

"How's it coming?"

Doug sighed. "Those guys are working as fast as they can. My biggest worry is that I haven't correctly predicted the line of the fire."

She understood his fear. In the end, he would take responsibility for the plan's success or failure, regardless of the fire's behavior. It was a tough place to be, knowing lives and homes depended on your best guess.

"Can you get out to the homes on Casson's Road and go door-to-door?" he asked. "The fire's driving straight toward that area and the wind's picked up again. I'm afraid we may lose the eight homes there. It doesn't look good at all. Tell those folks they need to be out immediately."

Josie glanced at her watch. It was 7:05 p.m.

"Realistically, how much time do they have?"

"I want them out within the hour," he said.

"We're on our way."

The landscape within Arroyo County varied from flat dusty desert to areas of grassland farther north that received rain from mountain runoff as well as water from underground springs. The locals called the area north of town the mudflats owing to a low depression in the desert that filled with rain during the monsoons and made a mud pit that the local kids and ATV riders descended on for a giant party each summer. It was designated public land, and as long as the party didn't get too rowdy, law enforcement let the revelers go.

Just to the east of the mud pit was a swath of prairie grass several miles wide. A road wound through the grassland where eight homes dotted the land. Josie loved her home and Dell's cattle ranch at the base of the mountains, but she thought the green grasses gently blowing in waves in the spring and summer were one of the prettiest sights in Artemis. The problem now was that with no rain for nine months, the grass had turned brown and brittle—perfect fuel for the fire.

Josie and Dell loaded Chester into the back of her Artemis PD vehicle, a four-wheel-drive retired army jeep that served her well on the gravel and dirt roads throughout the county. They were quiet on the drive as they watched the wall of smoke in the distance, stretching from ground to sky, swallow up everything in its path.

They pulled into the first driveway at 7:20 p.m. The home was dark, the homeowners apparently gone. Josie checked the front door and Dell checked the back to make sure both were locked and the family had actually left. A half mile down the road they pulled into the driveway of the second home, a sprawling ranch with an attached garage. A man and woman were outside, frantically throwing boxes into the back of an SUV. The man ran up to Josie, looking relieved to see the police.

"We heard on the radio, mandatory evacuation."

"That's correct. It's time to leave. You have pets taken care of?"

Josie noticed Dell heading up to the front of the house where the woman had gone back inside, apparently for another load.

"We don't have any. Just us and the kids." He turned and pointed to the SUV. The open back doors revealed two girls under the age of five strapped into car seats. Both of them were wide-eyed, gazing out the car door at their parents' panicked activity.

"You know the evacuation route?" she asked.

"I do. We're headed down Bull Run Road toward 67. The radio said the elementary school is ready with cots set up for the night."

"Excellent. You have five minutes and I want you out of the driveway. Okay?"

The man nodded and turned to see Dell helping his wife with one last load.

Josie and Dell left and wound their way down the road to the next house, owned by Smokey and Vie Blessings. Smokey was a city council member whom Josie had worked with for many years. He was a voice of reason whenever Mayor Moss tried to fight Josie's decisions. Josie was also friends with Smokey's wife, Vie, a nurse at the town's trauma center. Where Smokey was easygoing, Vie was passionate. She was often the only nurse working in an ER that shared rotating physicians because of the town's small size and remote location. Vie got things done.

When Josie and Dell got out of the car and approached the house, they found Smokey standing by their pickup truck, his face red and angry. Josie reached her hand out and shook Smokey's. "You heard about the mandatory evacuation? Fire chief wants you out immediately. The fire is too unpredictable right now."

"I know about the evacuation. Tell my wife! I can't get her out of that house. I don't know what's wrong with her." Smokey turned back and glanced toward the truck, where his sixteen-year-old son was sitting, staring down at his cell phone. "Donny's been sitting in there for fifteen minutes while she keeps dragging out more junk we don't need. I can't get her to stop and listen."

Josie was stunned. She'd never seen Smokey lose his cool. "Let me go talk to her."

Dell offered to help Smokey throw the suitcases situated behind the pickup into the bed, and she ran inside the house. It was a two-story stone house, decorated with Southwest fabrics and patterns. Josie heard noise from the hallway to the left of the front door and found Vie digging in a closet in what appeared to be a craft or sewing room.

"Vie, it's Josie."

Vie pulled out of the closet and Josie recognized the wide-eyed vacant look on her face as a combination of terror and shock. It was a look that Josie did not associate with the woman who remained in charge during whatever crisis was thrown at her at the trauma center. Vie said nothing, just stared at Josie, her eyes unblinking.

"Vie, you have to leave. The fire is headed this direction. None of this stuff is worth your life."

Vie reached back into the closet and pulled out a box that appeared to hold memorabilia—baby books and a child's blanket. "I can't leave all this. I have boxes from Donny's childhood. I've kept all this for him. I don't have our photos yet. They're in my bedroom."

Josie put her hand on Vie's arm to pull her from the closet but Vie jerked free. Josie reached for her again, this time grabbing hold in a tight grip. "Vie," Josie said, her voice loud, her tone firm. "You are putting your son's life in jeopardy right now. That fire is headed directly toward this house. Smokey and Donny are outside waiting on you."

She turned and looked at Josie as if she'd been slapped. Tears welled up in her eyes. "We came from nothing. We built this home, piece by piece."

Josie kept her hand on Vie's arm and guided her out of the bedroom. Vie clutched the box but walked with Josie down the hallway. "You won't lose those memories. You've made a great home for your family, and if you have to, you'll rebuild. But we have to keep you safe. We need you to leave now so we can move on to the next family."

They reached the door and Vie stopped again, staring at Josie for a moment before finally walking to the car without another word. She got into the passenger seat and Smokey backed out of the driveway without hesitation.

The next three homes were empty. As they reached the last home, Doug called and said it was time to get out. The flames from the peak of the fire were now visible. The fire was within a mile of the mudflats. The smell of smoke was strong now and the smoke completely blotted out any evening light.

Chester typically lay in the backseat and slept when he rode in a vehicle, but he was agitated now, whining, obviously alert to the danger they were facing. Josie was always amazed at the dog's innate sense of natural dangers, such as approaching storms or fire.

Lights were on in the last home to check, but the front door was locked. Dell ran from window to window to see if someone was inside. Josie finally found the man in his woodshop behind the house. He was sitting on a stool at his workbench, whittling a small piece of wood and listening to the radio announcer discuss the evacuation. She knew him as a cantankerous retiree from the local bank who was now in his late eighties.

She told him, "Mr. Beeman, the fire is within a mile of your home. You are in extreme danger."

He ignored her, refusing to look up.

Josie bent down, getting right next to him and speaking loudly. "You could die if you don't leave."

He swatted her off with his hand. "Get out and leave me be."

Josie felt her face flush with anger. "Mr. Beeman, the flames are visible from here. It isn't *if* the fire will burn your house, it's *when* it will hit."

He looked up and glared at her. "I'm not going anywhere. I got a storm cellar. That's where I'll go."

"That cellar won't do you any good if your burning house caves in on you!" She was furious at his unwillingness to help himself.

He turned back to his workbench and drew his whittling knife down the side of the piece of wood. Josie looked more closely at the piece and saw that it was in the shape of a heart, and he was carving the initial *B* in the center. His deceased wife's name was Beatrice.

After pleading with him one more time, she choked back tears as she turned from the old man and left. Ultimately, it was a person's right to choose death.

FIVE

After checking the most vulnerable houses in the mudflats area, Josie and Dell drove south to Lonesome Road, where a group of roughly sixty firefighters were spread across a three-mile span, widening the firebreak. Josie drove two miles toward downtown Artemis, down the side road that ran perpendicular to the firebreak, and found Doug's fire truck. Another group of firemen were using a water tank from a brush truck to fight the flames from the fire's flank, basically squeezing it in from the sides and preventing it from spreading any wider.

They approached Doug who stood at the edge of the road, talking on his cell phone. Once he finished he walked toward them, shaking his head. "We've got every road between here and Mexico closed. I just hope everyone got out of the south central part of the county."

"I hate to add this to your worries, but I couldn't get Mike Beeman to budge."

Doug shook his head, clearly angry. "He'll put my firefighters in danger trying to save his sorry ass." Doug ran his hands over his face as if trying to wipe away the thought. "I'll do what I can."

"What about the firebreak?" said Dell.

Doug held a hand in the air and tilted it. "The mudflats are in trouble up north, but this firebreak may save downtown. The guys have done a great job fighting this from the sides. Up north it was burning over eight miles wide. I just talked to the crew to the east of us. From where they're stationed, I think the fire's only burning about two miles wide. And it's headed straight for the break. This might work."

"What about west of town?" Dell asked.

Doug nodded, acknowledging that that was where their homes were located. "The fire across the river is contained. The wind direction up north is remaining constant. Anything west of the watchtower is currently out of the line of fire."

"What more can we do to help?" Josie asked.

"Your next job starts tomorrow. Go home and get a couple hours' sleep. As soon as we've deemed the homes and outbuildings safe enough to search we'll give you a call. We'll have a lot of ground to cover and you'll have people fighting to get back to their homes."

Josie nodded. "I already talked to Roy. Since the jail's cleared from having to evacuate, he's working with his officers to get barricades up on all the closed county roads. He'll take care of keeping back the residents tomorrow, and we'll help you check structures." Josie paused, thinking about Vie and Smokey. "Any idea when we'll be able to get in and check the mudflats?"

Doug frowned. "It's not good, Josie. We're doing what we can, but there's little doubt we'll lose some of those homes. Texas Forest Service is on their way with planes, but . . . " He looked away. "We'll need daylight to start assessing damages, assuming we can stop this tonight. I'll call you by seven tomorrow morning with an update."

———•———

Josie knew that the western area of the county had been spared, but she felt immense relief as they topped the hill and her home came into view. Dell exhaled like he'd been holding his breath. The relief made her all the more aware of what her friends and neighbors would experience over the next few days as they discovered their homes and possessions burned to ash.

She drove Dell down to his house, but he didn't get out. The inside of the car was dark, and they were both exhausted from the night. She wondered at the hesitation.

"You want to come in for a cold drink? Unwind before you try to get some sleep?"

She nodded and followed him inside. He was right. She was exhausted, but the intensity of the night would sit on her chest like a rock if she tried to go to bed without settling her thoughts.

He poured them both glasses of ice water and they sat out on the front porch in his old wooden rocking chairs.

"I can't get old man Beeman out of my head," Dell said. "I hate to say it, but that could be me in another ten years."

Josie grinned. "You're a pain in the ass like he is, but you've got more sense. Grit's one thing, but self-preservation has to count for something." Josie thought about the heart he had been whittling but didn't bring it up to Dell. There was already too much sadness to contemplate. She didn't want to imagine what might have happened to Beeman in the fire.

Dell drained his glass of water and set it down on the floor.

Josie felt the stress and emotion of the day pressing in on her chest, and her thoughts turned to Dillon. She wondered when she would be able to face a major event in her life and not think of him. He had been the calm voice of reason when her intensity needed a buffer. She turned to Dell, her best friend and occasional confidant. "I called Dillon yesterday to let him know about the fire. I left a message. I thought he might be worried, but he never called me back."

"Maybe he already heard about it on the news."

"I just thought he would have returned my call."

Dell sighed and Josie closed her eyes in embarrassment. She imagined herself as too tough to agonize over a man who clearly wanted nothing to do with her, but there she was, dragging him up again.

"You get why he left you. Right?" Dell said.

"I get why he left Artemis," she said. "I understand why he hated this place after the hell he went through. He said he was tired of watching over his shoulder for the next disaster. He said leaving was the only way he could ever find happiness again."

She could feel Dell staring at her in the dark. "You get why he left Artemis, but not why he left you?"

Josie was quiet, gazing up at the pitch-black sky, where the light from stars and the moon had been extinguished by smoke. Josie had mastered the art of deflection, but Dell knew her too well.

"You told me a couple of weeks ago that it was time to let him go," he said.

She leaned back into the rocking chair and heard the familiar creak of the wood against the porch. Over the past few years, the dangers required of her job had been an issue for Dillon, but he'd also understood her dedication. After the kidnapping, though, everything changed. He shut down. He quit laughing. They didn't argue, because they quit talking, but she'd believed that eventually things would return to some kind of normal. "He didn't give me the chance to leave with him. That's what hurts," she said. "He didn't even ask. He just ended it. He came to me one night and said he was selling the business and having movers pack up his house. He couldn't handle walking by Christina's desk one more time. He left the next day. That was it."

"Surely you can understand him feeling that way," he said.

Josie felt numb. "It sounds selfish, after the hell he went through. It's just that you think you're important to someone, and then you discover that other things matter more."

"You want my opinion?"

"I do."

"Certain people define themselves by their career. Teachers and nurses and cops are the worst. You go to work ten, twelve hours a day, but then you come home and it doesn't stop. Teachers're always trying to fix people, nurses want to heal the world, and cops want to solve problems. Well, you got dished up one hell of a problem with

Dillon. And you thought you solved it. He came home safe. Problem was, you had no idea how to make him better. And you can't handle that."

She absently twisted the ring around her finger that Dillon had given her the year before for her birthday, but said nothing. She knew Dell was right.

"Dillon's a smart guy. I always liked him. He was a little soft for my taste, a city boy, but he had a good heart and he loved you. I know that much for sure."

Dell stopped and looked at her until she nodded. He was right. There was little doubt that Dillon had loved her.

"I get that," she finally said. "But it obviously wasn't enough."

———————

In the middle of the night, Josie had received a text from Doug Free stating that the firebreak had worked, and that the fire was 75 percent contained. She'd finally been able to relax and get a few hours of sleep before her meeting at the firehouse the next morning. On her drive into town she called both Otto and Marta to confirm that their families were fine, and that the fire had spared their homes.

At precisely 7:00 a.m., Doug sat down at one of the training tables across from Josie and Otto. His eyes were glazed over from exhaustion and his face sagged from the stress of the night. "We're up to eighteen homes that were burned in Arroyo County over the past two days. Eleven of those homes are probably a complete loss." His expression showed his grief.

"How many of them have been cleared?" Josie asked.

"Nine were up north in Riseman and Hepburn. All those homes have been checked. No fatalities."

Josie hesitated, dreading the answer. "What happened with Beeman's house?"

"The fire started ripping through that area and one of my guys went and got him. He was sitting in his wood shop, shaking like a leaf."

"We oughta throw him in jail for putting your men in that position," Otto said.

Doug frowned and nodded. "It's maddening. He was awful glad to see us though, when the flames started lapping at his back door. He's fine, but his house is a complete loss."

"What about the Blessingses' place?"

Doug shook his head. "I'm sorry, Josie. I know they're friends of yours."

She closed her eyes for a moment against the news, imagining Vie trying to hold it together when she found out her home was gone.

"We've got some things to be thankful for. The fire that started across the Rio is completely out. And most importantly, the firebreak worked. Downtown and the most populated areas weren't touched. And other than minor injuries, none of my firefighters were seriously hurt."

Josie nodded. "You guys did an incredible job. This town owes you a big debt."

"I hope I get a few more volunteers out of this. It's tough to get people to put in the kind of time this job takes. Without a strong crew though, this town would have been lost last night."

"Are we free to check the remaining nine houses?" Otto asked.

"Not yet. I have a new crew out of Fort Stockton working the fire right now. I hope to have it ninety percent contained by noon. A group of guys went off the clock at three this morning to get some rest. They'll be out again at ten to check homes for structural damage. I can't send you in there to check for survivors until I know you'll be safe. At least not the homes up north."

"Where do you want us?" Josie asked.

"One of my guys said there were some structures, maybe a barn, burnt over on the western edge of the fire. We used Prentice Canyon Road as a firebreak. I didn't think anything burned west of that road last night. Check that area first."

Josie nodded.

"Just assure me you won't go poking around buildings that may still be smoldering. You could have a roof that looks fine collapse, or a floor cave in. I've seen it happen."

⸺

Several thousand acres of ground were intentionally burned each year throughout Arroyo County. Ranchers set fire to their lands to keep the dead brush to a minimum. The bigger ranches used spray rigs to water down their cattle and take care of small fires on their properties. Seeing burned land was nothing new, and with the summer rains the vegetation would come back in a matter of months. But to see homes and livestock buildings burned was a different matter. Neither Josie nor Otto had seen the affected areas of the county on their drive into town to meet with Doug that morning. Now, driving north along Prentice Canyon, the edge of the fire, they began to see smoldering barns and charred ground the color of coal.

"I'd hate to see what the mudflats look like," said Josie.

The road curved along through the desert hills, but she noticed that the fire hadn't crossed the gravel expanse.

"This road saved the western part of the county," Otto said, noticing as well. "Why don't we have mandatory firebreaks? We'd at least have some protection from smaller fires."

"Who's going to tell these ranchers they have to give up acreage for a firebreak? They use their own brush trucks and stock ponds to keep their land safe. They don't want the county telling them what to do."

"Not every rancher takes care of business. The fire finds the void and spreads."

It was an old conversation. What appeared to be a simple solution would turn into a court battle that no one was prepared, or had the money, to fight.

She pulled down the driveway of the first ranch they reached. A sign that read NEW MOON RANCH hung over the end of the driveway. She drove several miles down the dirt lane back to the ranch house before passing two buildings that were blackened, but didn't appear to be seriously damaged by the fire.

Josie pointed her finger out her side window. "You can see where the flames licked up the side of that barn. There just wasn't enough fuel to let it catch."

"Those grass fires burn like hell. But they burn so fast, they can pass by the big stuff."

Josie slowed her jeep. "There's somebody walking around the side of the barn."

They both watched a man walk through the dusty lot. Josie drove down the dirt lane toward him. He wore blue jeans and a ranch shirt, and both were covered in black soot. Josie pulled her jeep up beside him and rolled down her window. His face was streaked with black. He put a hand out and Josie shook it through the window.

"I'm Joe Gutiérrez. I'm a ranch hand for Mike and Shelly Morris."

"Chief Josie Gray, and this is Officer Otto Podowski. Your horses and cattle make it through the fire?" she asked.

"Every one of them." He pointed to a field that lay beyond the barn. "The horses, I stayed with last night. We got the cattle to a clearing. Kept the fire back with water from the stock pond."

"We're glad to hear it. You need any help checking outbuildings this morning?"

"No, we're fine. I heard the house up the road got hit hard. You might check there."

"Will do. Take care," she said.

Josie turned her jeep around in the barn lot and drove out along the ranch lane. "The next house up the road is the Nixes'."

"That's the country music people?"

"Billy Nix. He's a singer, plays guitar. You ever heard him play?"

Otto made a dismissive noise. "Everybody drinking beer and crying and leaving. I have to put up with that nonsense with the yahoos we drag to jail. I don't need it in my music."

Josie smiled. "He's pretty good. I've heard him at the Hell-Bent a few times. He's hardcore country. Tries to come off like Waylon

Jennings and David Allan Coe." She glanced at Otto and saw by his blank expression that he had no idea who she was talking about. "Anyway, his wife, Brenda, is also his manager."

"How's a boss lady for a wife work for a hard-core country guy?"

"I don't know. I hear she's all business, all the time. Rumor is she's negotiating a recording contract."

About two miles past the New Moon Ranch they saw that the road had not stopped the fire from spreading west as Doug had thought. Scorched earth slowly spread out from the edge of the road into the pasture.

"Doug said the wind was gusting from the northeast. And everything we saw driving over here supports that. How would embers jump the road against the wind here?" Josie pointed off to the other side of the road. "It's mostly sand and clumps of scrub brush."

"One ember blowing in a crosscurrent could catch a clump of that grass," Otto said.

As they drove another two miles down the road, the remnants of the fire spread farther into the field and down into a ravine. The steep valley made it impossible to see how far west the fire had traveled. This area of the county was sparsely populated, with no houses beyond the Nixes'. Another mile and the road ended at the base of Helio Mountain, which was part of the several-thousand-acre Oler ranch. The Nixes' home wasn't part of the ranching operation, and Josie was worried that it had been burned with no firefighters or ranchers to offer protection.

About five miles beyond the New Moon Ranch, around a bend in the road, the Nixes' one-story white home came into view. Josie slowed the jeep to a crawl. Over half of the ranch-style house had been severely burned. The front door was situated at the center of the house. Everything to the left of it appeared to have been spared. To the right was a large hole that opened up into what had probably been the living room. The house disappeared around jagged black edges like an abstract painting. To the right of the living room the building was completely gone. The gravel driveway led to the front of this burned-out area and Josie wondered if it had been an enclosed garage, but they were still too far away to tell. A pickup truck parked in front of the house was nothing more than a blackened frame.

Josie stopped the jeep before pulling into the driveway and considered the layout of the property. Once around the bend, the road straightened out for about a half mile, and the house sat in the middle of the straight stretch, sitting back about five hundred feet from the road. There were several trees around the house, now burned down to blackened stubs, but with no furniture or other yard ornaments, it didn't appear there had been much landscaping or many plantings to burn up.

"That's not a good sign," Otto said. He pointed at the burned-out truck. "You'd have thought they'd have taken both vehicles when they evacuated."

Josie pulled into the driveway. Even with half of the house burnt up, it was still apparent it had needed work. White paint had chipped off the siding; some boards were down to bare wood, weathered gray from the sun. There were no other vehicles parked around the house, and no other outbuildings.

She stopped the jeep and they got out of the car, saying little. It was obvious the fire trucks hadn't reached the home. No sloppy wet ash surrounded the house. It appeared the fire had burned hot and strong, and then had died out without taking the entire house. Josie knew Doug would take the loss hard. He thought the firebreak had been a complete success, and yet this fire on the wrong side of the break had been extremely intense.

Josie looked at Otto. He stood with his hands on his hips, looking perplexed at the jagged hole in the house.

"Looks odd, doesn't it?" she said.

"Looks like somebody blew a hole through there." He turned and looked around as if searching for something. "No sign of a propane tank, or something that could have caused an explosion."

Josie hollered several times and they listened for a response from someone who might be in the house and injured, but they heard nothing.

They split up to walk around opposite sides of the house, keeping their distance from the blackened interior. The smell was horrible, like a trash fire but more acrid. Around the back of the house Josie found a wooden picnic table charred and still smoking. She felt the metal back door for heat. It was warm, but not too hot to touch. Josie put on a pair of latex gloves she kept in her back pocket and tried to open the back door, but it was locked. There were no cars behind the house. She wondered if the truck out front was dead and they'd had to leave it behind. She was hopeful the Nixes had heeded the warnings and evacuated.

Otto met up with her behind the house and gestured beyond, to the rolling hills that stretched out as far as the eye could see. "The burned scrub brush disappears down into that ravine. From here, it looks like the fire spread maybe another two or three acres and fizzled out."

They walked back around to the front of the house and stood in the road directly in front of the property, appraising the damage, trying to understand the path of the fire.

Josie pulled her cell phone from her breast pocket and called Doug.

"This is Josie. You have a second?"

"I'm on the fire line, but go ahead."

His voice was loud and she heard commotion in the background so she made it quick.

"We're on Prentice Canyon Road, on the western edge of the fire. You know where Billy and Brenda Nix live?"

"Yes."

"Their house burned. It's about half gone. Do you know if you had any guys working their house?"

"That house isn't one of the eighteen I talked about. I didn't know it burned."

"Okay. I know you're on the line. Give me a call later when you have a minute."

"Will do. I'll check it out later today."

Josie put her phone back in her pocket and turned back to stare at the house again with Otto. "So the house burned like hell, and then the fire went out on its own."

"Appears that way," he said.

"Look here," Otto said. He was pointing behind them, to the edge of the road. "There's tire tracks in the ash." He pointed to where tires must have spun out and threw gravel as a vehicle took off.

"Probably some gawker driving by. They pulled off and stopped to look at the damage. The tire tracks are on top of the ash."

He nodded. "Could have been this morning even." He took his camera from his pocket and snapped several photographs at different angles and distances.

"You think Doug can look at the house, the burning trees, what might be burning inside, to determine when the fire started?" she said.

"Problem will be pulling him off the fire," Otto said. "Let's see how close we can get to the inside of the house."

Josie and Otto were both wearing rubber boots over their police shoes to protect the soles from hot embers. They both walked slowly, carefully examining the ground outside the home, and around the opening in the house, for footprints or signs of foul play. A concrete pad, probably used as a front porch, stretched about fifteen feet, from the left side of the front door to the right side of where the living room window once was. Shards of glass covered the concrete and the floor inside the living room. The wood siding on this part of the house burned down to the foundation, and the fire had reached up into the rafters. A ten-foot-wide hole provided access to the room, but they were reluctant to enter the structure because of the roof damage.

Isolated trails of smoke drifted up from charred pieces of siding and smoldering furniture inside the house. Otto pulled a handkerchief out of his back pocket and placed it over his mouth and nose. Josie heard him mumble something into his hand. The smell of burnt wood and fiber and man-made belongings was overpowering and Josie felt her stomach cramping.

From where Josie stood on the concrete pad, she could see the layout of the living room: square in shape, modestly furnished with a couch and loveseat. To the left of the hole, the front door opened up into a small tiled entryway with a coat closet and a hallway, most likely leading to bedrooms. The hallway appeared largely undamaged by the fire.

The furniture faced an entertainment center on the wall opposite where Josie stood looking through the hole. The center held a large flat-screen TV and a great deal of electronic stereo equipment. The shapes were still visible, but the equipment was severely burned and melted.

To the left of the entertainment center was a wide doorway that led from the living room into what appeared to be a dining room. That room had been burned, but the walls were still intact and structurally it was in slightly better shape than the living room, but that wasn't saying much.

"It's a complete loss," Otto said, still talking into the handkerchief.

Josie stepped gingerly into the living room, testing the floor to make sure it would hold her weight.

"I don't think you ought to go in there until Doug takes a look."

"I just want to get down the hallway if I can. Make sure there's no one inside. If the floor feels soft I won't go on."

Now that she was inside, Josie turned to check out the living room one last time. She had a better view of the couch now and took a deep breath, stunned at what she saw.

SIX

Dell stood at the end of his bed and laid a pair of dark slacks on the blanket. They were navy blue with a crease down the middle of each leg. He'd not had a crease in a pair of pants in thirty years. He didn't even think pants had creases in them anymore. It seemed like a ludicrous waste of time.

He walked to his closet and opened the sliding door. Three new button-down shirts hung on hangers, still stiff from the plastic packaging he'd unwrapped them from. He sighed, pulled one out, and laid it on the bed, too. He dug around in the hall closet until he found an iron he kept in its original box. He ironed the fold creases out of the shirt and moved on to his cowboy boots. It had been a while since he'd cleaned them, and they were showing their wear. He found the saddle oil to rub out the dirt, and then conditioned them.

After a quick shower, he stood in front of the steamy bathroom mirror to shave, something he typically did about once a week—once a month when he forgot. This was the third time this week he'd shaved, and it was grating on his nerves. By the time he'd dressed and was ready to go, the entire process had taken almost an hour. This is what females did to men, he thought. They turned them into sissies.

Dell drove his pickup thirty minutes to Presidio and parked in front of Lou Ellen Macey's house, located behind the mammoth stained-glass-clad Our Lady of the Angels Catholic church. Dell walked past the brick rectory to the little house behind it that Lou Ellen rented from the Church. Apparently that gave the priest, a man in his early thirties, the right to snoop around in her private life, or Lou Ellen just freely gave away her private life to the priest—either way it made Dell uncomfortable. He didn't share his business with anyone. He had lifted his hand to ring her doorbell when he heard his name being called from behind him. He turned to find Father Paul standing in a bed of thorny red roses, watering them with a garden hose. He waved cheerfully, and Dell tipped his hat.

Lou Ellen opened the door wearing a flowered skirt and a light pink blouse. He had to admit, she was a fine-looking woman, slim and smelling like soap and vanilla, with her white hair fixed and her teeth shiny. He'd met her a few weeks ago at the Texas Tractor Implements store where she worked as a clerk. She'd had to help him order a part for his tractor. It had taken three visits to the store before he finally got the part he actually needed. On the last visit she offered to buy him a cup of coffee for all the trouble he'd been through. He'd been so shocked that he'd not been able to say no. He'd been even more shocked four times since when she'd suggested new outings, and he'd simply agreed to the arrangements for lack of a better response.

This afternoon he was taking her to a musical being performed by someone she knew, or someone she wanted to know, or some such thing. He had no interest whatsoever in musicals of any sort and he'd begun to wonder what he'd gotten himself into. Except she smelled like soap and vanilla, a smell more intoxicating than he wanted to admit.

———————

"Otto. We got a problem," Josie said.

He stepped up to the edge of the living room, but remained outside on the concrete pad. "What's wrong?"

Josie turned her head away from the couch, sickened. "There's a body. Looks like a male. He's burnt up bad." She heard Otto exhale and saw him rub his hands over his face. There was nothing more horrendous to see than a body burned in a fire.

"Billy Nix?"

Josie forced herself to look again. "The face is unrecognizable."

"I thought we'd dodged the bullet. No fatalities." Otto started to step inside the house and took his leg back out. "You're sure this floor will hold my weight?"

She peered down at the floor and bounced on her toes, checking the give in the floor. She walked slowly toward the loveseat and stood behind it, as if it provided some measure of protection from the grotesque body on the couch. "I don't feel any give. I think it's okay." She glanced up at the ceiling where the rafters were burned. "The fire burned all the way through the roof. You can see daylight."

He frowned. "I think you'd better get out of there until we find out if it's safe."

"It's a smoldering house, Otto. We need to get details logged before we lose them."

"Not if it means a house falling in on us!" He beckoned with his hand for Josie to come outside. "Call Doug. Have him get the fire marshal down here to start an investigation. I'll call the coroner."

Josie started toward the opening in the living room wall and stopped next to the body. She looked at Otto for a moment. "If you were in your living room, and it caught fire, what would you do?"

He smirked, refusing to answer what appeared to be a stupid question.

"Let's say something inside your house exploded even, and caught your house on fire, what would you do?"

"Are you serious?"

"Yes."

"I'd get out."

"How would you get out?"

He stared at her.

"What do they teach every kid in school about a fire?"

Otto finally caught on. "Stop, drop, and roll."

She pointed at the couch. "Billy Nix, or whoever this is, is lying on his back on the couch. His hands are curled up around his head like he's trying to shield his face. Wouldn't he have rolled off the couch, onto the floor, tried to crawl out?"

"But if there was an explosion he wouldn't have had time."

She shook her head. "No explosion. Something burned through this part of the house. Look at the furniture in the living room." She walked out of the house and stood with Otto, looking back inside. "The couch, with its back facing us, is still intact. It's burned, the fabric melted, but not like it was blown away from an exploding living room wall. And, it's directly in front of where the outside of the house seems to have been burnt first."

"As if somebody put gas or an accelerant on the house and torched it," he said. "Which would have given Billy Nix ample opportunity to get off the couch to safety."

"Unless he was already dead."

———

Josie cleared the rest of the house for other possible victims. She found it odd that Billy would have stayed behind during the evacuation and his wife would have left. She thought of them as a team.

After completing an initial sweep of each of the remaining rooms, she and Otto stood near the road where the stench wasn't as strong in order to make their phone calls. She called Lou Hagerty, first-shift dispatcher at the PD, and asked her to begin the process of tracking down the Nixes. Josie instructed Lou to find them, but to provide no information. Josie wanted to talk with them first. Otto had also called Mitchell Cowan, the county coroner, who was on his way.

Almost an hour after Josie left a message for Doug about the body, her phone rang again. She explained the details they had discovered and their suspicions.

"Where did you find him again?" Doug asked.

"He's lying on the couch, on his back. His arms clenched up with his fists around his face. Maybe in fear?"

"If he was afraid why wouldn't he get out, at least try and crawl to safety?"

"That's just what we thought. We're assuming he was already dead when the house burned, but Cowan's on his way. We'll get the autopsy started unless we need to wait for the fire marshal."

"No, that's partly what took so long to call you back. I talked to him. He's in Odessa, covered up right now with all the wildfires in the area. It'll be at least tomorrow before he can get here. He asked if I would step in. You okay with that?"

"Absolutely," she said, grateful for the help. She knew very little about fire damage, and she'd never worked a fire investigation for a possible homicide. Those investigations were turned over to the state fire marshal. The local police typically had little involvement.

"When can you get here?"

She heard him cover the mouthpiece on his phone to talk with someone. He finally came back and said, "I'm on my way."

Josie received a call from Lou stating that she'd not been able to reach either of the Nixes by phone. Josie gave Lou the names of several additional people to call who might know their whereabouts, and asked Lou to text her a list of phone numbers and contacts that Josie would be needing.

Several minutes later Josie and Otto watched the white county hearse, a converted 1978 Dodge station wagon, wind its way down the road until finally pulling into the driveway. Mitchell Cowan got out of the driver's seat wearing brown dress pants and loafers with a plaid button-down shirt. He'd always reminded Josie of the sad-eyed donkey with the big belly from the kids' stories. Eeyore. Shaped like a bowling pin with a broad midsection and small head, Cowan was slow and methodical, and talked only when necessary to provide relevant information. Most people considered Cowan odd, but Josie had always liked him. He worked hard and he genuinely cared.

It took him several minutes to gather his medical bag and assorted other cases out of the back of the hearse. Josie and Otto stood behind him, filling him in on the basic information.

"We still haven't ID'd the body. Based on the patches of clothing I could still see and the cowboy boots, I assume this is a male, most likely the homeowner, Billy Nix. We've not touched the body, but I'm anxious to roll him over and see if he has identification in his pants pocket." Josie shuddered involuntarily at the thought. "I don't know if the fire burnt all the way through."

Cowan pulled two bags over his shoulder and handed a plastic briefcase to Josie. "Let's have a look then."

"Nobody's examined the house to make sure it's structurally safe," she said. "The fire burned through the roof. The fire chief should be here in the next fifteen minutes or so and he can check it out if you want to wait."

"Sounds prudent," Cowan said.

When they reached the opening in the house they stopped and scanned the inside of the living room as Josie described how she found the body. From where they stood, the body was hidden behind the back of the couch. "Since the body was on the couch, and not making an attempt to escape, time of death will be critical."

Cowan nodded. "Agreed."

"Can you tell if fire or asphyxiation was cause of death? Or, if he died before the fire?"

"That's a fairly simple matter. If the person was dead before the fire he was no longer breathing. He won't have drawn soot down into his lungs. I'll also do a simple blood test. If carbon monoxide was in his lungs we'll know he was breathing during the fire."

"Excellent," Josie said. "Can you get that to us today?"

"Shouldn't be a problem."

They heard a vehicle pull into the driveway and turned to find Doug Free driving his red pickup truck, which had the Artemis Fire Department logo painted on the door. Doug parked and got out of the truck, then surveyed the yard and the surrounding land for several minutes before joining them in front of the house.

He said hello to the group and asked if they had identified the body. Josie explained that they hadn't gotten that far in the investigation. "We're trying to locate the Nixes, but haven't had any luck yet."

Doug sighed. "The guys will be heartbroken. We were feeling good about only a few minor injuries. I sure didn't expect to find a fatality."

Doug gave an update on the status of the Harrison Ridge fire. "We're eighty-five percent contained. It's reached the Rio and doesn't have enough energy to cross. Fortunately, the forecast is clear for the next two days and we've got minimal wind today. I think we're out of the woods."

"You fellas did a heck of a job," said Otto.

Doug frowned and nodded. "I got a great crew. I just need more of them. Fortunately this didn't last for days on end. Those weeklong fires, or two-week fires? People forget these guys are volunteers. They have jobs to get to, paychecks to earn." He shrugged like he needed to get off his soapbox. "Anyway. Tell me what you have so far."

"We need to get Cowan inside to the body," Josie said. "Then we need to get the body transported for autopsy. We haven't gotten too far with the preliminary investigation because we're worried about the roof. Can you check it out?"

Doug retrieved a fifteen-foot stepladder from his truck and climbed up into the rafters in the living room to check for structural damage. While Doug worked, Josie called and spoke with Lou about tracking down the Nixes. Lou said she hadn't gotten anywhere because her phone was ringing off the hook with residents wanting to know about fire damage and road closures and when they would be allowed home. Josie thanked her and told her to refer people to the sheriff's department and to keep trying on the Nixes.

After Doug declared the structure safe, he gathered Cowan, Josie, and Otto on the concrete patio just outside the hole in the living room wall to talk about how they should approach the scene.

"Let's talk about how this investigation might differ from what you're accustomed to. With a death involved in what could possibly be arson?" Doug frowned.

"This'll end up at trial," Josie said.

Doug nodded several times and put a thumb in the air as if agreeing. "And, the insurance company, or companies"—he paused and looked at both officers as if stressing the point—"will be crawling all over us. As you know, a trial could be a year or two away. We need photographs, video, and detailed notes. The fire marshal really stressed that." He looked at Cowan. "You play the most crucial role right now. The body will tell us all kinds of things about the fire. When it happened, maybe even if something was used to start or accelerate it."

"Understood."

"The scene is well preserved," Josie said. "There's been no water damage, nothing to disturb the house, as far as we can tell. The only tracks we found were a set of tire tracks, on the other side of the road. With the road closures, no one should have been coming through here, though."

"Don't put too much weight on the tracks. There's always a few Peeping Toms after a fire passes. We're trying to do our job, and they want a first look at the disaster."

"What about evidence collection?" Josie asked.

He pointed a finger at her. "That's what we need to talk about. It's completely different at the scene of a fire. I don't want to insult your intelligence, but this is usually what the state fire marshal would take care of."

Josie waved his concern away and he continued.

"Here's my worry about you going in to take care of the body," Doug said, tilting his head toward Cowan. "We may have evidence around the body that's extremely fragile. Possibly unrecognizable."

Josie watched Cowan process the information.

"What do you suggest?" he said.

"I would like to limit foot traffic as much as possible."

Josie put a hand up to interrupt him. "My first priority is identification of the body and finding the Nixes. Can you and Otto take care of processing the scene in the living room so Cowan can get in there and hopefully find identification?"

Doug nodded. "What are you thinking?"

"For now, this is an unidentified body," she said. "Lou hasn't made contact with the Nixes. She would have let me know if they had returned her calls. I know they're good friends with Hank Wild, the owner of the Hell-Bent. I'd like to start there first. I'll talk to Hank about how to track them down."

"That makes sense," Otto said.

Doug faced Otto. "I'd like you and me to take the video camera and walk together. We'll start outside the house, then through the point of origin. We can make our way back through the dining room where the fire burned out. I want very minimal foot traffic on our first walk-through. Just observations. Then you can take it slower. Just be extremely careful when you reach for anything to pick it up and catalog it. It may look solid, and then disintegrate in your hands." He turned to Otto. "It's critical that you check for evidence before Cowan walks around the body. It's a different kind of investigation when everything you look at is charred gray and black and evaporates when you touch it."

SEVEN

The Hell-Bent Honky-Tonk drew well over a hundred people every Friday and Saturday night for live music, cold draft beer, and a packed dance floor. Located off Highway 67 in the midst of rolling ranch country, it drew people from all over far-west Texas. The owner, Hank Wild, had a knack for discovering talent and developing singers and bands into local celebrities. Over the past five years, two different local bands had been signed by Nashville labels, all because Hank had enough clout with the industry to get the scouts to make the long trip west.

It was hard not only to bring big-name acts to such a remote area, but also for the locals to travel several hours to see an out-of-town show: the band had better be worth the drive. The Hell-Bent was the solution. With its success, Hank became a local celebrity in his own right. Country singers in the area knew that if they wanted an audience, they had to develop a performance Hank would buy. If he didn't like your act, you might as well pack up and move elsewhere, because the Hell-Bent was where it was at.

No billboards advertised the dance hall; they weren't necessary. A metal sign hung between two massive poles at the entrance to the lane that read HELL-BENT HONKY-TONK, but an out-of-towner could easily mistake it for one of the surrounding ranches and drive on by. From the road, the building appeared to be a large hay barn, but a trip down the long drive revealed a gravel parking area large enough for several hundred people, with spillover parking in the desert beyond. At night, there was little doubt what the Hell-Bent was about: outdoor pole lighting and lanterns strung along the roofline lit up the building, and the bands and the rowdy crowd could be heard for miles.

At a little before noon Josie pulled into the parking lot and counted about fifteen cars, most likely people searching for solace among friends until information could be discovered about the status of their homes and their property. Josie knew they would be frustrated with her when she wasn't able to provide information. She grabbed her steno pad from the passenger seat and locked the jeep.

The barn was weathered gray and covered in handmade signs that local performers were invited to display to advertise their acts. The band signs had become more artistic, and more outrageous, as the years had progressed. Hank strategically moved the signs to keep the front-runners near the entrance. Josie noticed that Billy Nix's sign hung on the porch, just a few feet from the front door—a prime location. Billy's three-foot-wide sign was a carved replica of a rugged cowboy hat with the words "Outlaw Billy Nix" carved into the hat brim. Josie thought of how sad it would be if his life ended before he received the big break he'd worked so hard to achieve.

The barn's substantial wooden door opened onto a dance hall the size of a basketball court. After driving into the bright afternoon sun, Josie had to allow her eyes to adjust for a moment. The shiny wooden dance floor was empty and swept clean. A few overhead lights were turned on, but otherwise the space was barely lit. Hank served sandwiches and other greasy bar food, but it was secondary to the music. No one cared if the fries were cold as long as the bands were hot.

Opposite the front entrance, on the far side of the dance floor, was a raised stage where Josie and Dillon had last watched Billy Nix perform almost a year ago. She remembered having a conversation with

Dillon about how there was often a fine line between the great local bands and the stars who played on the radio. They had agreed that night that Billy and the Outlaws sounded as good as any band they'd ever heard at a larger venue.

Josie walked toward the bar, where half a dozen men sat on stools. Another ten or fifteen men and women sat at the tables. The TV on the wall was on, but the volume was down. Hank was talking to the men sitting at the bar and didn't notice her approach. When she reached the men, Sauly Magson, who was sitting on a stool at the end of the row, spotted her and called out, "Chief!"

Sauly was one of Josie's favorite locals. He was an old hippie burn-out who didn't have a mean bone in his body. He was dressed in ragged blue-jean shorts and a ripped T-shirt, and he wore nothing on his feet, allowing his leathered soles to serve as his shoes. The "No shoes, no shirt, no service" motto had never applied to Sauly, at least not in Artemis.

"Hey, Sauly. How you doing?" Josie patted Sauly on the back and felt the attention in the bar shift to her, the conversation die out to nothing. She knew people were desperate for information, so she backed up to see most everyone and raised her voice. "I'm not here to give an official report, but I know you all need answers. I just wish I had more to give you. The police haven't been given the authority to check homes yet. Unofficially, I can tell you the fire is close to contained. The bad news is, the firefighters haven't had the chance to check structures to make sure they're safe enough to allow people back in."

"How many homes were lost?" Hank asked.

"That number hasn't been confirmed yet."

"Let us check our own structures. We're not idiots," said a man Josie recognized as a local truck driver.

"Nobody said you were an idiot. But you and I both know, if we open up the roads, we'll have people who have no idea whether the roof is ready to cave in on them walking back into homes. I'm not willing to risk someone's life. Just try and be patient with us. I promise, our goal is to get everyone back into their homes as soon as possible. Keep listening to Marfa Public Radio. That's the best source of information right now."

Sauly asked, "You figure on getting in to check houses today still?"

Josie paused. She didn't want to commit to details, with the first responders facing such a huge task with no timeline yet established. "I honestly can't say, Sauly. I wish I could. Those firefighters worked through the night and they're exhausted. They just need time to do their job." Josie paused a moment and no one said anything so she turned and sat down next to Sauly.

"Rough night," he said.

Sauly lived on the other side of the mudflats and Josie was surprised when Otto had told her that Sauly had evacuated. She had figured him for a holdout. It had been a relief to hear he left.

"Where'd you stay last night?" she asked him.

"You really want to know?"

She laughed. "No, I guess not."

"'Cause I'll tell you."

She raised her hands, still smiling. "Nope. I don't really want to know." She had no doubt Sauly would tell her the truth. She assumed he'd trespassed, maybe slept in someone's barn or business for the night to stay close to town.

"Have you seen your house today?" she asked, knowing that the road he lived on was still closed.

Sauly grinned. "Yep."

"Did it make it through the fire?"

"Yep. Burned all around me. You see my plow job?"

Josie shook her head, having no idea what he meant.

"I been watching the fire since they first showed it on the news with the wind blowing our way. Night before last, I got my tractor out and I plowed up four acres of land, all around my house. Plowed up my garden and all my flowers. There wasn't nothing to burn next to my house. Wasn't a flame that touched me."

Josie nodded. "You're a smart man, Sauly. More people ought to think that way, but everybody figures the gamble's worth it. I'm the same as everybody else."

Josie waved at Hank, who was standing at the other end of the bar, pouring someone a draft beer. He put a finger in the air and grabbed his ringing cell phone by the cash register and answered it.

Josie faced Sauly again. "You heard anything about Billy or Brenda Nix? Where they might be?"

He screwed his face up in thought. "Can't say I have. You might ask John Lummin, sitting over there." Sauly pointed to a man with a smooth shave and a beer belly, laughing at the woman sitting across from him at one of the tables. "He and Billy are buddies."

Hank walked quickly down the bar. "Sorry, Josie. What can I get you?"

"You mind if we talk in your office for just a minute?" she asked.

He paused, his face instantly tense, the universal look of dread that people got when the police unexpectedly asked for a conversation.

"You bet. Come on back."

A waitress was wiping up tables and Hank waved a hand at her and motioned toward his office. She looked up and nodded.

Josie patted Sauly on the back and told him to stay safe.

Hank walked down to the end of the bar and led Josie back to where his office was located. He pulled a key out of his front pocket, unlocked the door, and flipped on the light switch. The office was decorated in classic cowboy style, with ropes and spurs and rodeo posters hanging on the wood-paneled walls. Hank's rolltop desk was a mess of papers that he didn't glance at. He motioned toward a small table and a pair of chairs next to the desk and they sat down.

Josie had known Hank for many years, but she still didn't have a good sense of the person he was outside of the Hell-Bent. He wasn't married and appeared to be devoted to his business and his customers, a nice guy who cared about the people and the town that he catered to. He was in his mid to late fifties, with thinning hair and a slight paunch that hung over his large cowboy belt buckle. Rumor had it that Hank had a fling with each new waitress he hired, but

Josie doubted there was much truth to the stories. Rumors were all part of the high-profile job of running a honky-tonk.

"What can I do for you?"

"I have some questions I'd like to ask you, but I'd like to keep our conversation confidential. Is that okay with you?"

"Sure."

"Have you talked to Billy or Brenda since the evacuation?"

He thought for a moment. "They stopped by on their way out of town yesterday."

"Here?"

"Yeah, sure."

"What time did they come by?"

His eyebrows drew together and he pursed his lips as if thinking. "Jeez, I don't know. Maybe six o'clock? It's hard to say. It was such a madhouse in here yesterday. People used it like an evacuation center. I had a few people bring sleeping bags and an air mattress and they slept on the dance floor last night."

"Can you think back and try and give me your best estimate on the time? It's important."

"What's this about?" he said.

"Let's just think through the timing first."

He looked worried now, obviously caught off guard by her response.

"Okay." Hank sat forward and placed his forearms on the table, crossed his hands in front of him, and concentrated his stare on the table. "Well. They came in to get Billy's guitar. Both of them came in together. We were serving food. It was in the middle of the dinner hour, but we'd been serving meals all day. People ordered just to sit down at the tables and talk to their neighbors and families. Trying to figure out where to stay through the evacuation. I had people crying, others calling the bar, trying to find out where people were."

Josie listened quietly, allowing him to process everything.

"I was behind the bar." He looked up at Josie, his eyes lost in thought for some time. Finally he shook his head slowly and said, "I just can't say. I wasn't paying any attention to the time. I talked to so many people, trying to connect family and friends. And, honestly, trying to keep up with orders. I called in all staff members who could make it." His expression changed and he pointed a finger at Josie. "I'll tell you who might know. Angela, one of our bartenders, had to get the keys from me to let Billy into the dressing room."

"Is she here?"

"No, she worked about a fourteen-hour shift yesterday. She's off today."

"Doesn't she live in the little brown adobe, along FM-170?"

"That's it."

"Do you know if Billy and Brenda stayed long?"

"I don't think so. Seems like after Angela let Billy in, he came walking out not long after with his guitar. I think Brenda was sitting down at one of the tables talking to somebody. I don't remember who though."

"I was at their house this morning. I didn't see any cars, just a pickup truck. Any guess where they might have spent the night?"

He gave her an apologetic look. "I'm sorry, Josie, I just don't know. Hopefully Angela can give you better information."

"We've tried to reach them via their cell phones, but they haven't returned our calls. Any ideas on how we could track them down?"

"I'd check with one of the band members. Maybe they'll know where they're staying."

———

Josie followed Hank back to the bar and saw that John Lummin was no longer in his seat. She asked Sauly about him and learned that John had just left. Josie said a quick thanks to Hank and left to try and catch up with John. She waved his truck down as he was backing out of his parking spot.

He rolled down his window. "What can I do for you?"

"I'm trying to track down Billy Nix. Sauly said he's a friend of yours."

"Is this about the fire?" he asked. "They didn't lose their house, did they?"

"I'm just here to track the Nixes down so that I can speak with them. Any idea where Billy was headed when he left town yesterday?"

"Yes, ma'am. I talked to him yesterday in the bar." John had a slow Southern drawl and a smooth-shaven face that reminded her of a young George Strait. "He and Brenda were going up north to Austin to see about booking some weekends. Brenda said she wanted to make use of the time. She told Billy, no sense laying around a hotel room for days when they could be booking dates." He lifted an eyebrow at Josie.

"You don't think Billy wanted to go?"

"I know he didn't. Billy was worried about the house. He was worried about their friends, about people losing their homes. Brenda don't think that way though. It's all about the contract."

"What do you mean?"

"I mean, getting Billy to Nashville. Signing with Gennett."

"Signing him to a record label."

"Yes, ma'am. Brenda used to live in Nashville. She thinks she's got big connections. She forgets it's Billy's talent that'll get that record contract."

"Have you talked to them since they left?"

"No ma'am. I got their cell phone numbers if you need them."

"We've already tried and left messages."

He frowned. "That's not like either one of them. They keep those cell phones on all the time. Don't want to miss a gig." He said the last statement in a falsetto, as if imitating Brenda.

Josie ignored the sarcasm. "Can you tell me what time they left the bar yesterday?"

He rested his hands on the steering wheel and looked out the front window for a moment. He finally looked back at her, shaking his head. "I don't remember seeing them leave. There was so much commotion I didn't pay any attention."

"I appreciate your time."

"I'll let you know if I hear from him."

Josie called Otto and told him about her conversations with Hank and John. He and the fire chief had just finished combing the living room for evidence. "Nothing of interest. Cowan's just beginning his initial examination. The only thing he's commented on is the position of the victim's arms and hands, all curled up. We thought it looked like he was trying to defend himself. Cowan called it the boxer's pose. He says when a body dies with intense heat present, the hand and arm muscles draw up. Makes them look like a boxer in the fighting position. Because of that, Cowan thinks the victim died either in the fire, or was killed just before the fire was started. If the body was experiencing rigor mortis it most likely wouldn't have curled up like that."

"Good. That narrows it a little more. I'll drive by Angela's place to see if we can get a specific time the Nixes stopped at the Hell-Bent."

"Call me back in an hour. I should have more from Cowan."

———•———

Otto stood just inside the living room with a clipboard and pencil, making a detailed diagram of the house, the furniture, the dimensions of the room, and the location of the body. Cowan stood in front of the body, dictating his observations into a microrecorder. He wore a white mask that made it difficult for Otto to hear what he was saying. Otto was anxious for him to check the victim's backside in hopes a wallet was still intact since the couch wasn't completely torched.

Cowan said, "Otto. Interesting find here. Come take a look."

Otto was intentionally standing behind the couch so that he could construct the diagram without having to view the body. As a police officer, he felt that his weak stomach was an embarrassment, but it was something he had little control over. Earlier, he had looked at the grotesque mask of death that was on the victim's face and had to turn away until his stomach settled.

Otto stepped carefully over the ash, still leery about walking on the burned floor. He was cautious by nature, and he was certain that his careful ways had maintained his safety through four decades of police work.

Otto stood next to Cowan and peered down at the blackened arm that he had lifted a few inches off the couch.

"Recognize this?" Cowan asked.

"An arm?"

Cowan turned his head to glance back at Otto and raised his eyebrows. "A bit more specific than that?"

Otto clenched his jaws. Cowan had the annoying habit of asking questions of the police officers he worked with instead of simply explaining what he was working on. Otto found it insulting. It made him feel like a student walking through rounds with a physician, being quizzed on his investigatory acumen.

"Why don't you just tell me what you've found?" Otto said, barely concealing his irritation.

"Come closer," Cowan said. He leaned out of Otto's way so that he could get a better look. "His wrist?"

"Hmmm. I see the watch now. Let's get pictures, and I'll note it on the diagram. It's located on his left wrist, the face of the watch on his outer wrist. Let's get that off him and see about the time."

Cowan didn't respond. Otto assumed Cowan was annoyed that he hadn't praised his discovery.

After Otto noted the location of the watch on the diagram of the body, Cowan handed Otto the watch, and he took it outside in the sun. The glass was black with soot and had been shattered from the heat of the fire, but Otto was hoping the face would still be intact. Cowan followed him outside and handed Otto a tiny screwdriver, which he used to pry the blackened pieces of glass away. The hands of the watch were melted into the white face at 7:38. Otto pulled his cell phone out of his shirt pocket.

Josie answered immediately.

"The victim was wearing a watch. The hands melted onto the face at seven thirty-eight."

"Any identification?"

"Not yet. Haven't gotten that far."

"I'll call Doug and tell him we need to speak with the firefighters who worked closest to this area immediately. If we know when the fire spread through this general location, we'll know whether the two fires are connected. I'd love to have this timeline pieced together when we speak to the Nixes."

"You sound optimistic it's not Billy Nix lying on this couch."

"Hank confirmed that Billy at least left with Brenda. I suppose he could have picked up his guitar and returned home while she drove to Austin. That seems unlikely."

"Maybe that's why the truck was parked at the house," Otto said. "Maybe Billy went back home. Couldn't bear to leave."

"Or, Brenda dropped him off and set the house on fire," she said. "The timing works. They made a public appearance at about six and she says they're headed to Austin so Brenda can establish an alibi. Then she drops him off, maybe knocks him out, sets the house on fire to make it look like it was all part of the wildfire burning through Artemis. She assumed the fire would burn through the area after she left."

"But, why? She managed his career. If he's dead, she's out of a job," he said.

"Maybe Angela can help us get a better handle on their relationship. I'm on my way."

"Good. I'll keep you posted on the timeline."

Otto put his phone away and Cowan called for him again. The inside of Otto's nose burned from the sharp smell. He'd been in the house for several hours and could feel his patience beginning to wane. He had no doubt that Cowan wanted an assistant, but he had his own job to do. He'd not even begun to fingerprint and sift through the bedrooms and hallway.

"Help me take measurements," Cowan said. "I'll do it again on a flat table at the morgue to give you more precise numbers, but this will be close."

Otto took the end of the measuring tape and held it at the top of the body's head while Cowan stretched the tape to its feet.

"I'd put him between five foot ten inches and six feet tall."

Otto jotted down the numbers on his diagram of the body.

"Let's take a look at his teeth. We won't get an exact match, but we can at least get an age range."

Otto turned his head as Cowan placed a metal tool inside the blackened skeletal remains of the jaw. As Cowan began to discuss the number of teeth, Otto saw a navy-blue pickup pull into the driveway. He both hoped and worried that the Nixes had just driven around the barricade and arrived home. He left Cowan, glad at least for the excuse to leave the body, and stepped outside through the hole in the living room wall.

A man in his midtwenties got out of the pickup truck carrying a clipboard. Otto noted the blue strobe light on the dashboard of the truck and realized he was most likely a volunteer fireman.

"What can I do for you?" Otto asked.

"I'm Derek Lanman. Doug called and told me to bring you the spotter records for yesterday."

Otto nodded, finally recognizing him. "You work over at the body shop?"

He smiled. "That's me. I do the custom paint jobs. My specialty's old Fords."

"I'll keep that in mind," Otto said. "I appreciate you coming over so quickly."

Derek had the baby face and pale skin of one who had been pampered as a child, although Otto doubted that was true. His dad owned the business, Bodies by Carl, and Otto knew that Carl was a hardnose with high expectations of his staff, including his son.

Derek tilted his head toward the house. "What's going on?" He pointed his thumb over his shoulder in the direction of the hearse parked behind them. "Somebody die in the fire?"

"We're not making any statements at this time. We'll get information out to people as soon as we can. Meanwhile, until we have facts and have spoken with family members, I need you to keep what you've seen here confidential."

Derek stared into the living room, obviously trying to see what Cowan was doing behind the couch.

"You'll keep this confidential?" Otto repeated.

Derek turned his head back toward Otto, an embarrassed grin on his face. "Sorry. I've never seen the hearse at a fire. Just kind of weird to see."

"The confidentiality?" Otto was beginning to wonder if Doug had made a mistake telling Derek to come to the scene.

The kid's expression turned earnest. "Yeah, sure. I won't say a word."

Otto pointed toward the road and they walked away from the house and the temptations of Cowan's work.

"What can you tell me about the fire that burned through here?" Otto opened his steno pad and propped it on top of his forearm to take notes.

"We keep spotter logs. I'm one of the newest volunteers. I haven't had much experience in the field, so Doug had me logging reports that were called in by the spotters. I keep the information for Doug. He uses it to predict the direction and speed of the fire."

Otto looked at the clipboard. "Is that the log?"

"Yeah. I don't have much for this area though. We had a crazy weather pattern blowing westward that finally connected with the Harrison Ridge fire. We were pretty confident the road would act as a firebreak to keep that fire from moving any further west. That's why I was surprised when Doug said the Nixes' house burnt. I didn't think the fire jumped the road over here."

"Can you look on your list and tell what time the fire reached Prentice Canyon Road?"

Talking quietly to himself, Derek studied the log, running his finger up and down the pages. "A spotter called in up north of here. He said the fire reached their ranch at nine ten. They called in to say the fire hadn't crossed the road. That means, I'd guess it crossed here around nine thirty."

"Can you explain what would have made the fire cross the road here when it didn't elsewhere?"

"Not really," he said slowly. "I'm not the expert, but I don't really get why the house is so burnt up. Don't make much sense."

"Could the fire have crossed here at around seven forty-five yesterday instead of nine thirty?"

He squinted his eyes like he just couldn't make the figures work. "There's just no way. Prentice Canyon runs north-south. So if the fire crossed that road at nine ten and then traveled south, there's no way this place could have burned at seven forty-five. The fire wasn't near this far south yet."

"Maybe your spotter gave you the wrong time. Or you logged it incorrectly in the book."

Derek narrowed his eyes and turned the corner of his mouth up in an irritated smile, obviously offended at Otto's comment.

"I'm just thinking that it's dark out. It's crazy and stressful," Otto said. "I'm sure mistakes happen."

Derek scanned down the page again and finally looked up, smiling as if he'd just been vindicated. He tapped his forefinger on the clipboard hard. "Right here. Skip Altman called from the Morris ranch and said they had the fire under control using their spray rig and stock pond. That place is just south of here. His call was at nine forty. No way it would take an hour to get from the Nixes' house to the Morrises' ranch."

"Okay." Otto nodded, pleased with the information. "I'll need to take your records and submit them as evidence."

Derek took a step back as if ready to protect his information. "Doug never said nothing about any of that."

"Why don't you give him a call? He can confirm we need the records."

Derek called Doug. After a quick conversation, Derek hung up and reluctantly relinquished his logbook to Otto. Derek took one more long look at the house and finally got into his truck and drove away.

Otto went back into the house and discussed the time frame with Cowan.

"I'm ready to release the scene to you," Cowan said. "I'll rule this a homicide with a preliminary time of death of seven thirty-eight p.m. I'll get back and start on the autopsy."

The recital ended, and after a miserable two hours of sitting in a hardback chair listening to four people screech away at violins and cellos and who knew what else, Dell could finally get up to stretch his knees and back. He stood in the back of the room as Mary Lou hugged and kissed each of the musicians, gushing over their brilliant performance. Dell was thinking about needing a new water source for his cows when she finally made her way back to him.

She patted his arm and he noticed the smile lines around her eyes. He wasn't sure how to handle a perpetually happy person. It didn't feel natural to walk around smiling all the time, but he felt compelled to at least try since she seemed so inclined.

"I have a surprise for you," she said, smiling. She gestured toward the door and they walked outside into the late-afternoon heat. "I know this wasn't your idea of a fun afternoon, so I'm going to make it up to you."

He opened the truck's passenger door for her and she slid across the seat, toward the middle. He walked around to the driver's side, not entirely sure he wanted her to make anything up to him at this point in the day. He felt guilty, but he had chores to do.

"I have chicken salad already prepared in the refrigerator, as well as fruit salad and chocolate cake made from scratch. I thought we'd have a nice light lunch since it's so hot out."

"That sounds nice." He started the truck. It had always been Dell's position that meat and salad did not go together in the same dish.

He rarely ate bread with his meat, preferring to allow the taste of the meat to dominate. The idea of mixing chicken into a salad did not appeal to him in the least.

"I thought we'd stop by my house and pick it up, then take it out to your place. Maybe you could show me around the ranch after lunch."

He nodded, and looked over at the smiling woman sitting next to him. She was beautiful and kind, and for some odd reason she wanted to spend time with him. But he was rapidly losing control of his life.

"You know, it would be nice to invite Father Paul out to have lunch with us. He's young and new to town. He doesn't get out much."

He gripped the steering wheel tighter.

"We'll have him out to dinner another night," she said. "Let's just enjoy the day at your ranch together."

EIGHT

Angela Stamos had been bartending at the Hell-Bent for as long as Josie could remember. Her heavy-lidded eyes and permanent smirk said she'd seen it all. Angela was in her early fifties, with auburn hair cut in a stylish pixie that framed her round face. She wore round wire-rim glasses with purple-shaded lenses. Angela was a striking woman with a reputation that kept the men at bay. For the most part, they treated her with a degree of respect that some of the other, younger women at the Hell-Bent didn't get. Josie wondered if bartending for so many years had tarnished her opinion of men.

Last Josie had heard, Angela was single, but when Josie parked her car in front of the bartender's home she saw a man standing on the side deck flipping hamburgers on a small charcoal grill. He turned slightly and waved, giving Josie a long stare, but he stayed where he was.

The house was a small brown adobe with deep-set window wells and a front porch over which the roof extended by eight feet along the front of the house. Two wooden rocking chairs sat on the front porch with a small table in between them. The table held an ashtray filled with cigarettes and two empty martini glasses. A small yard was landscaped with native plants like prickly pear, agave, and yucca. It was a comfortable, attractive home and it fit Josie's image of Angela.

Angela opened the front door and stepped outside before Josie reached the porch. Her face was pinched with worry, not the expression of the laid-back bartender Josie was accustomed to.

"Hi, Angela. Sorry to stop by without calling ahead."

Angela nodded. "No problem. Something wrong?"

"We're working on an investigation and I need to ask you some questions."

"Is this about Buddy?"

Josie recognized the name and remembered he was her brother, a perpetual troublemaker. "No. This doesn't have anything to do with your family. I have some questions about work last night."

She sighed, visibly relieved, and motioned for Josie to sit in one of the rocking chairs. Angela wore jean shorts that didn't cover much more than her underwear, a tight T-shirt and cowboy boots, and a necklace made of rattles from a rattlesnake that hung down her chest.

"Sorry. I haven't heard from the peckerhead since the evacuation yesterday. He was supposed to go to my parents' house in Houston, but he never showed up." She seemed to notice Josie's concerned look and waved a hand in the air. "No worry. Buddy's a jackass. He doesn't follow through with anything. He worries my parents sick." She sat down in the chair, picked a pack of cigarettes off the table, and lit one. She held the pack toward Josie.

"No, thanks. We're trying to put together a timeline of events that took place yesterday evening, and I hope you can help me with some details."

"This have to do with the fire?"

"We're not sure yet. Why don't you start by taking me through your day yesterday? What time you came on shift, went to lunch, and so on."

Angela squinted at Josie through her purple glasses. "Am I in some kind of trouble here?"

"I assure you, you're not in any trouble at all. You just happened to be working during a time frame we're trying to piece together."

She smirked. "Story of my life. I always just happen to be somewhere." She settled back in her rocker and took a long drag of the cigarette. "Okay, so I went to work at noon. Hank called begging for help. He was bartending so I ended up waiting tables and helping in the kitchen."

"What time did you get a break?"

"I sat down about four to have a sandwich. We had such a crowd I skipped lunch. I ate a hamburger and was back up waiting tables again by four thirty."

"Could you make a list of people you saw come through the bar?"

She raised her eyebrows. "Seriously?"

"It would be very helpful."

"I guess so. I could try."

"Did you see Brenda and Billy Nix that night?"

"Yeah. They came in for Billy's guitar. I had to unlock the dressing room for them."

"Can you tell me what time that was?"

She scowled and thought for a moment. "I guess about five thirty."

"Can you think back, give me a more exact time?"

Angela looked at Josie closely, obviously realizing that Josie had already zeroed in on specific customers. "Actually, I know it was five thirty because I remember walking into the dressing room and looking at the clock on the wall. I remember thinking that I'd be lucky to make it home by midnight. Which I didn't."

The man who had been grilling when Josie pulled up opened the front door and poked his head out. "Everything okay?"

Angela leaned forward in her chair so that she could see him. "It's fine. Give me a minute and I'll be in." The door shut and she faced Josie again, her expression troubled.

"Did both Billy and Brenda go back to the dressing room with you?" Josie asked.

"No, just Billy. I saw Brenda, but I don't know where she went when Billy and I went back."

"What did you and Billy talk about?"

Angela paused and squinted at Josie. "Why are you asking about Billy? Is he in some kind of trouble?"

"I'm sorry. I can't tell you at this point. I'm just pulling together information."

Angela's expression had grown guarded.

"What did you talk about?"

"We just talked about the fire. Billy wanted to stay home. Brenda was set on leaving. After he got his guitar we walked back out onto the dance floor and he was looking for Brenda. It was a madhouse in there. I think he ended up talking to John Lummin for a while. You might talk to him."

"You said Brenda was set on leaving. What do you mean by that? Didn't they both want to leave because of the evacuation?"

"She wanted to go to Austin, talk to some of the big-time bar owners. I felt sorry for him."

"Why do you say that?"

"She's just—" Angela paused and curled her lip up. She flipped ashes from her cigarette into the ashtray as if disgusted by the thought of the woman. "I don't know. I don't like her. I think she treats him like crap. He's the one with the talent and the heart for music, but she talks to him like he's nothing. Tells him what to do. I sure as hell wouldn't put up with it."

"Give me an example of how she tells him what to do."

Angela leaned her head back and drew on her cigarette as she searched her memory. Josie glanced out across the front yard and noticed the heat waves rippling across the sand under the scorching sun. She wiped the sweat off her forehead with the back of her hand and wished they could have had the conversation inside the air-conditioned house. Josie had heard that Angela grew marijuana for personal use and she figured that had something to do with the location of their conversation.

Angela finally turned to Josie and nodded her head as if she'd thought of a good one.

"Okay. Hank always has me deliver the band a round of drinks, on him, before they go onstage. One night I went back to the dressing room, and the door was partway open. I stood outside with the tray and a couple whiskeys for Billy. I was about to holler for him when I heard her literally yelling at him for wearing the wrong shirt and jeans. She was like, 'I laid out your clothes on the bed. You have an image, Billy, and this isn't it. This is soft. You look sloppy and soft.'" Angela laughed, her eyes wide at the memory. "I kicked the door with my foot and walked on in so she knew I'd heard what she'd said. She's such a witch."

"Did she say anything to you?"

"She didn't care. She just glared until I left. Didn't thank me for the drinks, either."

"Do you think they both left town together, after Billy got his guitar?"

She looked surprised at the question. "I don't know why they wouldn't have. That's why they stopped at the bar. Billy wanted his guitar before they left town."

"Do you think Billy could have gone back home, and Brenda left without him?"

Angela exhaled heavily, as if she was irritated by the question. "He's her meal ticket. She wouldn't go to Austin without him."

"What do you mean?"

"I mean she treats him like he's six. Tells him what to do. She'd be afraid he'd screw something up without her telling him every move to make."

"If she treats him so bad, why does he stay?" Josie asked.

She laughed. "Everybody at the Hell-Bent wonders the exact same thing."

"Do you have any idea who Billy's closest friends are? Maybe the band members?"

"Without a doubt, Slim Jim, his drummer, is his best friend. They grew up together in Alpine."

"Jim Saxon?"

She stubbed her cigarette out and stood. "Everybody knows Slim Jim. You want the dirt on Brenda Nix, go see Slim. He'll give you an earful."

———·—·———

Jim Saxon lived on the western edge of the county, just a mile north of the Rio Grande, in a house trailer sided with weathered gray boards and covered by an open shelter house that shielded the trailer from the brutal desert sun. The forecast for the day was 106 degrees down by the river, and she had no doubt it had been reached.

Most everyone in Artemis knew Slim Jim, either by reputation as a whiskey-belting, hard-living son of a bitch, or as a man thoroughly dedicated to improving life along the river. The trailer sat fifty feet back from a creek that fed into the Rio. Between his trailer and the creek was a garden that rivaled anything Josie had seen growing in the much milder Indiana summers of her youth. With a greenhouse off to the side of the garden that had been pieced together with cast-off windows, doors, and wood, much of it from the county dump, Jim made plants grow that others said couldn't be grown in West Texas. The garden was a thing of beauty, and the bounty fed anyone needing the extra rations.

Josie parked her jeep in front of the trailer and knocked on the front door. When no one answered she walked around the garden and greenhouse. Finding no one home, she dialed Angela's cell phone and asked if she had any idea where Jim might be.

Angela was quiet for a moment and then cursed. "I wasn't thinking. I know where he is. The kids are getting ready for the state-fair competition. He's at the high school. They have that maniac teaching high school kids how to play drums."

Josie left Jim's house and drove back toward town. On her way she called Otto for an update.

"Did Cowan find any identification?"

"No. The clothing on his backside where he was lying on the couch is somewhat intact, but there wasn't a wallet or any ID on him."

"Age of the body?"

"Cowan said he's older than twenty-five, and younger than fifty, based on what he could tell by his teeth. Billy's in his forties, so it doesn't help us much."

"How about height?"

"Cowan says five foot ten to six foot."

"Billy's at least six foot, don't you think?" she asked.

"I know he's taller than I am, and I'm five foot ten. Again, not much help. What about the timeline?"

"Angela confirmed what Hank said. She said they came in at five thirty and didn't stay long. She also described Brenda as a 'witch.' Her word, not mine. Brenda tells Billy how it is, and he listens. No one can figure out why he puts up with it."

"Unless he actually needs her."

"For what?"

"Maybe he loves her. Maybe he likes someone telling him what to do. She's his mother figure or some such Freudian thing. Maybe she has connections and he doesn't."

Josie acknowledged the point. "Love's a strange thing."

"What do you have for me?" he asked.

"It's nearly four o'clock and still no return call from the Nixes," she said. "Wouldn't you think with a fire burning through town they'd keep their phones on and return calls?"

"I think we just keep working the time frame until we get a hit on the body. I'll swing by the Morris ranch and see if the ranch hand can provide any more details on the timing for the fire. Meanwhile, Cowan ruled this a homicide and the body's in transport."

"Good. Can you start paperwork for the search warrant for the Nixes' house? We need to make it official."

"Will do."

"I'm on my way to talk to Jim Saxon, Billy's drummer. If the Nixes were headed to book performances, surely at least one of the band members would know something about their whereabouts. And Saxon is supposed to be his closest friend."

Josie was approaching the lone stoplight in Artemis when her phone buzzed.

"I got another call. See you in the morning?"

"See you then."

She hung up with Otto and immediately recognized the other number.

"This is Chief Gray."

"Hi, this is Brenda Nix, returning your call."

———————

Billy Nix walked into the Baker's Dozen, a popular biker bar in Austin that was best known for the amount of whiskey consumed every Friday and Saturday night, and the hard-core country bands that fired up the raucous crowds. Billy had played there once after another act had canceled last minute. Billy thought the crowd had loved the band and he had expected a call back, but it had been six months since they'd played, and not a word.

He stopped inside the door to let his eyes adjust from the bright late-afternoon sun. Billy took some time to scan the room. He was tall with wide shoulders and a narrow waist: in his boots and Stetson he gave the impression he could knock a guy out with a one-fisted punch, but on the inside he was mush. He took a long breath and exhaled, counting to ten, trying to still his nerves, trying to feel like he belonged there, not as a bar patron, but as a musician, as a head-liner. He realized he'd been standing by the door too long and forced himself to take the first step. He repeated the phrase he'd been repeating for the past five years. The phrase Brenda had taught him. "Fake it."

Billy walked up to the bar and a young woman wearing a white halter top and miniskirt turned from the cash register and flashed him a smile. "What'll it be, handsome?" Her teeth glowed as white as her top against taut skin tanned almost as dark as her brown eyes.

"Give me a double Glenfiddich, neat."

"You got it."

She reached up high on the shelf behind her, high enough to pull the halter top up her back and allow Billy a look at the tattooed butterfly wings that spread across the small of her back, just above her miniskirt.

She poured the Scotch and slid the tumbler to him, then walked down the bar to another customer. Billy sipped and turned to look around the bar. When they'd played at the Baker's Dozen, he'd arrived in Austin with his band at 6:00. They'd eaten a quick sandwich in the car, then set up and walked on stage at 8:00. He'd not had time to scout out the place and get a feel for the customers, something he and Brenda usually did together.

It was a nice setup. A square bar was located about twenty feet inside the door, but centered so that people could get drinks from all sides. Traffic flowed easily from all sides of the room. Beyond the bar was a large open dance floor with twenty tables flanking either side, and a space directly in front of the stage with another ten tables for the customers that liked it loud. Those were the hardcore fans Billy had played to. Brenda had told him, "That's where your fan base is made."

It was late afternoon, with only a handful of people sitting at the bar, but he could imagine by eight o'clock, even on a weeknight, the bar would be packed. Whiskey bottles were packed against both side walls, stacked in rows all the way up to the ceiling—empties that now served as wall art. He liked the look.

The waitress came back. "Seems like I'd know a face like yours if you'd been in here before," she said, flashing that bleached white smile.

Billy averted his eyes and grinned. Nothing better than a big rough guy brought to his knees by a pretty young girl. Brenda had taught him that too.

"I played here a few months ago. Billy and the Outlaws."

"And I just bet you're Billy."

"That I am."

"You coming back?"

"I hope so. Thought I'd check in with the manager, see if he had some openings this summer."

"You a local?" she asked, leaning forward now, her chest propped up on the bar.

"I'm from Artemis." He saw the blank look on her face. "West Texas. About seven hours from Austin."

"Ohhh. You came a long way." She smiled and winked, turning from him, then saying over her shoulder, "Let me see what I can do for you."

A few minutes later the woman came back. "Marla's in the office. She said to go on back." The bartender turned and pointed to the end of the bar.

Billy put a twenty-dollar bill in the tip jar. "Thanks, darlin'. I appreciate your help."

"You come back and sing me a love song? We'll call it even."

———————

Billy took another deep breath, counted to three, and entered the open door. He expected bar furniture and drinking paraphernalia that matched the bar decor, but the space looked more like an office at a car dealership: brightly lit, messy metal desk, a few posters on the walls held up with thumbtacks and some chipped metal filing cabinets. There was one chair in the corner with a case of Bud Light perched on the seat and the desk chair was filled by a woman who he figured had to be Marla.

Marla was short and heavy; she looked uncomfortable sitting behind the desk, her arms reaching up to the keyboard on the desk. She scowled at Billy and said nothing as he entered the room.

Billy leaned across the desk and offered her a hand. She gave him a dry, small hand to shake and then wiped it down her pants, apparently wiping away his sweat, or maybe his germs. He tried not to allow his misery to show on his face. He had not wanted to come. Brenda had insisted. He was no good at small talk, no good at begging for work. Brenda was the manager, as far as he was concerned, and she was the one capable of landing work. Not him.

"Billy Nix, ma'am. I appreciate you seeing me."

"Okay. I've seen you. Is that it?" She stared at him without a trace of humor.

"Actually, I was hoping to follow up on a performance my band gave a few months back."

She raised her arm and pointed up and behind her head. Hanging on the wall was a small metal sign that read DON'T CALL US. WE'LL CALL YOU. IF WE WANT TO.

Billy's face reddened and he smiled and nodded, trying to engage the woman on some level. "Sorry about that. I thought maybe there was a manager that took care of bookings. Maybe someone I could talk to about playing some dates this summer or fall."

The woman slumped her shoulders and her expression softened. She looked more tired than angry. "Look, Billy. I remember you. You guys were fine. You did a good job. But I got fifty other bands that are fine and do a good job. And each one wants special consideration. It wears me out. Okay?"

He nodded.

She pointed again to the sign behind her head. Billy left the bar wishing he could retrieve the twenty he'd wasted in the tip jar.

Josie listened to Brenda's story about traveling to Austin with Billy, and why the couple hadn't returned the phone calls. Josie didn't believe a word of it.

"So, you're saying a wildfire is devouring our town, putting your home and all your possessions in danger, and you and Billy both turned your phones off because you needed to focus on your work?"

There was a pause on the line. "Well, yes, that's exactly what I'm saying. I don't mean to be rude, but I don't think I owe you or anyone else an explanation for when I turn my cell phone off or on."

"Your house was burned in the fire, Ms. Nix. We've been trying to notify you."

"I didn't think the fire was coming our way. I thought it was moving east." Brenda stumbled over her words, either shocked or playing the part. It was impossible to tell over the phone. "How bad is it?"

"It's too soon to tell. We're gathering information, talking to people. Is your husband there with you in Austin?"

"Of course he's with me. Where else would he be?"

Josie sighed. It was a relief to hear he was alive. "How soon can you be here?"

"Was the house destroyed?" Brenda's voice had grown louder.

"We don't have all that information yet. Too many homes were affected." Josie heard a door slam in the background and Brenda cover the phone to talk to someone for a moment.

"You want me to come home, but can't tell me if I have a home to come home to?" Her voice was quieter now, but angry.

Josie ignored the sarcasm. "You'll run into a roadblock outside of town. The area is too dangerous to allow residents back into their homes until we've had a chance to make sure they're safe. Let the deputy know you have a meeting with me, and he'll escort you to the police station. I'll give you as much information as I can there."

"This is outrageous! You tell me my house has been burned but won't give me any details. What a terrible thing to do to someone!"

"I'll see you tomorrow. Let's make it one o'clock at the police department. That should give you time to drive from Austin."

Josie hung up and called Otto with the news that both the Nixes had been located and would be in town the next afternoon. Josie decided to talk with Slim Jim, hoping to piece together a clearer picture of the couple before meeting them the next day.

NINE

The Arroyo County Junior/Senior High School was located on the outskirts of Artemis. Dry level desert spread for miles on either side of the school complex, which also housed the elementary school. A paved road provided access to the flat-roofed elementary school, and then wound around a dusty patch of land that served as a soccer field, and ended in the parking lot of the newer junior/senior high school. Some students spent close to four hours per day on a school bus. An education in this part of the country was something a kid worked for, and Josie respected the people who made the decision to locate their families in a place that traded the luxury of "things" for the luxury of peace and space. If she ever had kids of her own, which was beginning to feel more remote by the day, they would attend this school.

Driving with the windows down, she heard booming bass drums and the rapid-fire rhythm of snare drums a mile away from the school complex. With no vegetation to hinder the sound, the drums carried along the hot night air and reverberated against the school buildings along the access road.

The marching band stretched in ragged rows across the parking lot, instruments up but silent, the band director yelling, "One, two, three, four," through his megaphone as the kids moved like an amoeba down the hot pavement.

She parked her jeep alongside the parking lot and got out. With the evacuation order she was surprised to see a practice taking place, but for the kids in the county that were left, she figured the practice was a safe place to forget about the drama going on all around them.

Josie heard the drums but couldn't see them. She followed the sound to the other side of the high school building, where she found four kids standing with the drums strapped over their backs, and another kid playing the bass drum. They were standing in the shade of the building but sweat dripped down their faces as they pounded their mallets in rhythm. Slim Jim stood in front of them, eyes closed, beating a drumstick against the side of the building. He was yelling a rhythm as they played. "Rata tata rat tat. Rata tata tata rata tat tat." The kids noticed her round the corner, zeroed in on her police uniform, and lost their concentration, breaking the rhythm. Jim's eyes flew open.

He looked first at the kids, and then behind him to find the source of the interruption. He recognized Josie and tried to reel in his anger, waving his hands in the air for the kids to stop playing. Their expressions were guarded, assessing their instructor's possible trouble.

He faced the kids. "All right. Ten-minute water break. Be back here, instruments ready. Exactly ten minutes. Not eleven! *Ten!*" He watched them lift their drums up and over their sweaty heads and set them on the ground, already chatting, ecstatic at the few minutes of freedom, their instructor and his troubles forgotten. Josie smiled. Ten minutes was a lifetime at sixteen.

"Sorry to interrupt, Jim. I just need a few minutes."

"What'd I do?"

Jim was tall and skinny, wearing long mesh basketball shorts and a tattered T-shirt with the sleeves cut off.

"Why so paranoid?" she asked, smiling at his resignation.

"Look. They told me, I clean up the language or I'm out. On my ass." He said the last word quietly between clenched teeth. "You know what that's like for a guy like me? If I didn't like these knucklehead kids so much I'd tell the principal to ram a drumstick up her ying yang, and I'd go back to the bar where I belong."

"I'm not here to cause you grief."

"Ohhhh! Really?" He opened his mouth and eyes wide, his expression incredulous. "Don't they teach you in cop school that all you have to do is show up somewhere and you cause a guy grief?"

She grinned and held a hand up in the air to stop him. "If the principal gives you grief, you tell me and I'll talk to her. Agreed?"

"Yeah, whatever."

"What can you tell me about Billy and Brenda?"

"I got ten minutes, not ten hours."

"Give me the short version."

"He's a musician. She's a wannabe. She couldn't make it in Nashville on her own, so she's using Billy to get there."

"She's a musician too?"

"Hell no!" Jim blew air out slowly and then drew more in through his nose as if he were conducting a deep-breathing exercise. Josie assumed he was trying to control his temper. Finally, he said, "Okay. Here's Brenda's deal. She comes from a long line of Nashville royalty. But here's the kicker, she has no musical talent herself. Zip, zero, nada. Her daddy was a famous bluegrass fiddler. Ever heard of the Netham Sisters?"

Josie nodded.

"That's Brenda's sisters."

"No kidding?"

"Kid you not. Better than that? Her own sisters kicked her out of the band. Brenda left home to make a name for herself as a solo singer and couldn't do it."

"You think she's using Billy to make up for own failure in country music?"

"You said it. Billy, bless his dumbass self, is too stupid to believe it. And he's been told. Multiple times. By yours truly."

"I hear she's negotiating a record deal. She can't be all that bad, right? The band would benefit as well."

He laughed. "You give her way too much credit. She'd sell us out in a heartbeat. Billy's her concern. Not us. If it suits the record company that Billy's band comes with him, then we're gold. But if they want us gone?" He shrugged.

Josie saw the kids wandering back outside from the air-conditioned school, their ten minutes dwindling. Before she left she asked, "Can you imagine anyone wanting to cause trouble for either one of them?"

He looked taken aback at the question. Jim wasn't the type of person to be at a loss for words, but he wrinkled his forehead. "Why would you ask me that? Come to think of it, why are you asking me any of this?"

"Do they have any enemies? Somebody who would want to end Billy's career before it got started? Somebody who would want to frame Brenda to cause her grief?"

His eyebrows furrowed and his expression turned dark. "What's this about?"

"There's been some trouble. I can't get into it at this point. I'm sure you'll find out soon enough from Billy, but for now, I'm trying to understand who's connected to the Nixes."

The kids were quietly pulling their drum carriers back over their heads, obviously trying to catch the conversation. Jim motioned Josie away from them and Josie followed him into the parking lot. He turned to her, his expression earnest.

"Look. You know what it's like out here. Two-hour drive to the closest Walmart? This is a great big pond with a lot of little fishes trying to get noticed. Everybody wants their big break. And finally, our band's close. There's some jealousy out there. If we make it to Nashville, that means somebody else doesn't."

"Who specifically is jealous?"

He turned from her in frustration. "Come on, man. Don't go there."

"It's a fair question. I'm sure it's no big secret."

"The Calloway Boys. They talk smack. They're a Tex-Mex band with a hotshot guitar player and a singer who thinks he's God's gift to the world. Problem is, nobody outside of the locals is interested in their *alternative* country." Jim rolled his eyes and made a face to show he wasn't impressed, whatever "*alternative* country" meant to him.

"So there's some competition between the local bands?"

"I wouldn't call it competition. Here's what it is. They like to bash Billy and the Outlaws like we're commercial and they're some authentic piece of art." He rolled his eyes again and looked back at the kids. Josie noticed the band director crossing the parking lot toward them, probably making sure Jim wasn't in hot water with the police.

"Damn. I gotta go," he said.

Josie chatted with the band director to assure him that Jim wasn't in trouble and left the school. She had one more stop before going home for the night. Doug Free had left a message on her phone asking her to call or stop by before she went off duty.

Josie saw his truck parked in front of the fire department and pulled in behind it. She found him in the training room, sitting behind his desk with a fan blowing hot air directly on him. The police department wasn't fancy, but at least it had air-conditioning. Doug looked up from his paperwork and smiled when he saw her.

"How's it going?" she asked.

"I've sure had better weeks."

"You get any sleep yet?"

"A few hours. I'm about ready to check out for the night." He stood and gestured toward a folding chair in front of his desk and they both sat. "Otto called and filled me in on the conversation he had with my spotter, Derek Lanman. The timing's off."

"That's what we were afraid of."

"I met with Otto today and made a copy of the records he took as evidence," Doug said. "I combined that log with everything else I've got here. Assuming the victim's watch was correct, and he died at seven thirty-eight, that fire was set intentionally."

"Otto found another analog clock in the kitchen stopped at seven forty. I think we have our time of death."

Doug raised a finger. "Department of Public Safety's sending us a helicopter in the morning. We'll fly out at seven. We'll be doing a damage assessment, but first area we fly over is the Nixes' house. I want to see the burn patterns. You game?"

"Absolutely. I appreciate the offer."

"I'll see you at the Marfa airport at six thirty tomorrow morning."

———————

It was after seven o'clock before Josie arrived home. A year ago Dillon would have had supper waiting for her; he would have been putting the final touches on some dish and pouring himself a glass of the perfect wine to pair with the meal. He would have been doing all of the things that she knew nothing about. Without him, her dinner consisted of ramen soup and a bagel, or takeout from the Hot Tamale, or a frozen dinner zapped in the microwave.

She parked her jeep and walked inside, where she fed Chester and then microwaved a bag of popcorn. Even after two months she missed Dillon: sharing her day with him, talking through a quirk in a case she was working on, hearing about his day at the office. She thought about her conversation with Dell, but she was still surprised Dillon had not returned her call about the fire, and she wondered if he'd received it. She was certain he'd be concerned about the town—at least about his friends and former neighbors.

Sitting at the kitchen table, she stared at her phone for a while before mustering the courage to call. He answered on the third ring.

"How are you?" she asked.

"I'm doing okay, how about you?"

"It's been crazy. I thought you might want an update on the fire. I saw Arroyo County made the news on CNN, so I thought you might be worried."

"Yeah, I've been following it on the news. Sorry I didn't get back with you." His tone of voice was friendly, but detached.

"The fire came through the mudflats. That area got hit hard."

"How about Smokey and Vie?" he asked.

"They lost the house."

He sighed. "I'm sorry to hear that."

Josie talked a little about the Billy Nix case, but when Dillon wasn't responding she stopped and changed the subject. "Any plans yet on your business?" Her voice felt cheery and false and she wished she hadn't called.

"Not yet. I'm looking at options."

"Okay, well, I'll let you go. I just thought you might want an update."

"Josie, it's not that I don't care. I'm sure this seems callous to you, like I've given up on everyone."

"It's okay. You don't have to explain."

"Please, hear me out. I have nightmares about what happened. I still love you on some level, and I always will, but I can't maintain a relationship with you anymore. It's too hard right now."

She tried to focus on what he was saying, but the only words that stuck were *on some level*.

"Dillon, you know that what I want more than anything is for you to be happy and to get your life back again. If it's too hard to talk to me right now, then I will respect that. You focus on getting better, and someday down the road if you want to talk, you give me a call."

They ended the conversation and Josie stared at her phone. Was this just part of the healing process? she wondered. There was no rulebook. No one had said, This is how long a person should suffer after a major trauma. These are the steps you should take to help bring that person around: tough love, words of encouragement, silence. What was the right response? She had no idea. The counselor had wanted her to talk about her own feelings, but the experience had felt false, and she'd left feeling worse.

Josie walked back into the bedroom, where she took off her uniform and hung it in the closet. She needed out. She grabbed a pair of running shorts and a T-shirt from her dresser drawer, slipped them on along with a pair of flip-flops, and walked out the back door.

Josie and Chester walked behind the house and up the lane to Dell's. He was the person she went to for advice when the rest of the world made no sense. Josie's father had been killed in a line-of-duty accident when she was eight, and her mother had stopped being a parent at that point. After an unsuccessful stint at college, Josie had moved to Texas from Indiana, and she'd never looked back. She had virtually no contact with her family. Instead, she had Dell.

Chester loped up from behind and shoved his muzzle up into her hand as she walked, forcing her to pat his head. Josie stopped and kneeled in the dirt to rub his velvet ears and bury her head in his neck. He was an affectionate dog who seemed aware when things were out of sorts in Josie's life.

She finally stood and took a long breath. At this time of the evening the creosote and sage opened their pores and the extra moisture in the air caused a pungent, tart smell like no other. The sun was slipping below the horizon line now, trailing a swath of purple and orange across the floor of the desert. It was Josie's favorite time of the day, when life slowed to nothing, no sound but a few crickets and the wind brushing through the scattered cedar and piñon pine.

She began the quarter-mile walk to Dell's place, ready to take her mind off Dillon.

As she approached the cabin she saw Dell standing through his sheer living room curtains, most likely ready to settle into his chair with a book for the night. She walked up onto the porch, tapped twice on the door, yelled hello, and stepped inside.

Josie knew immediately that something wasn't right by the look of shock on Dell's face. She had entered his home the same way as she had hundreds of times before, with just a quick knock and a yell. As Josie registered his expression she sensed motion and turned to see a woman walking out of Dell's kitchen carrying two glasses of red wine. The awkward moment was quickly made worse as Chester pushed in behind Josie and rushed the woman, causing her to spill wine down the front of her top and onto the floor.

Josie clapped her hands and yelled for Chester, who was as shocked at the stranger in Dell's home as Josie was. Dell stood silently watching the two women and the dog fuss around each other.

"I'm so sorry. I'm Josie, Dell's neighbor. I didn't realize Dell was having company." She looked at Dell accusingly, as if irritated that he'd not bothered to tell her of his plans.

"That's quite all right," the woman said, setting the glasses on the end table beside the couch. Her eyes were wide and she looked at Dell, who seemed unable to speak. The woman was clearly shocked by Josie's presence. "I'll just get some water on this and it will be fine."

She walked down the hallway into the bathroom and Josie looked at Dell, dumbfounded. She'd lived next to Dell for years, and to her knowledge he had never once invited a woman to his house. And this woman seemed to know her way around Dell's cabin. Josie realized with a start that he was wearing a new pair of jeans and a button-down shirt that she'd never seen and his cowboy boots were clean. He still said nothing and instead looked down at Chester, who was demanding his attention. He avoided looking at her and Josie realized he was more embarrassed to be caught with this woman in his house than Josie was at barging in.

"I'm sorry. I should have knocked. We'll get out of your way." Josie walked toward the door and snapped her fingers for Chester. He lumbered over to her, always ready for a walk outside.

"That's fine," Dell said, his tone gruff but, Josie thought, also apologetic. "I'll talk to you later."

Josie left with Chester at her heels, hoping to get beyond the door before the woman returned in her wine-stained shirt. Dillon was gone and trying to move on with his life, and she couldn't accept that. Dell had apparently come out of a thirty-something-year rut, and she wasn't sure she could accept that. She walked down the lane wondering if the common denominator in her various troubled relationships was her.

TEN

The Marfa airport was located on US-90, about forty-five minutes from her home. When she arrived she found the pilot readying the copter and Doug standing twenty feet away, hands in his pockets, looking anxious to get going. Just a few minutes later the low thump of the rotor started and the pilot beckoned them forward. They boarded, belted into the bench in the back, and adjusted their headsets to allow communication with the pilot.

About five miles into the flight the blackened earth suddenly spread out beneath them like seawater, covering everything in its path. The ash appeared painted with long black brushstrokes. What surprised Josie were the stretches of beige grass dotted with scrub and trees untouched by the fire, tiny island oases in the middle of the ravaged land.

The pilot spoke into the headset and turned his head back to look at Josie. "We're approaching Prentice Canyon Road directly ahead of us. The chief did an excellent job predicting that firebreak. You can see where the trucks were down below. They fought the fire from the flanks and had it about closed off by the time it reached the road."

Josie looked out her side window and saw exactly what the pilot was referring to. Small fingers of black burned up to the road along Prentice Canyon, but the fire had obviously burned out there.

Doug spoke into the headset. "The wind finally cut us a break. We had the Bomberos de Piedra Lambrada fire squad out of Mexico giving wind and weather patterns throughout the night. They were a huge help."

As the pilot flew farther west, Josie noticed the change in the burn pattern below.

"Check that out," Doug said, sounding anxious even through the headset. "There's the Nixes' house, surrounded by black on all sides though the fire had all but died out across the road."

Josie nodded. The proof was there. She looked at Doug and hoped the photographs he was taking now would tell the story. The land around the Nixes' house was charred black, the trees burned almost completely down to the ground. A half-mile away from the house, on all sides, the fire damage was minimal.

"It's a good thing the wind died down or we could have lost the entire western part of the county," said Doug.

Josie couldn't help looking farther westward in the direction of her house, directly in the line of fire.

———————

When the helicopter landed she saw the smoke jumpers standing around by the jump plane. The group of ten or fifteen guys wore rumpled navy-blue Montana Fire and Rescue T-shirts and work boots. They stood around talking, in no hurry to take off. She ran over to check in with Pete. He was standing beside his jumpsuit and a pile of gear, talking with the other guys. He noticed her approaching, waved her over, and gave her a hug.

"I don't want to keep you," said Josie. "I just wondered if you'd have an evening free before you head back to Montana."

"Tonight. I already made plans for us. You free?"

"Oh!"

"We're working with Doug today, but we're headed to Big Bend for a practice run with the Mexicans this evening. I want you to come with us."

"I'd love to watch you guys train. What time are you leaving?"

"Be here at five. Wear jeans and boots. You drive and I'll ride with you. We'll follow the van."

"As long as I can get away from the investigation, I'll be here."

———

At one o'clock that afternoon Josie and Otto sat in their office, discussing the strategy for the questioning as they waited for Billy and Brenda Nix to arrive. While the two were the prime suspects in the murder investigation, she and Otto decided not to interview them separately during their first meeting. Because the couple came back freely to talk with the police, Josie didn't have to Mirandize them. Once their rights were read the attorneys would be brought in and the conversation would stop. The goal for now was to get as much information as they could before the Nixes clammed up and requested counsel.

When Lou buzzed the intercom to announce the Nixes, Josie went downstairs to greet them. They stood side by side in the waiting area just inside the front door. Billy wore a plaid Western-style shirt, dark blue jeans, and cowboy boots. Josie thought he looked like the country singer Trace Adkins, with the same large build and good ol' boy stance. Brenda stood next to him wearing white capri pants and a navy-blue short-sleeved top with a silver necklace and matching earrings. Josie thought she looked like a sturdy woman who could handle tragedy in complete control, doling out instructions and maintaining order. Maybe the outsider status she had within her own family had given her a tough façade.

As Josie approached the waiting area, she noticed the marked difference in the couple's expressions. Billy had the wide-eyed expectant look of one bracing for terrible news. Brenda's features looked pinched, her mouth forming a stern frown, her eyes small and determined. Billy was imagining the worst while Brenda was already preparing to take care of the aftermath. Josie wondered how many times this dynamic had played out in their marriage.

Josie pushed open the half door separating the waiting area from Lou's dispatch station. Lou sat behind her computer talking on the phone, paying no attention to the drama. Josie stretched a hand out to Billy first.

"Thanks for coming in, Billy. We're going to head upstairs where we can sit and talk." Josie motioned toward the back of the office and then Billy shook her hand and tipped his head but said nothing. He walked past her and Josie stretched her hand out to Brenda. "I don't believe we've met before. I'm chief of police, Josie Gray."

Brenda shook Josie's hand. "Pleased to meet you." Her tone was curt, as if she were meeting a business rival.

Josie led them upstairs to the office where Otto was setting coffee cups in the middle of the conference table. Otto introduced himself and the group briefly discussed the long drive from Austin before settling into chairs around the table. Josie asked if they would mind if she recorded the interview. Neither of the Nixes objected, so she set up the recorder and stated the date, time, location, and people present.

"I appreciate you coming in today," she said. "As you know, the wildfire that swept through Arroyo County has caused a great deal of damage to Artemis. Downtown was spared but the northeastern part of the county was hit hard. The fire reached the west side and died out. Unfortunately, your house wasn't spared. The fire chief and the fire marshal are working as fast and as carefully as they can to assess damage and get people back to their homes, but safety is first priority."

"Can you tell us anything about the damage?" Brenda asked.

"I'm sorry. At this time we don't have enough information to do that. To begin, I'd like you to start by telling us about the evacuation. When did you leave, what route did you take, and so on."

Billy glanced at Brenda, who spoke first, looking directly at Josie. "We'd been listening off and on to the public-radio station about the fire up north. Then Hank called Sunday afternoon and gave us an update on the evacuation. Billy and I talked it over and decided we should go ahead and leave before it got too late."

"Is Hank a close friend to you and Billy?" Josie asked.

"Yes, he's a good friend. He takes care of his musicians. He was calling everyone, the bands, regulars at the bar, just letting people know what was going on. The Hell-Bent ended up the gathering place for everyone. It was far enough out of the fire's path that we were all hoping it would remain safe."

"What time did you decide to leave town?" Josie asked.

"Hank called about noon. We finally decided to pack up at about two and left around five that evening."

"Did you pack many belongings?"

Brenda glanced at Billy as if passing off the baton.

"We mostly grabbed the instruments, the guitars and amps," he said. "We got them and some suitcases packed for a couple days away. We were worried but I never thought it would actually come through our area. You just never figure it'll happen to you."

"When you left at five, where did you go?" Josie asked.

"We went to the Hell-Bent to pick up my guitar. She's my favorite. An old Fender I've had for twenty years. I couldn't leave without her."

"Who did you talk to at the bar?"

Billy drew his eyebrows together as if questioning her motives. "Why's that matter?"

"We'll get to that," Josie said. "Right now I'm just gathering information from as many sources as I can find."

"For a wildfire?" Brenda asked.

"We'll get to that shortly. Let's stick to the evacuation. Tell me what happened when you left the house that evening."

Josie glanced at Otto, who was sitting quietly across from Brenda with his hands folded on a legal pad in front of him. His expression was kind and nonjudgmental. He hadn't picked up his pen since they sat down, signaling that it was a friendly conversation, not an interrogation.

"We drove straight to the Hell-Bent when we left home," Brenda said. "I saw Yvonne Ferrario and sat down to talk with her while Billy went back to the dressing room."

Josie looked at Billy and he continued. "I told Hank I was going to grab my guitar and he sent Angela back to unlock the door. We just talked a minute about the fire and how awful it all was. Then we left. I found Brenda talking to Yvonne and we left the bar by about six."

"Where did you go after that?" she asked.

"We drove to Austin," he said.

"Why not stay in Presidio or somewhere closer?"

"Billy's been playing the bars in Austin," Brenda said. "We had to leave home anyway, it made sense to drive on to Austin. Check in with the bar owners and book a few gigs."

"What hotel did you stay at?"

"The Hampton Inn. Downtown. We stopped at Gilly's for an hour or so to have a drink before we checked in."

Josie deliberately avoided asking how they paid for the bill. She would track down credit card receipts later. For now, she just wanted a basic time frame. As she requested more specific information, the Nixes would most likely feel threatened, and the details would dry up.

"Do you know roughly what time you arrived in Austin?"

"It was one in the morning," Billy said. "I remember because the bars close at two. We drove by the Hampton and could tell there were rooms available. The parking lot wasn't full so we just drove on to Gilly's. We checked into the hotel sometime after two."

"Did you book any gigs while you were there?"

"Billy talked with a couple bar owners." Brenda glanced at him as if requesting confirmation but didn't wait for him to speak. "He went to the Baker's Dozen and Mick and Eddy's yesterday. And, we both met with the owner of the Sage. We booked a few dates in November."

"Did you talk to anyone from Artemis before you returned my call yesterday?" Josie asked.

Brenda looked surprised. "No." She turned to Billy. "Did you?"

Billy shook his head no and frowned.

"Was anyone staying at your home when you evacuated?"

"No, of course not," Brenda said.

"Do you have friends who might drop by unannounced and stay overnight without telling you?" Josie asked.

"What are you getting at?" Brenda said.

Josie glanced at Otto to make sure he didn't have anything else he wanted to slip in before the bombshell. He tipped his head for her to proceed.

"A body was found, burned to death, lying on your couch. We found it yesterday morning when we went to your house."

Both of the Nixes pulled back into their chairs, as if trying to distance themselves from the news. Their eyes were wide, unbelieving, confused, all expected responses upon hearing such traumatic information, but Josie had learned not to put too much faith in the initial physical reaction of a suspect. Their reactions as the questions got tougher would be more telling.

"Who was it?" Brenda said.

"The body hasn't been identified. We're hoping you might be able to help us," Josie said.

Brenda looked at Billy, who continued staring at Josie in apparent shock.

"Billy, can you think of a friend, maybe a band member or a fan, who might have stopped by your house after you left? Maybe they needed a place to crash for the night?"

He opened his mouth as if to speak but said nothing.

"We don't run a flophouse!" Brenda said. "And who would stay at our house in the middle of an evacuation with a wildfire raging across the county?"

Josie kept her attention on Billy. "Can you think of anyone? Maybe someone you asked to stop by the house and check on things while you were away?"

He cleared his throat and shifted in his seat. "No, nobody. You don't know anything about the body? A man or woman?"

"A male. We believe he was between the ages of twenty-five and fifty."

Josie watched Billy struggle to swallow and clear his throat. "Do you have a drink? Some water?" he asked.

Brenda looked over at Billy, and Josie noted that her expression had changed slightly. She seemed irritated with him. Josie remembered Angela's comment about Brenda calling Billy weak.

Otto stood and retrieved a bottle of water from the small refrigerator at the back of the office. Billy removed the lid and drank half the bottle.

Josie faced Brenda again. "If not friends, do you have family members who might have stopped by unannounced?"

Brenda's face flushed and she sat up straight in her seat. "I'm not sure how else to say this to you. We don't have people stopping by to sleep on our couch. I have no idea who that person could be."

"The police found a dead man in your living room. We will do everything in our power to determine who that victim is. You also need to understand that you could be in danger as well. The death has been ruled a homicide."

"What?" She whispered the word, her expression shocked again.

"Why would someone kill someone in our home?" Billy looked

confused. "You're saying that the man wasn't killed in the fire? That someone killed him?"

Brenda's face had turned bright red and a sheen of sweat covered her forehead. "I want an attorney. We're done talking here. This is outrageous."

ELEVEN

Once the Nixes requested an attorney the interview ended. Josie had already called Manny and booked a room at his motel for the Nixes. The room had just been vacated by a family who had stayed during the evacuation but whose home was not caught in the fire. Josie wanted the Nixes close by for questioning, and fortunately, they didn't resist. The couple had left angry and thoroughly unstrung but agreed to remain reachable via their cell phones.

After the Nixes left, Otto and Josie drove back to the house to reexamine the scene. The Arroyo County judge had granted approval for the search warrant and Josie was anxious to get ahold of the computer and various files in the home office that might provide a glimpse into the Nixes' personal life. Otto drove his jeep and Josie rode beside him.

"Anything surprise you from Billy or Brenda?" Otto asked.

"Not really. I'd hoped for more. You?"

"Considering what we learned from the band and bar interviews, I'd say they were both predictable in their answers. Brenda struggled not to dominate the interview. She pulled back to allow Billy to talk."

"And he didn't seem to want to talk." She paused, recalling the conversation. "I kept thinking how I might feel, sitting down to learn that the police had found a burned body, dead on my couch. I realize because of my law enforcement background I'm not your normal suspect."

"You think?"

She ignored the sarcasm. "But I think after the initial shock I'd be angry. I'd want to know what the police were doing. I'd want to know who was inside my house. Who the police had talked to, and what they were doing to find out who this person was. I'd want answers."

Otto stopped the car so Josie could get out and take down the yellow crime-scene tape at the end of the Nixes' driveway. He pulled up the driveway, parked, and joined Josie, who was now standing on the concrete pad just outside the front of the house.

"So, what's your point?" he asked.

"I know Brenda isn't well liked, but her reaction seemed right to me. She's mad as hell. Her house is destroyed. Some guy not only got into her home, but he was murdered there. And now the police are asking questions that make her feel like she's a suspect." She turned and faced Otto. "And what did Billy do?"

"He clammed up. But doesn't that fit his personality?"

Josie narrowed her eyes. "It was more than that though. I thought he looked scared. He got choked up and he had to drink water before he could even talk. That's a sign of fear, not worry."

"I'm still not sure what you're getting at."

Josie stared at the gaping hole in the living room. "I don't know yet. I'm just thinking out loud."

They spent the next hour searching through the rubble in the house for something that might explain Billy's reaction, but they found nothing more than personal mementos, music paraphernalia, and the bills and paperwork typical of any other married couple. They retrieved several boxes of charred evidence, including a desktop computer and a file cabinet full of business and personal files, and tagged and loaded the evidence into Josie's jeep before going back into the house.

They stood outside for a water break, sweaty from the exertion and nauseated from the stench.

"You took prints in the bedroom the day of the fire?" Josie asked.

He wiped his hands on a cloth and tried to rub the black soot off of his skin. "I did. Everything's logged."

"I was thinking about Billy's question. What was the first thing he asked after he found out about the body?"

"Remind me."

"He asked whether the victim was male or female."

Otto shrugged. "He wants to know who the victim is."

"But we already told him we don't know who it is. And if Billy didn't have any idea who was lying on his couch, then why would he care if the body was male or female?"

"He's wondering if the body belongs to someone he knows after all. Maybe there's a woman he's seeing on the side?"

Josie nodded. "Let's check the bedroom and bath again. Maybe it was a crime of passion. Maybe that's where it started, and ended up with a dead body, and a married couple seven hours away in Austin."

Otto walked into the master bathroom to search the cabinets and countertops for something more telling than what his original search had turned up. Josie stood in the bedroom, observing the space as a place of intimacy, shared by a married couple. The room was painted white with a few department-store framed paintings of flower arrangements in vases. The furniture was a matching set from one of the discount chains. There was nothing ornate or original to distinguish it from a hundred other bedrooms. Josie figured it fit Brenda's sensibilities. Her focus seemed to be on Billy and his career, not material possessions or fostering a homey place to live.

The alarm clock was located on the right side of the bed, closest to the bathroom. Josie figured this was Brenda's side. She couldn't imagine Brenda allowing Billy to set the alarm. Next to the clock were a box of tissues and a hardback novel by C. J. Box. A small pad of sticky notes and a pen lay underneath the table lamp. Josie picked up the pad and found several notes Brenda had apparently jotted down to herself.

The first note said, "Call L. Lester follow-up recording."

Underneath that she found another note with what appeared to be a phone number. She jotted the number down in her steno pad to call later from a restricted phone line that would protect her identity.

A drawer underneath the tabletop revealed a pile of jewelry pitched haphazardly into a glass bowl and a pile of odds and ends from earrings to lip balm and pens and pencils. Underneath the drawer was a pile of paperback mysteries and romance novels. Nothing of consequence. No photos or letters.

Billy's side of the bed held mementos, from a CD case signed by Willie Nelson to several concert tickets signed by people Josie didn't recognize. She found a pile of coasters from assorted restaurants. She flipped over one coaster with SAMUEL ADAMS BOSTON LAGER on the front, and on the back saw the scrawled message "Love you man." None of the other coasters bore any writing.

After an hour of digging turned up little of consequence, they gave up the search. They were walking back down the hallway when Josie's eye settled on a tiny brightly colored piece of paper lying on top of the edge of the baseboard. She asked Otto for a plastic bag and tweezers from the evidence kit he was carrying. He went back into the bedroom and opened up the case on the bed. The hallway and bedrooms hadn't been burned, but the fire in the living room had left a thick coating on the tiled floor and the hallway. Since the bedroom door had been closed, the ashfall there wasn't nearly as heavy.

Otto handed Josie the supplies, and she bent down and retrieved the piece of paper. She stood, pressing the tweezers tightly between her fingertips, holding the tiny piece of paper out for Otto to look at, a wide smile on her face. "Recognize this?"

He studied it for a moment and then laughed. "I think we have ourselves a murder investigation."

TWELVE

Josie and Otto spent a half hour sifting through the ash on the Nixes' hallway floor with small soft brushes, looking for more of the confetti-like pieces of paper, and plotting them on a diagram to determine the starting and stopping points of their trajectory. The brightly colored pieces of paper were ejected from a certain model Zaner stun gun when fired. Each piece of paper carried a set of numbers that a law enforcement agency could use to track down owner registration for the gun. They found several dozen pieces, which made it clear they weren't left there from a prior use. The gun had no doubt been used to stun the victim before killing him: a brutal, premeditated murder.

On the drive back to the office Josie received a call from the coroner.

"What do you have for us?" she asked.

"It's clear the man didn't die of asphyxiation. There was no smoke damage to his lungs. He was dead before the fire burned him."

"Any idea yet what caused his death?"

"I'm not finding any blunt-force trauma. My gut feeling is an overdose, but I can't say. I was able to pull enough blood for toxicology, but that could be two weeks or longer."

"But what about his arms pulling up to his face? You called it the boxer's pose. If he overdosed that wouldn't have happened, would it?" she asked.

"Think of it as shrink wrap. When you apply heat to shrink wrap it shrinks up. When intense heat is present, or the soft tissue burns, it causes the muscles to contract and pull in. The victim could have died of an overdose while lying on the couch. As long as rigor mortis hadn't set in, his muscles would have contracted when the fire started."

Josie ended the call and filled Otto in.

"The pieces aren't quite fitting together. Let's say Cowan is right and the victim overdosed. Why would a stun gun be necessary?"

"Someone used a stun gun to disable the victim, then they knocked him out and laid him on the couch." Josie drove, absently watching the sandy desert roll by as she put the pieces together. "If Cowan is correct, someone shot him full of enough drugs to cause him to overdose, and then used accelerant to set the house on fire. There's no way this is anything but premeditated murder."

"So they took advantage of the wildfire to commit murder," he said.

"Meaning the victim and the perpetrator most likely knew each other. The killer knew the victim would be there so the killer came prepared with the drugs and accelerant."

"What if we switched up the order?" Otto asked. "Maybe the victim had already shot himself full of something. Let's say heroin."

Josie stopped him. "If he was shot full of enough heroin to overdose, the stun gun wouldn't have been necessary."

"I think you're closing in on it."

"If only we had the murderer."

"And knew the victim."

Back at the office Josie logged on to the Zaner Web site. She filled in an online form and submitted her department information. Two hours later Zaner International called her to confirm her identity and provided her with registry information for the Zaner gun. Armed with this new information, Josie hung up the phone and faced Otto, who was sitting at his computer typing up case notes from their visit to the Nixes' house that morning.

"The gun is registered to Brenda Nix. Purchased in 2009 from a dealer in Houston," she said.

"Ah," Otto said, grinning. "That narrows the list of suspects considerably."

"Let's talk about timing. We know the body was burned at seven thirty-eight, so let's work backwards."

Otto went to the whiteboard and wrote:

5:00/5:10—Nixes left home
5:30—Arrived at Hell-Bent
6:00—Left for Austin (7-hour drive—arrived at 1:00 and went to Gilly's bar)
6:00—Or went back home. Home by 6:20-6:30

Otto turned around to look at Josie. "Let's make some educated guesses on the Zaner. It obviously was used before the fire since the ash was covering the paper. I think it's safe to bet it was used between six thirty and six forty-five. That would allow enough time for someone to kill the victim, lay him on the couch, start the fire, and take off." He raised his eyebrows at Josie for confirmation.

"That works."

He returned to the board and finished writing the timeline.

6:30-6:45—Zaner is used
6:45-7:00—MURDER?
7:15—Start the fire
7:20—Leave home for Austin

Otto turned to face Josie. "Give me the times again for the fire." She consulted her notes and read the times to him as he added them to his list.

7:38—Body burned

9:30 - 10:00—Fire burns through that part of the county

2:00?—Nixes check into the Hampton

"That works. If they were checked in by two o'clock, they would have had just enough time to burn the body and escape," she said.

"We need to confirm what time they checked into that hotel," Otto said.

"And if they used their credit card at Gilly's that night. We also need to know if both checked in, or just one of them. If they don't have proof they were both there by two that morning, they're screwed."

"What's the latest they could have left?" Otto said. "If they took Interstate 10 and hauled ass all the way to Austin, they could make it in six hours. Let's say they wanted to get to Gilly's by one thirty to make an appearance. They would have to leave by . . . " He calculated the time in his head. " . . . by seven thirty."

"Let's call them in for questioning." Josie considered Otto for a moment. "Who gets Brenda?"

"Let me have a crack at her. I think Billy might do better with you. He seems to like strong females."

"Otto. I think you just gave me a compliment."

He ignored her smirk. "It's already four o'clock. There's no point calling them tonight. Call first thing in the morning."

"We call them in tonight. What can it hurt?"

He tilted his head and looked at her like she was being foolish. "Look. We obviously can't charge them yet. Anyone could have used the stun gun, even though it's registered to Brenda. We're close, but not close enough. So why antagonize them? They won't come in without an attorney. And they won't get an attorney here this late. Just call in the morning. Go home and clear your head for the evening. Hell, let me clear *my* head for an evening."

Josie felt agitated. She wouldn't sleep knowing a murderer was sleeping in a hotel bed downtown with the opportunity to flee at any moment. But for now, she didn't have enough evidence to charge either of the Nixes. The Zaner hadn't killed the burn victim, but it certainly played a part in his death. And Otto was right. Anyone could have used it if they knew where it was located. She also had to acknowledge that just because the timing worked didn't mean the Nixes killed the man found dead on their couch. She needed Cowan to provide the cause of death, and she needed a subpoena for the Nixes' credit card information for the night of the fire.

Josie glanced at her watch and considered Pete's offer to watch the smoke jumpers train at Big Bend. It would be nice to spend the evening with him and watch the jumpers in action. She sent him a text and said she'd be there by five. She had brought jeans and boots to work with her that morning, just in case she was able to make it, and she changed in the office.

She thought about checking in with Dell, but figured he was entertaining his new girlfriend. He'd not called and left a message for her like she thought he would. Call her stubborn, but she'd be damned if she'd go down to his house again before he filled her in on his new arrangements. He'd always kept tabs on her relationships, offering unsolicited advice through the years that she occasionally appreciated but usually ignored. But Dell had never so much as mentioned a woman in all the years she'd known him. So what had changed?

Josie arrived at the airport and found the guys loading into the van that would take them to Big Bend. She pulled her jeep in next to where Pete was standing and rolled down her window.

"You sure you don't need to ride with the guys?" she asked.

"Hell no! I got this all worked out." He climbed into the passenger side of her jeep. "So, you know the area? Big Bend National Park?"

"I know it well. Dillon and I camped there a lot. It's a beautiful place."

"You're the guide then. The van can follow you. We're working out of Boquillas Canyon with the Mexicans. They have their own hot-shot crew training with us. Your gear's already loaded on the plane."

"What gear?"

"You didn't think I was going to drag you down there and make you watch me, did you?"

"That's exactly what I thought."

Pete stuck his arm out the window and gave the "OK" sign to the driver of the van, who waved back. "Head out. They're ready."

Josie, still reeling from his comment, backed the jeep up and said, "You're talking about me parachuting?"

Pete laughed. "I already got this cleared with my crew boss. He owes me a favor. He's got the gear. He said he'll let you tandem jump with me today."

"It'll be dark by the time we get there!"

"Sunset's at nine. We'll be there by eight. No excuses."

"I've never parachuted! I don't have any idea how to jump."

"This isn't something you'd normally do," he said.

She laughed. "Obviously! I've never even had a lesson!"

"I got this figured out. I call it jump therapy. Someday I'll patent my idea and make a million. My old shrinks will be furious.

"Here's the trick. You go live a little. You do something that gets you completely out of your head. You break free of whatever night-mare you're living. Even if it's only for ten minutes, it's a start. And, suddenly, you want ten more minutes. And ten more minutes after that. And one day you realize you've moved on from whatever hell you've been living."

Josie laughed. "I don't think it's quite so easy as that."

"How's that shrink working out for you?"

"She's not a shrink. And she's trying to get me to see the situation from a different perspective. To change my thinking."

"That's exactly what I'm doing for you. Except I'm free. And I'm a hell of a lot more fun."

After a three-hour drive along FM-170, and a nonstop stream of Pete's observations about life and love, they approached the far east side of Big Bend National Park.

"You get into this?" Pete asked, pointing out at the miles of sun-baked hills and mountains.

"Get into what?"

"All this desert and rocks and sun? We've driven over two hours on a marked road and not passed one car. Not one. That doesn't happen anywhere. And I live in the boondocks."

"That's the beauty of it. You want to get lost? Come to West Texas."

Pete was quiet for a time, taking in the canyons and the vast sky and the lack of people. "I guess I can see you here. In a quiet place. You were always the quiet one."

She smiled at his reference to their high school years. "You made enough noise for all of us."

"Don't you miss that old pickup truck?" he asked.

"All four of us crammed into the front seat. I'm not sure how I'd have survived high school without you guys," she said.

"It's a wonder we all made it out alive."

"You and Dave got us into some crazy situations."

Pete propped his feet up on the dashboard and pointed at her. "You were no angel. Me and Dave would come up with some dumbass idea, Lisa would try and talk us down, and then you'd convince Lisa to do it. You were the one who convinced Lisa to swim in the town water tower."

Josie grinned and looked over at Pete. "That was fun. You have to admit."

"Even if it was stupid-crazy, if you said we'd be okay, we all believed you."

They drove for thirty minutes through Big Bend, reminiscing about high school, before they reached the turnoff for the border crossing to Boquillas, Mexico.

Pete pointed to the sign. "You got a border crossing in a park?"

"It's an unmanned border crossing. You park and cross by boat."

"What's in Boquillas?"

Josie smiled. "About eighty people. Maybe more now that they opened up the crossing again. It's a hard town to earn a living in; no industry, and ranching is tough. Some of the people that live there cross the river and set up their art around the canyon trail with coffee cans to collect money. They make money from the tourists that come through. They use the honor system to collect the money people leave when they buy the trinkets."

"Tough way to live."

"A good friend of mine is a river guide on the Rio. He and his wife both guide. They don't make much money. Hot as hell in the summer. Four-hour drive to any major shopping. Scarce water, power outages. But they wouldn't trade it. He lives on his own terms."

Pete looked at her, his expression skeptical.

"He's got his own irrigation system rigged from the creek behind his house. He shares his food with others. For him, it's not about a fancy house. It's about the outdoors that stretch around him for miles, and the plot of land he and his wife cultivate. He sees beauty in the rock formations, not in a ten-thousand-dollar slab of polished granite countertop."

Josie could feel Pete staring at her, and she grinned, realizing she sounded like a zealot. "Don't get me wrong. I'd be happy to have a granite countertop in my kitchen. But I get where he's coming from. People think living like this is crazy, but this is paradise to others."

Once they finally arrived at Boquillas Canyon, things moved quickly. The plane was already prepared for takeoff. Since it was a practice run the guys moved rapidly, as they would during a real fire run. Josie stepped into the harness Pete gave her and tried to focus on the good-natured banter of the smoke jumpers standing around her. They'd made hundreds of jumps together and were obviously a close-knit group.

"It's like riding a bike. But it's easier. Pete'll do all the work for you," one of the guys said. She tried to smile and nod, to not look terrified. She would be strapped to Pete's chest, staring down at the earth some fifteen thousand feet below them, free-falling for almost a full minute before Pete pulled the cord.

She adjusted the harness around her legs and groin and straightened to find Pete smiling. He tightened the harnesses around her chest. The other men were wearing padded jump jackets and pants that looked like a set of Carhartts, but Pete had said they were lined with Kevlar to protect the men when landing in rough terrain. Each man had two bags strapped to the front of him, and another on his back. She figured they were wearing close to a hundred pounds of gear.

Pete stepped back and examined her equipment. On the drive to Big Bend, he had spent ten minutes explaining how the tandem jump would work. Basically, she would be a passenger for the trip down. Enjoy the ride. Nothing to worry about. She had repeated that phrase in her mind over and over. She rarely flew. She wasn't afraid of heights, but this was beyond high.

"So, here's a summary," Pete said. "We'll get up to about three thousand feet and the pilot will circle the canyon and drop a couple sets of drift streamers to watch how they fall. The wind coming out of that canyon can be tricky. We also have a crew from Mexico that's training across the river. They'll be observing, communicating with our pilot. You'll get to watch the crew jump. Then we'll get out to the open field and get up to about fourteen thousand feet to make our jump."

"That's almost three miles high." Josie felt a surge of panic.

Pete smiled but ignored her comment. "My gear will get dropped separately with the heavier tools since you'll be strapped to me for the jump. One of the van drivers will pick us up and take us over to the training area when we're done."

He talked on about the jump and what to expect, obviously trying to keep her mind occupied. She was glad for the effort.

She pointed to a pouch strapped around Pete's calf. "What's the bag on your leg?"

"That's my let-down rope. You land in the top of a hundred-foot pine tree, you need something to rappel down with."

She laughed. "You guys are insane."

"I've been told that my whole life." Pete patted her roughly on the arm and motioned toward the plane the other men were boarding. She took a long breath and blew out slowly. She tried to look the part of the confident tagalong, hitching a ride for a free fall.

She climbed a rusted ladder and through a large door that opened into the belly of the Cessna. The engines were roaring and it was almost impossible to hear. Pete sat first on the floor of the airplane and then gestured for her to sit down between his legs. The other men sat along the sides of the plane, apparently in a predetermined order. The plane shuddered and groaned as it gained speed down the makeshift runway. Once in the air, she could see out the door to the land beneath them, spread out like a patchwork quilt of brown and beige shapes.

Pete yelled into her ear, "Two thousand feet."

Josie tried to distract herself as the plane continued its ascent. And then someone yelled "Three thousand" and everything began happening fast. The men were up and moving, with two men approaching the door, heads out, watching, and then disappearing, then another in quick succession, each one getting a hard tap on the back of his calf from the crew leader. With the crew gone, the plane made its ascent higher into the sky. The jumpmaster held a hand in the air with his fingers spread, indicating five minutes. Pete yelled something in her ear but the engine noise and the roar of the wind were so loud she couldn't hear. Pete began tightening the already snug harness. She felt constricted, her clothes and equipment tight and bulky, and then Pete pressed the front of his body up against hers. He yelled, "Three minutes."

Finally, they moved up to the opening and she realized it was going to happen. She was strapped in and facing a three-mile fall from the sky, the earth impossibly small beneath her. The next moment Pete was moving behind her, yelling something, and they were out the door, falling into a cushion of air, the wind roaring by, her mind full of everything and nothing all at the same moment. She clutched the harness at her chest but had the powerful sensation of needing to reach out and grab something. It was the sensation of falling. Her mouth was dry and her eyes watered under the goggles as warm air blasted her face. For brief moments she thought they were going to spin out of control all the way to the ground.

A moment later the parachute opened with a mighty jolt and everything slowed and quieted and a beautiful calm overcame her. Josie smiled and then laughed.

"Jump therapy, man. Nothing like it in the world," Pete yelled.

She couldn't get over how peaceful it was. Completely still.

They floated slowly toward earth and took in the grand landscape, the flat mesas and the knife's-edge split into the rock that allowed the Rio Grande access to the towering Boquillas Canyon a thousand feet below. The sun was dipping below the horizon and the view from so high up looked fantastic. She took in the rugged mountains and the hundreds of miles of chocolate-brown rock and desert sand. And with a stunning moment of clarity, she realized, *I only get one shot at being a part of this.*

THIRTEEN

After the late-night drive from Big Bend left her with just a few hours of sleep, Josie got up early and drove to work at 6:30 with a task to complete. When she arrived in Artemis she drove down Seminole Street and pulled up in front of the Office of Abacus. A sign hung on the front door that simply read CLOSED, and provided a phone number to call Dillon Reese for further information. She left and drove through town, turning in to Dillon's old neighborhood. She drove slowly by his house and scanned the street. Most homes were lit up with families getting ready for work and school, making the hectic last-minute push to get out the door on time. Dillon's home was silent and empty.

Josie headed to the police department and parked in the space designated for the police chief. Instead of going inside, she walked across the street to the park bench in front of the courthouse and sat down.

Downtown was silent. It was a half hour before sunrise and too early for county employees and shop owners. She watched the stoplight complete a full rotation: green to yellow to red and back to green again without a single car driving by. She imagined Dillon driving to work in downtown St. Louis through the frantic streets with honking horns and people on every corner, all of it so different from the pace in Artemis. She tried to imagine herself driving to work in that kind of madness and the thought alone made her feel anxious.

Spreading her arms across the top of the bench, she leaned her head back to stare at the navy sky pinpricked with stars and a sliver of moon, already fading in preparation for the searing heat of the morning. She solved problems for a living, but recently her own life had felt like a twisted-up mess.

She thought about the jump with Pete the day before, and the idea he was trying to communicate to her, and she knew he was right. There was too much living for her to do to remain stuck in the past. It was over. There was no changing it or bringing Dillon back.

At seven o'clock, with the sun pushing up over the distant horizon, she stood and walked across the street to the police station. She had confronted her personal demons—or at least had started to. Now it was time to confront Brenda and Billy Nix.

———

Knowing there was nothing more to be gained by keeping the murder from the public, Josie drafted a media statement with the basic details of the homicide. She e-mailed Bev Woodruff, reporter for the local paper, as well as the manager for the Marfa public-radio station.

At 7:45 a.m. Josie called Brenda Nix at the motel and woke her. Josie explained that the police had new information that was critical to the case and asked that she and Billy come to the station as soon as possible. Brenda said she needed to consult her attorney and would call back.

A little before eight, just as Otto was stirring creamer into his coffee and discussing the list of questions he'd drawn up for the interview, Lou buzzed and said Brenda was on line one.

"This is Chief Gray."

"This is Brenda Nix. Our attorney said she can be at the police department at eleven. We'll see you then."

"Who's representing you?" Josie asked.

"Jenna Turner."

Josie rolled her eyes and turned to Otto as she hung up the phone. "Turner's representing her."

"Isn't she that hard-ass out of Presidio?"

"That's the one."

At precisely 11:00 a.m., Turner walked in with Brenda and Billy following behind her. It was clear the three had already met and prepared. Josie was certain that Turner was well informed about the case and knew as much as the Nixes could afford to tell her. Turner was hard on prosecutors and judges, but she was equally hard on her clients. She demanded the truth, and she'd been known to relinquish a case if a client held back pertinent information. Josie had watched her ream out a client in the hallway outside the Arroyo County courtroom just last month. The twenty-something-year-old kid had stood meekly in front of her, wearing his orange prison scrubs, saying nothing.

"You will not make a fool out of me again. Never again. You understand?"

The kid hadn't responded fast enough and she'd jabbed her forefinger into his chest and stood on tiptoes to get her face within inches of his own. "Do you understand me?"

He had backed away and said, "Yes, ma'am," and followed her back into the courtroom looking like a scolded child.

Josie wished she could have watched Turner dish out the rules to Brenda. She couldn't imagine Brenda taking a scolding sitting down, especially from another female.

The local law enforcement community referred to the attorney simply as Turner, no first name necessary. Sitting in a bar on the weekend, buying a round for a group of off-duty cops to say thanks for a job well done, she was both liked and respected. But in the courtroom, she could slice up a state's witness as finely as a paper shredder. Josie had been at several social functions with her and found her to be a great deal of fun; she just didn't want her stalling out the interview.

In her midforties, with short ash-blond hair, Turner wore a pair of black slacks and a classy cream-colored top with low heels and minimal jewelry. She carried a leather briefcase that looked near to exploding. She smiled grimly and put a hand out. "Chief."

"Good to see you, Turner." Josie turned to the Nixes. "Thank you for coming in this morning. Let's all get situated upstairs."

In the office, they sat down at the conference table and Otto joined them. Billy, Brenda, and Turner sat across from Josie and Otto. Josie faced Turner. "How familiar are you with the basics of the investigation?"

"The Nixes have shared the basics, but I'd like to hear it from you."

Josie nodded and sat with her hands folded on the table in front of her. "We discovered a male, thought to be somewhere between twenty-five and fifty years of age, dead on the Nixes' couch in their living room. Their house was severely burned the same night as the wildfire. The body was burned too severely to identify. The body was discovered the next morning by Officer Podowski and myself. I tried calling the Nixes at that time to notify them of the body but they did not return my calls or messages."

Turner looked shocked at the last statement. "I beg to differ! Ms. Nix absolutely returned your call! The same day you called her, she returned your call."

"There were six hours between the time I called and the time Ms. Nix returned my call."

Turner smirked. "Really? Are we doing this? Disparaging remarks thirty seconds into your summary statement?"

Josie let it go. "The first piece of troubling news, from our standpoint, was that the fire that spread through the western part of the county, where the Nixes' home is located, had moved through that area almost two hours past the time the body was burned on the couch. The wildfire had not reached the Nixes' home at the time it burned."

"How do you know?"

"The hands of the watch on the victim's hand were melted into the face at seven thirty-eight p.m. According to spotter records, the fire didn't roll through there until after nine thirty."

"How do you know his watch wasn't dead?"

Josie raised her eyebrows.

"His watch could have *quit* at seven thirty-eight, and the fire melted the face of the watch at nine thirty."

"We found a clock in the kitchen that was stopped at seven forty p.m." Josie paused and looked directly at Brenda. "The coroner also provided additional information today after the autopsy. He's confirmed that the victim was dead before the fire that was intentionally set burned his body."

"And he knows this how?" Turner asked.

"There was no smoke damage to the lungs as there would have been if he had asphyxiated during the fire."

"My clients were out of town. I'm still not sure what this has to do with Brenda or Billy," Turner said.

"Yesterday, after searching the house again, we found evidence that a Zaner stun gun was discharged in the house before the victim was burned in the fire."

"And?"

"And the Zaner is registered to Brenda Nix."

Brenda looked from her attorney to Josie, her expression confused. "What do you mean my Zaner was discharged? I haven't even had it out of the box in months."

"Out of what box?" Josie asked.

"I keep it in a box in the bedroom. Go look for it. It's a wooden box with a carved lid. Sitting on top of my bureau drawers."

Turner raised her hands in the air and dropped them on her lap. "Well, there you go. Anyone who knows the Nixes could have gotten into the box, used the Zaner to disable the victim, and then killed and staged the body. Again, no clear connection to the Nixes."

"The body was lying on their couch."

"They weren't home at seven forty when you just stated the man died!"

"That's not what I said. He died sometime *before* seven forty. This is premeditated murder. He was disabled with a stun gun, murdered, then staged on the couch. His body was burned so severely at that time that the hands of the watch melted," Josie said.

Turner rolled her eyes. "Please spare us the melodrama."

"Here's the timeline as we know it," Josie continued. "The Nixes left home at about five, arrived at the Hell-Bent at five thirty. After picking up Billy's guitar out of the dressing room they both left a little before six."

"And?"

"From here things get a bit vague," Josie said.

"Because?"

Brenda leaned forward and clicked her fingernails on the table to get Josie's attention. "Excuse me." Her voice was low and quiet, her eyes angry. "I'm sitting right here. Since you're talking about my husband and me, wouldn't it make sense to address us as if we were a part of this conversation?" Her tone was flat but the muscles in her face were taut with fury.

Josie locked eyes with Brenda. "At six p.m., you either left for Austin, or you returned home and committed murder."

Brenda sat back up in her seat and withdrew her arm into her lap, her face bright red.

"You're way out of line, Chief," said Turner. "They've already told you they drove to Austin and went to Gilly's, and then checked in at the Hampton."

"Did you use your credit card at Gilly's to buy your first round of drinks when you arrived at one?"

Josie could tell by the three expressions sitting across from her that the answer was no.

"They paid with cash. A legal form of currency last time I checked," Turner said.

"What time did you check in at the hotel?"

"Two twenty-five in the morning, just after the bars closed," Turner said. "Just like they told you." She opened up her briefcase and shuffled through it for a moment. Finally she shoved a piece of paper across the desk and Josie read the hotel name across the top of the paper.

"If the Nixes checked into the Hampton at two twenty-five, that would have allowed plenty of time for them to have murdered a man and set fire to the house before making the six-to-seven-hour drive to Austin."

Billy looked bereft. "I don't understand why you would suspect us of murder. What could we possibly gain by killing someone and burning down our own house?"

"What kind of homeowner's insurance do you carry?" Otto asked, picking up his pencil as if ready to write down the policy number.

Billy wrinkled his forehead and looked at Brenda. "I don't know. We rent the house," he said.

"Okay. Let's cut to the chase," Turner said. "Are you charging my clients with a crime? If you are, let's get it over with. Otherwise, we're leaving until you come up with something more than circumstantial pondering."

"I would suggest trying to find someone who can vouch for your whereabouts Sunday night from the hours of six until one in the morning. We're not filing charges, but you are the primary suspects." Josie paused for a moment. "If you didn't commit this crime, then help us figure out who did."

After the Nixes left, Josie and Otto spent the afternoon working in a companionable silence. Otto cataloged evidence they had collected from the Nixes' home the night before, and Josie caught up on phone calls and e-mails until 12:45, when she left to interview the lead singer for the Calloway Boys. Mick Sinner owned an upholstery shop behind the fire station in Artemis and had agreed to talk with Josie after lunch.

The shop was a small clapboard bungalow painted navy blue with white trim. A covered front porch was decorated with a vase of flowers on an end table with a wicker rocking chair sitting beside it. A framed sign on the table read, *If you are here for upholstery business, please walk around to the garage in back. We are open M–F from 8:00–3:00. Thank you!* It was a homier setup than Josie would have imagined.

Josie followed a sidewalk around to the back of the house, where she found a two-car garage with the door closed. An OPEN sign hung on an entrance door to its right. Josie pushed the door open and found a man and woman standing in front of a tattered couch on a large worktable that put the couch about three feet high. They were both prying staples out of the wood and removing fabric that looked to have once been a flowered print. Patches of the fabric were disintegrated and faded to light shades of gray, brown, and yellow.

The man continued working but the woman looked up and smiled. She was petite, barely over five feet, with a slim frame. Her black jeans, white V-neck T-shirt, and short haircut gave her the look of a young girl, but the fine lines around her eyes made Josie guess she was in her early fifties. She wiped her hands on a towel draped over her shoulder. "Hi! I bet you're Chief Gray."

They shook hands. "That's correct."

"I'm Vicki. Good to meet you." She pointed toward a kitchenette in the corner of the room where a table and chairs were located. "Let's have a seat."

Josie sat down as Vicki pulled a pitcher of water from the refrigerator and filled three glasses. Josie felt air blowing on her and noticed ductwork in the open ceiling area for central air and heating. She also noted several other pieces of furniture sitting along the far side of the garage, waiting to be worked on.

"I would have never guessed there was such a market for upholstery work in a small town," Josie said, making small talk and hoping Mick would join them.

"We have a nice little niche here. People don't have a lot of furniture options in town, what with being so far from the city. So we buy up classic furniture at flea markets in El Paso and reupholster. We have clients now that send us pictures of what they want and we find it for them, then find a fabric they love. It's turned into a good little business."

Mick finally moved away from the couch and brushed the lint and stray pieces of fabric off his T-shirt and jeans before coming over to the table. Black hair hung in loose ringlets down to his shoulders and gave his pale angular face a softer appearance. He was thin and dressed in the same uniform of black jeans and V-neck T-shirt that the woman was wearing.

"Mick Sinner," he said, hand outstretched. The corners of his mouth were downturned. He had the look of a person who took life very seriously.

Josie stood and shook his hand. "I heard you at Hell-Bent last year. I enjoyed the show."

"Awesome." His expression remained unchanged, as if he'd heard it too many times and was no longer impressed by compliments.

They settled around the table and Josie began. "I'd like to talk with you about the country music scene in Arroyo County and some of the bands you play with. I'm working an investigation and the information you provide will help me understand who I need to talk with."

"Sure."

"You play at the Hell-Bent. Are you regulars?"

He tilted his head and gave her a look as if he thought the question was odd. "What constitutes a regular in your mind?"

"Do you play there frequently? Several times per month?"

"Sure. We got a good name around West Texas."

"You ever open for other bands?"

"Here? No." He shook his head, frowning again. "We headline."

"You never open for Billy and the Outlaws?"

He laughed. "Seriously? You said you've seen our band. Did we sound like we'd open for Billy?"

"I don't know. Someone at the Hell-Bent told me you opened for them." That wasn't true, but she wanted his reaction.

He lifted up his arms and shoulders, his face puckered in mock confusion. "So you just stop by today to insult my band? I'm not sure where you're headed with this. Do clue me in."

"Why is that an insult? I thought Billy and the Outlaws were a big name in West Texas. About ready to hit it big in Nashville."

He opened his eyes wide now, his face animated. "Oh, really? Is that their story? It's that monster wife manager who spreads shit like that. True or not it makes them sound big. That's what it's all about for her. Generating buzz. It's not about original sound or compelling music."

Josie said nothing and waited a moment for him to continue. She could tell he was holding back.

He finally leaned forward in his seat and squinted at her as if trying to get her to understand the situation. "They're a mediocre band trying to snag a recording contract."

"It sounds like it's working for them," Josie said.

"It's not working for them, and here's why. You find the band of the moment, you emulate the sound, and by the time you get enough name recognition for your own band the moment's gone. It doesn't take a rocket scientist to figure that out."

"Okay. Let's change gears. I want to talk about the fires that moved through the county. Where were you the night of the evacuation? Sunday evening from about five until about midnight?"

"What the hell is this? Now I'm being interrogated?"

"This isn't an interrogation. It's a homicide investigation, and I have some questions for you."

His eyebrows rose. His expression was still animated, but the anger had been replaced with shock. "Homicide? In Artemis?"

"Where were you Sunday evening?"

"I stayed with Vicki and her husband Bill. They live on a ranch headed toward Fort Stockton."

Vicki placed her hand on the table in front of where Mick was sitting, protectively, Josie thought.

"Mick got to our house Sunday afternoon around three," she said.

"I ate dinner with them and stayed the night."

"You said homicide. Who died?" Vicki asked.

"A man's body was found burned to death in the Nixes' home Monday morning. There was no identification on the body."

"No kidding? In their house?" Mick asked.

"Have you heard of anyone in the music community or around town who's missing? Maybe someone who left during the evacuation and hasn't returned?"

Vicki returned her hand to her lap, and studied Mick with her eyebrows drawn together as she contemplated the question. She finally looked back at Josie and said she couldn't think of anyone.

"Burned to death?" He winced and shook his head as if to clear the image. "I haven't heard anything. Rumors spread like the plague around here. We'd have heard if someone was missing."

Josie had no doubt that by dinnertime the Hell-Bent would be buzzing.

"I didn't think the fire moved through that area of the county," Vicki said.

"You know where the Nixes live?" Josie asked.

She looked surprised by the question. "Well, yes. We redid a couch for them last year. Mick and I both delivered it."

"I thought your two bands didn't like each other."

"I don't dislike Billy. I just don't think he's God's gift to country music," Mick said.

"Can you imagine Billy having the kind of house that someone would stop by and crash for the night? Maybe some guy's wife kicked him out and he needed a place to stay. Can you imagine someone going to the Nixes for help?"

Mick laughed out loud and Vicki grinned. She spoke first. "I can't imagine Brenda giving anyone the impression that they were free to stay at her house without an invitation."

"What about close friends?"

"They know everyone," Vicki said. "Brenda networks like a politician. That doesn't mean they're friends with anyone though."

"There's a kid who hangs out whenever Billy's playing. He's probably late twenties. Cocky little shit. He tries to play himself off as a personal assistant for Billy."

"Brenda's the manager though, right?"

He nodded and looked perplexed. "That's the weird thing. I can't figure out why Brenda hasn't put an end to this kid. Maybe she's tried and can't. He'll even sit with her sometimes when they're playing. You can tell she can't stand him though."

Vicki made a face as if she wanted to say something.

"Go ahead," Josie said. "This is a private conversation."

"I don't think Brenda would put up with someone, no matter who it was, if she didn't have something to gain."

"What's his name?"

Mick sneered. "Ferris Sinclair. What a name, right?"

"Do you know where I can find him?"

Mick glanced at Vicki and they both shrugged. He said, "No clue. I don't really think he's from here. I've only seen him hanging out at the bar."

FOURTEEN

Josie found Otto sitting at the conference table, surrounded by piles of file folders and a stack of what looked like billing statements.

"What's the word, Chief?"

"I talked with Mick Sinner and his business partner for a while," she said. "Vicki Macke provided Mick a solid alibi for the night of the evacuation. The only odd piece to the interview was that they were both in the Nixes' house in the past year to deliver a couch they had reupholstered for them."

"Didn't Hank say they hated each other?"

"I think they dislike each other intensely. It seems odd you'd let someone you hate fix your couch. You'd have to think about them every time you sat down to watch TV."

"Maybe Billy's clueless," Otto said. "He might not have any idea Mick hates him. He doesn't strike me as someone who's very self-aware."

Josie walked over to her desk and pitched down her notepad. "You're right. I wouldn't read too much into it."

"Nothing more?"

She sat down and faced him again. "This is a little better. Some kid named Ferris Sinclair hangs around the band. Apparently Mick's seen him in the bar."

"A fan?"

"Something like that." Josie said. "Mick says the kid's infatuated with Billy and the band. And he's a 'cocky little shit'—Mick's words, not mine. And Mick says Brenda doesn't like him."

"Better get an interview with him." Otto pursed his lips in thought. "I went out to the Nixes' to search for the box containing the stun gun. Want to guess what was inside the box where the Zaner was supposed to be kept?"

"Nothing?" she asked.

"Exactly."

Otto spent the next four hours logging information from the Nixes' computer files. When Marta came on duty at 3:30 p.m., she systematically checked each document on the Nixes' computer. The files were extremely well organized, with expenditures tediously noted. Fortunately, like most people's, the Nixes' information was woefully unprotected. She found a spreadsheet under "Home Files," with tabs that contained an identity thief's gold mine. One tab contained credit card numbers, expiration dates, and security codes. Another tab included all of the online sites they frequented along with logins and passwords. One of the tabs included all of the family's insurance policies and health-care information, all wide open to any hacker in the world.

Marta called each credit card company and found a total credit card debt, at least using the cards listed on the spreadsheet, of $9,467. Not too out of line for a couple trying to grow a small business. Payments were up to date and on time each month. Incredibly, Marta even found the Web site and password for their online free credit check. She logged in and discovered that their credit was within the "Good" classification, not surprising given Brenda's managerial skills.

Otto found life insurance policies in the manila file folders that were paid up. Each carried $100,000 in insurance, with the spouse as the sole beneficiary. No new insurance had been obtained over the past eleven years, assuming they would have kept paperwork on such a policy. Otto also finally made phone contact with the landlord of the Nixes' home. He lived in Idaho and hadn't even heard about the wildfire, and was shocked to discover that his old family home had been demolished.

Otto also found a ledger with information about booking dates and earnings. There were notations about how much each band member made after each performance. It appeared that Billy made about thirty to fifty percent more than the other band members for each gig, but it also appeared that his money paid Brenda's managerial fees. Otto intended to ask other band members their opinions on Brenda's role as manager and keeper of the finances.

While Marta and Otto worked on the Nixes' files, Josie ran a background check on Ferris Sinclair and found nothing of consequence. Since Ferris's connection to Billy was the Hell-Bent, she opted to try there first for background information on him and his relationship with the Nixes.

She pulled into the parking lot of the Hell-Bent just before 3:00 p.m. She figured two cars in the parking lot were probably typical for a Wednesday afternoon. It was too late for the lunch crowd, and too early for the after-work crowd. She found Hank sitting in his office pecking two-fingered on his computer keyboard. He looked up and stood from his chair when she knocked.

"Come on in, Chief." He came around to the other side of his desk and cleaned a stack of rolled-up posters and what appeared to be mail and magazines off the two chairs next to a small table.

"What's the word on Billy and Brenda? I finally got ahold of them yesterday and Billy was a mess. He said you think they killed someone in their own home. Killed him and set their house on fire. That's insane! You ought to know Billy better than that."

"No one has been accused of a crime. Our first priority is to find out the identification of the victim."

He looked relieved. "You oughta tell Billy that. He's convinced it's a witch hunt and he's headed for jail."

"If he didn't kill the victim he has nothing to worry about."

Hank grimaced. "Tell that to the guy who fried on death row an innocent man."

Josie had no intention of talking politics. "Do you know a man by the name of Ferris Sinclair?"

Hank rolled his eyes. "He's a hanger-onner."

"A what?"

"Ask any bartender with live music. They know the type. The kind that takes up seat space and never buys a drink. They come in hoping to connect with the band and get someone to buy them shots along the way. You ever heard of moochers?"

She laughed. "You don't think much of the hanger-onners."

He smiled. "Okay, that was a little rough. This kid gets under my skin though. He takes advantage of Billy and Brenda both."

"How so?"

"Brenda catches a lot of hell for some reason. I really don't get it. She's fair to deal with. She doesn't come in here making unreasonable demands. She and Billy don't walk around like prima donnas. I know people don't like her, but she's a manager. Plain and simple."

"What's that have to do with Ferris?"

"His latest stunt was to tell people he was Billy's personal assistant."

"Is he?"

"Not hardly." Hank chuckled and shut his eyes at the thought. "Do you know Billy very well?"

"Just through his music."

"He's a big kid. He can't take conflict. He can't say no. So Brenda deals with anything negative in Billy's life. I couldn't do what she does. And I guarantee Ferris couldn't."

Josie gave him a quizzical look, still not understanding why Hank said Ferris *got under his skin.*

"Ferris loves the scene. He loves to hang out with the band. He likes for people in the bar to know he's close to Billy, a personal friend, and Billy doesn't have the heart to tell the kid to take a hike. He's obnoxious, overbearing, lies when it benefits him."

"Why doesn't Brenda deal with him?"

"She's tried! I've heard her tell him she's saving a seat when Billy and the Outlaws are getting ready to take the stage, but Ferris laughs it off. Sits next to her anyway. It's just bizarre." Hank's expression changed, his eyes narrowed in suspicion. "What's this about?"

"I'm just collecting information right now. Do you have any idea where I can find Ferris?"

"He lives in Presidio. That's all I know."

"Does he ever stay with Billy and Brenda? At their home?"

Hank pulled air in between his teeth and gave her a look as if that idea was a stretch for him to believe. "I can't imagine Brenda would allow that."

Josie imagined dusk as the time when the dust and drama of the day, worn down by the unrelenting sun, settled over the desert. Mentally, the sun took a toll on people. The heat of high noon in the desert was like no other, and when the sun tipped over the edge of the horizon the relief was physical and emotional. Driving home, she noticed the orange fade on the horizon and she sighed with relief as she pulled onto Schenck Road.

Josie pulled her jeep into the driveway and found Chester already waiting for her on the front porch. He typically waited to leave Dell's barn until he heard her engine as she came down the road. He was a large dog, weighing about eighty-five pounds, with the typical coloring and ears of a bloodhound, but he had a gallop that reminded her of a horse. She wouldn't have imagined that a bloodhound who spent half his time outdoors with his nose to the ground could run with such grace.

She got out of the car smiling. He stood on the edge of the porch wagging his whole body in delight, but he refused to come down the steps to greet her. As much as he wanted a pat on the head from Josie, he wanted his evening bone and a nap on his rug even more. He was a dog of habit, and when Josie's schedule became too messed up with work, it made him irritable.

After scratching his ears and nuzzling his neck she stood to unlock the front door and found a piece of notebook paper taped to the sidelight window.

She pulled the paper off and read: "Supper's on the stove. Corn bread. Beans been cooking all day. See you when you get here. —Dell"

She sighed and smiled. She missed Dell. She had been selfish and unreasonable the other night when she found the woman in his house. If Dell had found love, then good for him; it was well deserved.

Josie hung her gun belt in the pantry and followed Chester into the living room, all part of the nightly ritual. She watched as he lay down on his rug and turned expectant eyes up to her. She set a rawhide chew between his front paws and he continued to stare at her until she said, "Well, go ahead," and then he picked it up and spent the next ten minutes chewing excitedly like a kid with a piece of bubble gum. She'd grown up with dogs and cats, most of them strays, but none of them had a personality like Chester's.

After she changed into shorts and a T-shirt, she and the dog walked to Dell's house at 7:00. It was still ninety-five degrees out, but the hard edge of the heat had dissipated and a slight breeze made it a comfortable walk.

She stepped onto the front porch and knocked on the screen door. This time she waited for him to yell, "Come in." Chester beat her through the door and ran into the kitchen with his paws scrabbling against the wood floor. Dell laughed like Chester was a long-lost grandchild instead of the dog that spent every afternoon following him around the ranch.

Dell had been sitting at the kitchen table reading the newspaper.

He pitched his glasses onto the table and went to the stove to dish up the bean soup.

He opened the pot and steam billowed up. "That's got some flavor in it. A ham hock and onions and peppers and a shot of butter and mashed beans for substance." He whistled like he was looking at a pretty girl.

Josie joined him at the stove and watched as he dished up the soup. "It smells like heaven."

"I thought maybe you disowned me after the other night," he said.

"I'd never disown you. You're my best friend."

"Me and the dog."

They carried their soup to the table, where a plate of corn bread was sitting. Halfway through dinner and small talk, Dell said, "Tell me about your dead body."

"How'd you hear about the body?"

"Otto said you had a homicide."

"When did you talk to him?" she asked.

He glanced up from his soup, his eyes bright.

"He called you, didn't he? That's what dinner is about. He told you to babysit me tonight. Didn't he?"

"I ran into him in town. He said he thought you were still feeling blue since Dillon left. How can you fault a man for watching out for your well-being?"

Josie shook her head, her expression incredulous. "Dell, I'm a cop. Have been for years. I can handle a little stress in my life without falling apart."

"Fine, you badass, what if I just wanted to have dinner with you?"

She laughed. "Badass?"

"Since you brought up the subject of the missing boyfriend, give me an update."

Avoiding the question, she asked, "You have any beer in the fridge?"

"No beer." He looked embarrassed. "There's a half bottle of wine in there that'll never get drank. It's all yours."

She raised her eyebrows.

"Just pour yourself a glass and tell me about Dillon. I don't feel like talking tonight. Tonight I listen."

Josie convinced Dell to let her clean up while he started a fire outside. She wanted to sit beside the fire and finish the conversation without the face-to-face scrutiny and harsh lights of the kitchen. And Dell never missed an opportunity to sit outside by a fire.

Josie washed up the few dishes and dried them. She opened the cabinets for the plates and bowls and found them as orderly as they had been any other time she had opened a cabinet. Dell was as predictable and stable as anyone she knew, and those two traits alone made him a hero in her eyes. She'd found very few people through the years that she could say that about.

She washed the countertop and found him standing over orange flames with two camp chairs set up. Once they were seated, Josie suffered through half a glass of dry red wine, and then said, "Things are getting better with Dillon. If I didn't have this nagging guilt that I'd destroyed his life, I'd be okay." She put her hand up, not wanting a lecture. "But I get it."

"You were both out of your league, Josie. The only way you two were going to survive is to move on. He's got way too many nightmares here to do that. And you have too much guilt to ever be able to help him. I'm glad he left. I'm glad for both of you. You've been moping around for two months. It's time to stop it."

They sat quietly staring at the flames and Josie said nothing.

Dell finally spoke. "Besides, you've been such piss-poor company I had to go find a lady friend to talk to."

Josie grinned. "And? Where's the lady friend?"

"She's back in Presidio where she belongs."

"Dell! You didn't give her much of a chance, did you?"

"It's got nothing to do with chances. She didn't like you, and she didn't like Chester, and I didn't like her."

"You could just go out as friends. Someone to hang out with every once in while."

"Look. I don't hang out. I'm not cut out for relationships. I've been a bachelor my whole life and I can't go changing that now. No sense dragging her along for something that won't work out in the end."

She smiled. "Every breakup should be so easy."

"Absolutely. If people'd quit acting like such pansies and have an honest conversation every once in a while, all of humanity would benefit." Dell extended his legs out in front of him and crossed his arms like he was settling in for a good story. "Now, down to business. Homicide."

"Okay." She downed the rest of her wine, shuddered, and set the glass on the ground. "Here's the basics. When the wildfire blew through Artemis on Sunday, most of the town evacuated. That included Brenda and Billy Nix."

"The country singer?"

"That's the one. They left town after stopping in at the Hell-Bent to pick up Billy's guitar. They claim they left at about six and got to Austin at about one, when they got a drink at a bar and then checked into a hotel a little after two."

"Easy enough to check, right?"

"They checked into the hotel at about two thirty in the morning. But they used cash at the bar."

"We all oughta use cash. All this electronic tracking will be this country's demise. Mark my words."

"Meanwhile, the fire chief, Doug Free, asked Otto and me to check out the west side of the county. He'd heard some outbuildings were damaged. We drove out to check structures and make sure no one was injured or in need of help. We drove down Prentice Canyon Road, which was the west edge of the fire."

"The firebreak?"

Josie nodded. "Doug thought it had been the perfect firebreak. By nightfall the wind had died down. By the time the fire hit that north-south road, it had lost fuel. That area of the county is mostly barren desert and clumps of scrub. Strategically, it was a great move on the chief's part."

"Don't the Nixes live on the other side of the road?" Dell asked.

"Exactly. No structures were lost on that side of the road except their house." Josie paused. "It's true, there aren't many structures out there to burn, but from the flyover, it became clear a fire was intentionally set at the house."

"They set it for the insurance?" Dell asked.

"Nope. It's a rental. The body we found on the Nixes' couch was burned before the fire ever crossed that part of the county."

"Meaning someone set the fire at their house on purpose. To make the murder look like an accident."

Josie smiled. "You get better and better at this. I should hire you as a consultant."

"What do you pay?"

"Nothing."

"Figures. So who put the body on the couch?"

"That's the question. Sounds like there's some jealousy among the local bands. A small group of people competing for the stage and the record deals."

"What's a body on the Nixes' couch have to do with that?"

"You want to end someone's career, what better way to do it," she said.

Dell narrowed his eyes like he wasn't buying the explanation.

"Remember that trial last year in El Paso?" she asked. "Some guy hated his divorce attorney so bad that he set him up for murder. He convinced his ex-wife, whom he also hated, to meet him at some office building. It was actually a vacant office. He killed his ex and planted evidence to make it look like the attorney was having an affair with her and killed her. The guy almost got away with it."

"All right. I get it. Hatred is a hell of a motivator. Wouldn't the Nixes make more sense though?"

"They're our primary suspects. But I can't imagine why you'd choose your own house to murder someone. The man was dead before he was burnt up in the fire. So if they were going to go to the trouble of arranging a body on their couch, why not drive him over to the east side of the fire where things were really cooking? Dump the body. They wouldn't have lost their home either."

"They probably thought no one would believe they'd torch their own home. Makes them look less suspicious. Besides," Dell said, "I don't know too many people who could stuff a dead body in their car and dump it along a roadside."

"You don't hang out with the right people."

At midnight, Billy Nix quietly rolled out of bed and stood without moving over his wife's body. He listened to her rhythmic breathing and watched the white sheet rise and fall. Her jaw was slack against the pillow, her face pale and delicate in the dim light cast from the streetlamp outside their motel window. She'd always been a heavy sleeper. Back when they still talked about having kids he teased her about sleeping through the delivery. Now, as he checked on her before sneaking out of the hotel in the middle of the night, the thought of having kids seemed a lifetime away. It wasn't that she'd be angry that he left, but he didn't want to disturb her. Even as he stood staring at her, repeating those words inside his head, he knew it was a lie. He didn't want to explain to her why he couldn't sleep.

Billy pulled his jeans and shirt and boots off the chair next to the desk and dressed quietly in the bathroom. He went back into the room and felt around on the desk for the pen and motel stationery and took them into the bathroom. He wrote her a quick note saying, "Couldn't sleep. Went for walk. Love you—Billy." He left the note on the bedside table and quietly unlocked the door and opened it. He stood outside the room and took a long slow breath, trying to clear the noise from his head. He felt his shirt pocket for the pack and lighter. He tapped the pack of Marlboros, pulled out a cigarette, and lit it, watching the red ember flare as he inhaled the smoke, listening to the paper and tobacco sizzle, glad for the familiar sound, for something reliable. He hadn't slept in days but he couldn't shut down his thoughts long enough to relax. He thought he might walk down to Mickey's, just a few blocks away. He knew the bartender. He could hang out for an hour or two and figure out what the hell had gone wrong with his life to make him a suspect in a murder investigation.

Brenda stood at the window watching Billy just five feet from the door, smoking a cigarette, thinking about God only knew what. He'd snuck out of the motel room to stand in front of the window with nothing but a sheer separating him from her view. Part of her wanted to smile at his innocence; another part of her wanted to kill him for his stupidity. Was he really that guileless or was he just not very bright? It was a question Brenda continued to wonder even after twelve years of marriage. If a man was going to sneak out of a motel room, wouldn't he slip down a side street and get on with his business?

She watched him raise his arm, draw on the cigarette, throw it onto the ground, and twist his boot to extinguish it. And then he walked off, most likely in search of a bar, but she really had no idea anymore. Their life had turned into secrets and veiled conversations whose meanings seemed to be more in what was not said than the embarrassed words they spoke. She watched his handsome backside as he, so utterly confident in his long-legged swagger, walked down the street and disappeared.

She drew the curtains closed to block out the streetlight and turned on the bedside lamp by Billy's side of the bed. She picked up his cell phone and turned it on. She checked for text messages out of habit, but she was certain there wouldn't be any. His hands were too big and cumbersome to use the keypad. She checked for voicemails and found none. Finally, she scrolled through his received and missed calls, recognizing every one of the numbers, her disappointment now complete. Like so many times before, she cleared the screen and shut off his phone, setting it back down and grabbing from her purse the Xanax that would finally allow her to sleep.

FIFTEEN

By the time Otto arrived, at eight o'clock, Josie had delivered two chocolate doughnuts from the gas station to the middle of his desk, made coffee, and run Ferris Sinclair through NCIC to discover his address was indeed in Presidio. Otto smiled when he got to his desk and saw his treat.

Josie was on the phone with Junior Daggy, a local real estate agent who knew almost every parcel of land in far west Texas and enough gossip to put most informants to shame.

"His name's Ferris Sinclair," Josie said, and read Junior his address.

"Oh, sure. That's the old Winferd station house. The railroad conductor had a stop-off house there. Somebody bought it years ago, fixed it up, and then sold it. Real cute place. Nice tall ceilings."

Josie cut him off. "You think Ferris owns it?"

He whistled into the phone. "Oh, yeah. He paid a pretty penny for that little gem."

"Do you know Ferris?"

"I know who he is. That's about it."

Josie thanked Junior for the information and shared it with Otto.

While he ate his pastry Josie called the Presidio County Sheriff's Office and asked for Deputy Susan Spears. Presidio was a small town located thirty miles southeast of Artemis. Josie had known Susan for years and knew she had a good handle on the locals. Now in her late fifties, she was called Grandma by half the kids in Presidio. She had a big heart for cast-off kids. She had started an intramural sports league that allowed all kids equal playing time about ten years ago and it had grown so large that she had people visit from all over Texas who wanted to start similar programs.

"You heard of a guy named Ferris Sinclair?" Josie asked her.

"Looks like a weasel?"

Josie laughed. "I don't know. I've never seen him. I hear he lives in the Winferd station house."

"That's him. Yep, I know him."

"How so?"

"He's made several complaints. Someone's always harassing him. I swear to you, he called one night because people were calling him names. I was like, come on, this ain't grade school. You're a grown man. If you don't like these people quit hanging around the bar. Pick a different place to drink your beer."

"Why were they calling him names?"

"Probably because of his smart mouth. He said some guys were calling him gay and hassling him. He wanted me to charge them with a hate crime."

"Anything come of it?"

"No. He wanted me to understand he wasn't gay. He was emphatic about that. But they *thought* he was gay, said hateful things, and so they should be charged with a hate crime."

"Seriously?"

"I know. There's plenty of hate crime out there to deal with. This just wasn't it."

"Can you give me a physical description?"

"Late twenties. Tall. I think some of the women think he's a looker. He's got these pinched features, narrow face, thin body. He just reminds me of a weasel. I can take about anybody but a whiner, and that's Ferris. I wanted to tell him to grow a pair."

"He ever get in any trouble himself?"

"Nope. He causing trouble in Artemis?"

"I'm not sure. I hear he hangs around Billy Nix, with Billy and the Outlaws?"

"That doesn't surprise me. He seems to want people to notice him."

"Would you do me a favor this morning?"

"Sure. Name it."

"Would you drive by his house and see if he's there? If he is, I'll drive over and talk to him. The only phone number I can find for him goes immediately to voicemail when I call."

"You bet. I'll give you a call back before lunch."

Josie hung up and told Otto about her conversation with Susan. "I'll follow up on Ferris as soon as I hear back from her."

Otto nodded and pointed toward the conference table. "You see the note Marta left you?"

Sitting on top of the Nixes' laptop was a note that said, "Still need to check the e-mail. I didn't get that far. Too busy. Took a car full of drunks to jail. What a night."

After logging in to the Nixes' computer, Josie scrolled through e-mails and discovered it was almost all to and from Brenda and dealt primarily with band business. There were several old e-mails from a woman named Patty who seemed to be her sister or family of some kind, filling Brenda in on her father's liver cancer. Brenda's responses were curt, obviously wanting the facts, not the emotions.

Almost two hours later Josie had skimmed through every e-mail in the system and found nothing of consequence. She did, however, figure Brenda earned her money as manager for the band. She spent an enormous amount of time cultivating contacts, setting up shows, and pitching different executives at several big houses for interviews and demos. Josie also discovered that the rumors were true: the Gennett deal looked as if it might come through, and not just for Billy but for the whole band.

Josie opened Internet Explorer and found that the search history had been cleared just two weeks ago, which led her to believe that either Brenda or Billy was hiding something from the other. It obviously wasn't a public computer, so why go to the trouble? Josie checked the sites that the Nixes had left opened in tabs: an online music store, a blog for country bands, a forum for guitar players where Billy was a member but had never posted anything, and a Budweiser site that explained the rules for a "Battle of the Bands" playoff in Los Angeles next month.

Next, she checked out searches that had been performed on Google. The first site to catch her attention was searched less than twenty-four hours before the Nixes had evacuated: mayoclinic.org. She clicked on the link in the recently searched history and was taken to a page titled DISEASES AND CONDITIONS: HIV/AIDS. Another twelve Google searches led to similar sites; three searches led to links that dealt specifically with symptoms. Josie turned her chair to Otto. "Come check this out."

Josie clicked through the links in the order that they had been searched. She learned that someone started with a vague search about HIV, then progressed specifically to symptoms, testing, and life expectancy. The searches were conducted between the hours of 10:45 p.m. and 11:57 p.m., on Saturday, the night before the evacuation.

Otto rolled his chair back from Josie's desk. "One of the Nixes has a healthy curiosity about a disease, or maybe Billy's worried he has HIV?"

"Might give Billy a motive for murder," she said. "He found out somebody gave him HIV and decided to get even."

Otto frowned. "Strange coincidence that Susan said Ferris wanted her to press charges against the guys that called him gay at the bar."

"Hmm. Maybe Billy and Ferris had a secret affair going on and one of them passed along HIV to the other one."

Otto narrowed his eyes at her like he was trying to follow her logic. "I don't know. Hard-core country singer, married, having an affair with a guy Susan described as looking like a weasel?"

Josie shrugged. "Just because you're hard-core country doesn't mean you can't be gay."

Otto gave her skeptical look.

Josie studied Otto for a moment. "The relationship and HIV diagnosis might give Brenda a motive too."

"How so?"

"If you found out your wife was HIV positive, you'd probably want to kill the person who gave it to her too," she said. "Hypothetically speaking."

Otto cocked his head and smirked. "Hard to imagine Delores with HIV."

"Okay, you get my point."

"I do," he said. "The interview with Ferris Sinclair should be a doozy."

Susan called Josie back on her cell phone just before lunch. "I drove by Ferris's house. I don't think he's been there in a couple days. I found mail in his box postmarked back to Monday."

"Thanks, Susan. I appreciate you looking. One more question. You ever hear any gossip about Ferris being HIV positive?"

"Oh, that's not good. From the bar-scene gossip around town, I hear he's pretty promiscuous. I haven't heard anything about HIV though. Want me to check around?"

"I'd appreciate it. He may be a homicide victim in a fire that took place at the Nixes' home during the evacuation. The fire that came through Sunday night. That's premature on my part, but let me know if you hear anything."

"Wow. Homicide. Burned in the fire? Or killed by other means?"

"Both. The victim was killed first, then intentionally burned. Ferris is a pretty big leap though."

"I'll ask around and get back with you."

As Josie hung up the phone Lou buzzed her from downstairs. "Pete Beckett is here to see you."

Otto raised his eyebrows. "Who's Pete?"

Her face grew red. "He's my friend from high school. The smoke jumper."

"Why the funny look?" he asked.

Josie played it off as nothing. "That's the problem with cops. You're too suspicious. I'll be right back."

She went downstairs and saw Pete waiting by the front desk of the PD, chatting with Lou.

"Hey, Josie! I wanted to stop in before we take off."

Josie smiled and pointed outside, not wanting to have a personal conversation in front of Lou. They walked outside and Josie saw the two vans that the smoke jumpers had traveled in parked in front of the courthouse across the street.

Pete's face was animated, his big brown eyes wide. "We just got a call to head back to Montana. Just wanted to stop and say bye."

"I owe you one, Pete. The skydiving was amazing. I think you have a winner with the jump therapy."

He grinned. "See? Old Pete's not as crazy as everybody thought all those years."

"You're as sane as anyone I know. You be safe out there," she said.

Josie reached out and they hugged for a long moment. He finally pulled away and ran for the van. She watched as they pulled out and the driver blasted the horn in a final good-bye.

———✦———

When Josie reached the top of the stairs she heard Otto talking on the phone. By the time she entered the office he was hanging up, his forehead creased with worry lines.

"Susan just called back," Otto said. "She was talking about Ferris to one of the other young deputies in the office who knew Ferris from hanging out at the bars. She told him that there was a victim burned in the fire and that we were concerned that it might be Ferris. Susan mentioned getting a warrant for the apartment and so on. Anyway, the deputy starts telling Susan about Ferris. He said Ferris was always telling stories about his life, most of which the guy figured were lies. Ferris told the deputy he was in the army right after high school and the deputy told Ferris he wasn't tough enough for the army. Ferris opened up his mouth and showed his teeth. Said the U.S. Army capped five of his back teeth with silver crowns. The deputy remembers him saying, who else but Uncle Sam would screw up somebody's mouth like this? The deputy brought it up thinking it might help ID the body."

Josie raised her eyebrows in recognition. "Good! We can check the fire victim's teeth for identification."

"Better than good. Remember I said Cowan checked out the victim's teeth to get a basic estimate on his age?"

"We may have just identified our victim," she said.

Otto rolled his chair around to face his desk and called Cowan. After a brief conversation he hung up and turned back to Josie with a smile. "Get this. I asked him if there was anything unusual he noticed when he examined the victim's teeth. Cowan said, 'Somebody butchered the guy's mouth. He's got five crowns.'"

"Excellent. Will you follow up with Susan to get contact information for Ferris's family? And can you get started on a full search warrant for his house and a subpoena for his medical records?"

"We could confirm his identity by tomorrow with dental records," he said.

Josie pointed to the laptop sitting on the table. "Okay. Walk through this with me. Let's suppose Ferris is HIV positive. He's staying the night at the Nixes' house. Maybe one of them sees his medication. Brenda hates him. She's searching through his bag for something to convince Billy that Ferris is bad news. Instead, she finds drugs she's never heard of. She goes on the Internet and discovers Ferris is being treated for HIV and reads up on it. She starts thinking about the band's big recording contract and decides this kid is trouble. He's terrible for the band's image."

"Let's go back to the idea that Billy and Ferris are having an affair. We've heard from several sources that Ferris is infatuated with Billy. Maybe Billy was infatuated too. Maybe Brenda began to suspect that Billy and Ferris had something going on. She wanted Ferris out of the equation before he ruined their marriage."

Otto said, "There's a fire raging through West Texas and she thinks, This is my chance. She convinces Billy to go get his guitar at the Hell-Bent to set their alibi. They go back to the house where they've told Ferris to wait. Maybe they told him to wait there and they'd come back and pick him up after they ran their errands."

Josie took the story back up. "Brenda convinces Billy that Ferris has to die before he ruins their marriage and Billy's plan for becoming a star. They get into the house and Brenda uses the stun gun on him. He drops to the floor and Billy kills him. Strangles him? He's big enough to choke a man out. Then they lay him on the couch, start the fire, and take off for Austin. Let him burn to death to make it look accidental."

"That works. There's motive, means, and opportunity," he said, ticking each word off on his fingers. "I'm not sure how plausible it is, but it works."

"We need the dental records. We need to know for sure how he was killed. And we need to know how the fire was started." Josie sat down at her desk. "I'd sure like to talk to the Nixes. Think there's any chance we could get them in here again?"

Otto looked doubtful. "Unless you're ready to file charges, I can't imagine Turner would allow it."

"I think our best bet is through Billy." She pulled her cell phone out of her shirt pocket and found Billy's number. She dialed and received no answer. She tried Brenda, who answered on the first ring.

"Brenda, this is Chief Gray."

"Yes?"

"We have some troubling news, Brenda. We'd like for you and Billy to come in and talk with us."

"I have to . . ." Her voice faded off and she paused for a moment. "I have to call our attorney. She said we need to take all this through her now."

"I understand. That's typical with the attorneys. I want you to let her know we believe we have the identity of the person who was killed in your home. We'd like to talk with you about it."

"Who was it?"

"I need to talk about that in person. I can tell you that it's someone you know. I'd like to give you an opportunity to explain things to us before we look at filing any charges."

"File charges? Against Billy and me?"

Josie knew she had to draw her in carefully and repeated her statement. "I'd like to give you the opportunity to come in to the department of your own volition to talk with us. I'll be honest, Brenda. I don't believe you and Billy committed murder. But right now every bit of evidence we have points your way. Come in and help us make sense of this. If someone is setting you up, then help us figure out who and why."

She hesitated for several seconds. "We'll be there at three." And she hung up the phone.

Josie grinned. "We got 'em."

Josie and Otto walked to the Hot Tamale, the local diner and their favorite lunch spot, to eat and plan their strategy. Lucy Ramone, owner, stood on a ladder outside the restaurant, retouching the sign that hung outside the diner: THE HOT TAMALE: QUICK SERVICE, AUTHENTIC RECIPES, AND THE MOST ACCURATE GOSSIP IN TEXAS.

"How's my favorite police officers?" She spoke with a paintbrush clenched between her teeth while she cleaned a smudge off the edge of a letter with a towel.

"We're better now that food is on the horizon," Otto said.

She took the paintbrush from between her teeth and climbed down. "One minute!" She opened the diner door and yelled, "Nina! For Otto, fresh bologna just came in this morning. Add some kraut and make him up a master sandwich. Give Josie a cold tamale with extra hot sauce."

Otto patted her on the back and called her a saint. She laughed and went back to her task.

Fortunately, they'd missed the lunch crowd and sat down at the front of the restaurant to plan their afternoon. It was decided that Josie would question Billy, and Otto would take Brenda. They had just begun to generate their list of questions when Josie's cell phone rang.

"Josie Gray."

"It's Lou. You better get back here. Now."

———————

Josie and Otto ran back to the department and entered to find Brenda Nix standing inside, her face in torment. It was 2:10 p.m., almost an hour before she and Billy were supposed to arrive for their interview, yet here she was without her husband. Her attorney wasn't with her either.

"What can we do for you?" Josie asked.

"I can't find Billy." Her face puckered up as if she might cry. Her eyes were already red and swollen.

Josie pointed toward the stairs at the back of the department. "Let's go upstairs and sit down. We'll talk this through. Would that be okay?"

Brenda nodded and put her hand over her mouth to stifle a sob.

Once they were upstairs and seated around the conference table, Brenda started talking with no mention of her attorney and no prompting from Josie.

"Billy left the motel room last night at around midnight. I heard him get up and get dressed. I figured he was going out to get a drink. He can't sleep when we're away from home. He'll get up and find a bar to have a drink or two and then come back to bed."

Josie interrupted her. She turned on the digital recorder and asked Brenda if she wanted to call her attorney before speaking with them.

"I don't need an attorney right now. I just need Billy."

"Did he tell you he was leaving?" Josie asked.

"No. He left me a note though." She passed the note across the desk and Josie read it.

"Is that typical?"

She tilted her head and shrugged. "I guess. Sometimes he'll sneak out without waking me. Especially if there's a bar at the hotel. Maybe since there was no bar to go to he thought he should leave a note. I don't know."

Josie saw her face starting to crumple and wanted her to keep it together. She changed course. "Has he ever stayed out all night?"

Brenda's eyes grew wide in what appeared to be an attempt to look sincere. "Never. He has never been gone more than a couple of hours. This is just not like him."

"Is your vehicle missing?"

"No. It's parked down the street in front of the motel."

"Could he be with a friend? Maybe he called a friend last night and they came and got him?"

Brenda teared up again. "Hank called me this morning. From the Hell-Bent?"

"Sure."

"He said Billy called him last night at about two in the morning. He said Billy was drunk and talking stupid. Hank told him to go back to the room and sleep it off. Billy said he would and hung up. Hank called me this morning to check on him. I was still asleep. That's when I realized Billy wasn't in bed."

"What time was that?"

"Nine."

Otto spoke up, his expression skeptical. "You slept until nine without realizing Billy wasn't in bed with you? You hadn't gotten up to go to the bathroom or anything earlier and realized he was missing?"

Tears now fell from her face and Josie pushed a box of tissues toward her.

"When Billy left I got up and took two sleeping pills. I couldn't sleep. This has all been so stressful on both of us. I was sound asleep when Hank called."

"Have you called your other friends, the band members, to see if he called them last night?" Josie asked.

"I've called everyone I can think of. Billy called Slim Jim last night too. He had the same conversation as Hank had with Billy."

"What time was this?"

"Slim said he called at about two. Slim told him to quit drinking and get to bed. He offered to come in to town and Billy told him no, that he was going to bed. No one else has heard from him."

"Have you searched anywhere?"

"No. I told Manny before I left and he was going to check all the rooms to make sure Billy didn't enter the wrong one last night." Brenda glanced sideways at Josie, as if ashamed that it could actually be an option.

"Mickey's Bar and Grill is the only place in town open after midnight. Did you try there?"

"I called Mickey this morning. He worked last night and said Billy never came in."

Josie was running out of options. She looked at Otto. He knew where she was headed. He nodded once in agreement for her to proceed.

"Brenda, I need to tell you why we wanted you and Billy to come to the department today. It may have something to do with Billy not coming home. Okay?"

She nodded, her face expectant.

"Do you know a man named Ferris Sinclair?"

She closed her eyes and sighed heavily as if even the name was a burden. "Yes. I know him."

"We have good reason to believe he is the man who died in your house. Who was burned on your couch."

Her mouth fell open and then she shut it suddenly, apparently stunned by the news. "Why on earth would someone kill Ferris in our home?"

"We're wondering the same thing. We've heard that you don't like Ferris. In fact, we heard that you hate him," Josie said.

"Well, I won't pretend that I like him. You're sure that it's Ferris?" she said.

Josie nodded. "We believe so, but we're waiting for a positive identification."

Brenda shuddered.

"What kind of a relationship do you have with Ferris?" Otto asked.

"Relationship? That's a bit too strong. He's a fame seeker. He sees Billy as someone who's going to make it big in Nashville, and he wants to ride his coattails."

"So you don't like him?" Otto asked.

Brenda stared across the table at Otto for a moment before speaking. "I always imagined him as one of those guys who marries some older woman and takes all of her money before leaving her or killing her off for insurance. That's the kind of person I think he is. So no, I don't like him. Billy doesn't have money for Ferris to take, but I believe he's after something. He's after his fame."

"I'm going to ask you a question, and I want you to think about it before getting angry and responding," Josie said. "This is a terrible thing that's happened to you. I'm not here to point fingers or accuse you or Billy of anything. I'm here to solve a murder."

She nodded once.

"Could Billy have gotten frightened and left town? Maybe he figured out the body was Ferris and panicked for some reason and left."

To her credit, Brenda didn't answer immediately. She was quiet, her mouth pulled in a grim flat line. She finally said, "Billy getting frightened and leaving would not completely surprise me. He is not a strong person. But when he left the motel room last night I watched him stand outside the window and smoke a cigarette before walking off. And the note he left me wasn't written by someone who was panicked." She leaned across the table and pointed to his signature on the note, "Love you—Billy." "That's not Billy in panic mode. I've seen that side of him. That wasn't him last night."

Josie nodded and looked at Otto. "Okay. Let's get some officers to scout out downtown. Without a car he couldn't have walked too far unless someone picked him up. I'd like for you to go back to the motel room and wait there for further instruction. You call my cell the minute you hear from him."

SIXTEEN

The search team that Josie assembled met at the courthouse at 4:00 p.m. and included Otto, Marta, and two sheriff's deputies, Dave Phillips and Juan Jiménez. Dave and Juan both wore brown-and-beige sheriff's uniforms with silver stars pinned over their breast pockets. Their heavy belts were weighted down with a gun, extra ammo clips, a nightstick, a flashlight, and assorted handcuff gear. Dave was in his midtwenties with an easy smile and the trim build of a lifetime athlete. Juan was a decade older, a foot shorter, and built like a linebacker with a scowl to go with it. The rough exterior paired well with a profane sense of humor that occasionally got him in trouble with the sheriff.

"What's the word, boss lady?" Juan asked.

"A missing person. But it's a little more complicated than that."

"Ah." He rubbed his hands together and gave her a grin. "Fill us in."

Otto pointed to the live oak tree on the courthouse lawn. "Let's get out of the sun here first."

The five officers moved into the shade and Josie filled them in on the homicide and the probable identity of the victim.

"You guys know anything about Ferris?" Josie looked at Juan and Dave.

Juan smirked. "Ferris is a whore dog. Man, woman, or beast."

"Come on, surely he's not that bad."

Dave laughed. "Yeah. He's that bad."

"How do you know?" she asked.

"'Cause I've seen him at Mickey's. If nothing's going on at the Hell-Bent he'll go down to Mickey's to find somebody to buy him drinks. If it's a lucky night he follows somebody home." Dave made a face as if he were gagging. "Let's just say he's not too discerning."

"You ever hear anything about Billy hooking up with Ferris?" Josie asked.

Dave made a face like he thought she was crazy. "What? As in Billy and Ferris together?"

"Hey, if I had to go home to that sourpuss wife every night I might look for another option too," Juan said.

"I don't know," Dave said. "I can't see it."

"Hey, I've known Billy for a lot of years," Juan said, "and he's not exactly Mr. Motivation. You know what I mean? If he didn't have his wife barking at his backside he'd still be pulling grunt work at the sanitation department. That's what Billy was doing when Brenda convinced him he could be a megastar. But she's a drill sergeant. She cuts that guy no slack. Maybe he liked Ferris saying nice things to him on the side." He raised his eyebrows as if to say, *You never know about people.*

Josie let the innuendo slide. "Is he known for taking off when things get rough?" she asked.

The two officers glanced at each other and shrugged.

"Brenda said Billy took off in the middle of the night to go get a drink and never came home. The car's still parked in front of the motel. None of their friends or bar owners have seen him. He called two friends last night while he was out drinking somewhere. Hank and Slim Jim. That was at about two this morning. Both guys told him to go back to the motel and he told them he would. But he's not shown up yet. I wouldn't think much of it, except we found a dead person in Billy's house."

"Still no ID on the body?" Juan asked.

"Not yet," she said.

"So we're doing a walking sweep of downtown?" Dave asked.

"We'll each take an area within a few blocks of his motel. Think like a drunk."

Juan socked Dave in the arm. "Ain't no problem, is it, buddy?"

The officers split up, focusing on dumpsters, alleyways, and corners where Billy might be sleeping off a bad drunk. Josie walked north of the courthouse, behind the police department and into the nearby neighborhood. Drunks had wandered into this neighborhood before, searching aimlessly for their homes, wanting nothing more than a bed, and waking the next morning having no idea how they ended up passed out beside some kid's swing set.

Josie walked down the alley that ran behind a row of homes, searching beside and behind garages and toolsheds. With the sun as hot as it was, she couldn't imagine Billy would still be passed out. She imagined he had most likely called another friend last night, too ashamed to call Brenda, and was sleeping off a massive hangover in someone's spare bedroom. Billy's life was spiraling out of control and Josie predicted that Ferris Sinclair was probably linked to whatever mess Billy was currently in.

Marta, who had taken the street south of Manny's Motel, called Josie.

"It's not good."

"Did you find him?"

"I think so. I'm not sure yet."

"Where are you?"

"I'm in the little park area behind the trauma center." Josie could hear scratching sounds in the background and then Marta's intake of breath. "I found him, Josie. It's him. Oh, dear God. I think he's dead."

"I'll be right there. I'll call the trauma center and get a doctor out there."

Josie and the other officers reached the trauma center within a few minutes. A nurse and the ER doctor, Mike Begley, were bent over Billy, who lay on his side underneath a bench covered by an arbor and shaded by trees.

Josie looked at the other officers, all of whom appeared as shocked as she was at finding Billy's lifeless body sprawled out in the open. There was little dignity in death. The muscles relaxed and body functions loosened, allowing bodily fluids to escape, and then within hours the body's muscles contracted and became locked in place, causing rigor mortis. It was clear by the awkward positioning of Billy's stiff legs and arms that he had been dead for several hours. Josie bent down to examine his face and saw that the blood had already begun to pool in the soft tissue in his face. His cheek, lying against the ground, was already turning a maroon color. After several minutes Dr. Begley stood and turned around to face the officers.

"No vital signs. I'd estimate he's been dead since early morning. There's vomit on the ground. Probably killed by alcohol poisoning."

Josie winced. The smell coming off his body was horrible.

She pulled out her phone and dialed Mitchell Cowan at the coroner's office.

"We've got a dead body," Josie said. "Behind the trauma center. How soon can you be here?"

———

Dave and Juan set up a perimeter around the park and marked it with crime-scene tape while they waited on Cowan to complete his initial exam. Josie and Otto took photographs and examined the area. They found an empty fifth of Jack Daniel's and a plastic baggie with several pills. Josie scanned the pills with her cell phone and used an app to identify them as OxyContin and Ambien, a deadly combination if mixed with enough alcohol.

Once the body had been removed for transport to the coroner's office, Josie and Otto finished processing the scene while Marta walked the perimeter of the park and the parking lot, looking for anything else that might tie into the case.

The bag of pills and the bottle were both lying within two feet of Billy's body. He appeared to have been sitting on the bench when he passed out, dropping the pills and bottle as he fell to the ground. There was nothing about the scene that appeared suspicious. Sadly, it looked like a straightforward and successful suicide attempt.

Josie placed the bag of pills into an evidence bag and Otto filled out a tag with date, time, and location.

"Suicide?" he asked.

"You think Billy killed Ferris and then killed himself over the guilt?" Josie said.

"Sure. If Ferris was HIV positive, he could have passed the virus on to Billy. Billy killed Ferris in anger, but couldn't take the guilt so he drank himself to death."

Josie felt something gnawing away at her, but couldn't put it in words yet. "Part of this feels a little coincidental."

"How so?"

She put a hand up and ticked off several points one at a time. "Ferris is found dead in Billy's house. Ferris has some issues with homosexuality. Someone at Billy's house is digging into research on HIV and AIDS. Billy shows up dead too. That's a lot of drama."

"Who has the motive to kill Billy?"

"If Brenda thought Billy contracted AIDS from Ferris?" Josie curled her lip up. "I'd want to kill him. That'd be motive enough for me as his wife."

"What about the meal-ticket theory. Everyone who knows her says her primary goal in life is to make Billy a star."

"I don't know. Maybe we're too focused on the HIV/AIDS theory."

Otto didn't respond and Josie noticed him giving her an uncomfortable look. "What about Brenda?" he asked.

She sighed. Their work at the park was finished. She had a job to do.

———•———

Manny's Motel was just two blocks from the trauma center. Josie found Brenda and Manny sitting on a bench outside the motel.

"Did you find him?" Brenda asked, standing when Josie reached her.

"Can we talk inside your room?" Josie asked.

Brenda paused, her expression already searching. "Of course, yes, come in."

Manny walked quietly back to his office, no doubt sensing the news was not good. Josie shut the door behind her and noted that the room was clean, the suitcase zipped up in the corner, the bed neatly made, the TV running on mute on top of the dresser. She imagined Brenda pacing the room waiting to hear from her husband. Manny, good man that he was, most likely came down to sit with her until she heard back from the police.

"I've come with terrible news."

"What? What's happened?"

"We found Billy's body in the small park behind the trauma center. It appears he passed away from alcohol poisoning."

"What?" The word came out in a strangled whisper. Brenda sank down onto the bed and stared at Josie.

"I'm so sorry," Josie said.

"I don't believe it."

"I'm sorry, Brenda. Do you have some family I could call for you? Someone who could come be with you right now?"

"Billy drinks whiskey. He's not a kid. Do you know how much he would need to drink to pass out?"

"We found an empty fifth of Jack Daniel's and a plastic baggie with a few pills in it. It appears he took a combination of prescription drugs and alcohol."

Brenda looked confused and then hopeful, as if there had been a mistake. "Billy doesn't take any medication. He doesn't take any pills. Even for a hangover he doesn't take anything. He's perfectly healthy."

"Prescription drugs are fairly easy to get. Billy could have gotten them from any number of people at the Hell-Bent."

"No!"

Josie leaned toward the bed, trying to get Brenda to listen to reason without going into details that she didn't want to hear. "We don't have blood results. We'll wait until an examination has been done, but it looked like a combination of Ambien and OxyContin. If he combined the pills with a fifth of whiskey, the result would be fatal."

"He doesn't have access to pills like that."

"Sometimes a spouse can have an addiction to drugs that their partner doesn't even know about. It happens more often than you might think."

"It did not happen to Billy! When you sleep in a hotel room with a person for days on end, there aren't many secrets. Billy is my husband and I love him very much. But he's also my job. I know everything he packs, everything he buys, who he talks to. He is not responsible." Something made Brenda stop talking. Perhaps she realized she was referring to her husband in the present tense. Maybe it was the accusatory tone of her words. She put her face in her hands and cried until her body shook. She finally curled into a ball on the bed and sobbed. Josie tried to touch Brenda on the shoulder, to offer comfort, but she pulled away and moaned in response. Josie walked to the front window in the motel room and looked outside, unable to watch the woman's private anguish.

Brenda finally stopped crying and Josie was able to find a phone number for her sister, Patty, by flipping through numbers in Brenda's cell phone. Josie told Brenda she was going to call Patty and Brenda simply nodded. Josie used her own phone and Patty answered. Josie explained the situation and that she was worried about her sister's state of mind. She explained that it would be a good idea for someone from the family to come stay with her for a day or two. Josie noted that when she spoke Patty's name into the phone Brenda closed her eyes and began crying again into her pillow. Patty assured Josie that she would be in Artemis by 8:00 that night and would stay as long as Brenda needed her. Patty had been shocked and concerned for her sister, saying she would come immediately, but Josie hadn't been able to glean much about Patty's relationship with her sister, or her feelings toward Billy.

When Josie hung up the phone she sat beside Brenda on the bed and explained that her sister would be at the hotel by eight that night. Brenda nodded without speaking. Josie left reluctantly, worrying they would have another suicide on their hands by morning.

SEVENTEEN

Josie pulled into her parking space the next morning at 7:30 to find Turner sitting in her car in front of the PD, talking on her cell phone. When Josie got out of her car, Turner rolled down her window and beckoned for her. She finished her conversation and hung up her phone but didn't set it down.

"Take a look at this," she said.

"Would you like to come in the office?" Josie asked, slightly annoyed that Turner expected their business to be conducted outside, next to her car, and predictably on her terms.

"Can't. I'm due in court this morning. Check out this video." She passed her phone to Josie. "Press the play button."

Josie did as instructed and watched a grainy black-and-white video, showing what appeared to be the entrance to a store or commercial building. After several seconds of seeing nothing she looked at Turner. "What am I looking at?"

"Don't look away! It only takes about thirty seconds. This is video surveillance taken at a Quick Mart just off Interstate 10 at nine thirty Sunday night. The video is time-stamped. Want to guess the location?"

Josie said nothing. She watched as two people walked up to the building. Even on the small screen of Turner's phone Josie could identify Billy and Brenda Nix walking side by side up to the door.

"That video's taken in Sonora, Texas. That means they left the Hell-Bent at six p.m., just like they said they did. That's a three-and-half-hour drive. No way they could have left their home at seven fifteen and made it to the Quick Mart by that time."

Josie nodded, impressed. "I'll need the original tape as evidence."

"Already done. I e-mailed you the store manager's contact information. I told him you'd be calling. I wanted to show you it this morning though before I got stuck in court all day. Brenda called me last night. She's a mess." She put her hand out of the car window to take her cell phone back from Josie. "I don't know who killed Ferris Sinclair. But somebody is playing hell with my client. Brenda Nix is an innocent woman."

"Do you think Billy committed suicide?" Josie asked.

Turner pointed a finger at Josie. "That's why *you* get paid the big bucks." She rolled her window up and backed out of the parking space.

Josie smiled. Turner often pissed her off, but she couldn't help liking her at the same time.

Lou had just taken over the computer from the night dispatcher and was catching up on messages when Josie entered the PD. Before Josie could say good morning to Lou, the bell rang and she turned around to see Doug Free walk in.

"Morning," he said.

"Hey, Doug. How's it going?"

"The fire marshal, Ned Franklin, just arrived this morning. He drove into town late last night. We're headed over to the Nixes'. I apologize for not letting you know sooner."

Josie put her hand up to stop him. "You don't owe me an apology. You have enough on your plate right now."

"It's been a tough week. We're still dealing with the aftermath at the mudflats. Ned would like to have you with us this morning if you can make it."

"Absolutely. I'll let Otto know where I'm headed, and I'll see you over there."

Josie walked upstairs to the office, where she found Otto digging through his filing cabinet. He turned and looked at her, his face slack and his eyes tired.

"Good news, Otto."

"We could use a bit of good news about now."

"The fire marshal is in town. I'm headed over now to meet with him and Doug at the Nixes'."

Otto shook his head, obviously hoping for something a bit more positive than that.

"Also, Turner stopped by this morning on her way to court. This case gets stranger by the day," she said.

"What did she want?"

"She showed me a convenience store video of Brenda and Billy entering the store in Sonora at nine thirty p.m. That means Billy and Brenda left the Hell-Bent by six, exactly when they said they left. They're off the hook."

He looked at Josie for a moment, obviously wrestling with something.

"What is it?" she asked.

"What if they killed him earlier in the day, before they went to the Hell-Bent?"

"Doesn't make sense. That would mean two different killers. If they killed him earlier in the afternoon, then someone else would have had to have driven to their home to start the fire later that evening. And why would they kill Ferris, and then have someone else come set their house on fire? Doesn't work."

"Well, I'll be damned. I thought for sure they were connected to Ferris's death."

"Yep. We're back to motive," she said. "Do me a favor and check on the subpoena for Billy's phone records. We need to know who he talked with the night he died. I'll be back, hopefully before lunch."

By the time Josie pulled into the Nixes' driveway, Ned Franklin was walking around the outside of the house, surveying the damage. He wore navy pants and a white short-sleeved shirt with the gold fire marshal shield above his breast pocket, gold corner pins over his collar tips, and a red and black insignia patch over his arm. He was a trim man in his fifties who walked through the blackened surroundings as if the territory were familiar to him. Josie watched his eyes travel over the house and grounds, surveying everything, cataloging the details as he listened to Doug summarize the time frame for when events took place. Josie overheard Doug explaining the spotter logs and the flyover in the helicopter as they walked around the side of the house.

"I feel very confident that the wildfire and the Nixes' fire were two separate events," Doug said.

"I would agree completely at this point," Ned said.

After the two had circled the home and arrived back at the front yard, Doug introduced Ned to Josie. He had silver hair, neatly trimmed, with deep lines across his forehead that signaled a life spent outside in the bright Texas sunshine. He smiled openly and shook Josie's hand.

"Under normal circumstances the Texas state fire marshal would assist, but the wildfires have every agent working overtime. The state marshal asked if I'd come down and offer a hand."

"We appreciate you coming. I'm paranoid every time I walk inside that I'm destroying evidence. Everything is so fragile," Josie said.

"That's the right approach to have. It'll be good to have you here with us. You might be able to fill in some holes for us."

"Any thoughts on what you've seen so far?"

He pointed toward the hole in the front of the house. "It's obvious an accelerant was used to start the fire. Accelerants burn hotter and faster." He pointed at the couch. "I'm surprised the synthetic material on the couch wasn't completely consumed." He then pointed to the floor just inside the living room where the center of the hole was located. "Notice the tile floor here? That's partly what kept this fire in place." He bent down on his hands and knees in front of the tile and sniffed. He finally stood back up and pointed to where the front doorway had been located. "The accelerant, and by the smell of it, I'm guessing kerosene, was poured directly in front of this tile floor. It caused the fire to burn up into the rafters rather than directly out."

Josie nodded, impressed with the information.

Ned stood on the porch facing the gaping hole into the house. "Look here. Fire typically burns in the shape of V so we can often trace back the exact origin. That's what's happened here. There's about a three-foot area where accelerant was poured onto the outside of the house around the doorway and left to pool on the ground."

"Makes sense," Josie said.

"See the black mark on the concrete here where it started?"

She nodded.

Ned got down on his hands and knees again and pulled a tool that looked like a wide screwdriver out of his pocket. He pried up the aluminum flashing under the doorjamb. "Take a look. See the black charring?"

Josie bent down closer. "Yeah, I can see it."

"The wildfire that whipped through here wouldn't have burned underneath this metal flashing. The puddle from the accelerant burned and caused that wood underneath here to catch." He used the tool to point to the concrete around the door. "This is called spalling, where the layers of concrete break away from the intense heat. Notice this is the only area on the patio where that happened?"

"That's excellent," she said, impressed with his knowledge.

"Doug already suspected this and collected evidence. I'll get it to the lab and get you a report as soon as I can on the liquid that was used. Let's move on inside and take a look where the body was found."

Once inside the house Ned stood in front of the couch and crossed his arms over his chest, staring at the charred mess in front of him. "Here's where I'd like your help, Chief Gray."

She nodded.

"The fire was either arson with a specific motive, or it was set by an arsonist who may have a set of motivations that are more complicated than you would first think."

She raised her eyebrows. "Can you explain the difference?"

"Arson is fire intentionally set to destroy property."

She nodded.

"An arsonist is the person who commits arson. If the person fits the characteristics of a typical arsonist we'd be looking at a young male, under the age of twenty-five, who comes from a single-parent family with no father figure. Fire becomes a sense of pride and way to control situations."

Josie nodded. "So you would approach the investigation differently if you thought the fire was set by an arsonist versus someone who burned the house down with a specific motive. Such as covering up a murder."

"Exactly."

Josie glanced at Doug and frowned. "Yesterday I would have told you that this fire was set with the sole purpose of covering up the murder of Ferris Sinclair. Today, I'm not so sure. The two suspects we thought might have had a motive for murder have a tight alibi. Ferris wasn't well liked, but I've not found anyone yet with the motive to want to kill him and burn his body. This was brutal."

Ned squatted down to get eye-level with the couch. He seemed to be surveying the fabric, inch by inch. After several minutes he stood and moved directly in front of the couch, performing the same visual scan.

He stood again. "Have you moved the couch?"

Doug shook his head. "We didn't want to move anything until you came on scene."

"Good. Get on the other side and let's move this couch directly back."

Doug and Ned lifted the couch up, moved it back about four feet, and set it down. All three looked down at the bare space under the couch, largely untouched by the fire. Sitting about five inches from where the bottom of the couch would have been was a plastic syringe. They all approached it at the same time and bent over to see that the needle was still attached.

Ned looked at Josie. "Were either of the Nixes IV drug users?"

"I don't think so. Highly unlikely."

"What about the victim?"

"I can't answer that."

"I have some pull with a toxicology lab up north," Ned said. "I'm sorry you had such a wait getting a fire marshal out here. I'll put a rush on the toxicology. I have a great lab I work with. They may be able to get us results in forty-eight hours if we're lucky. We'll hopefully know whether we're looking at recreational drug use, or the method of death."

When Josie arrived back at the office she found Otto just about to walk in. "You need a shower, Chief."

Josie looked down and noticed the black smudges on her uniform pants and shirt. "Think that comes out in the wash?" she asked.

"Call Delores. No doubt she'll have some vinegar remedy."

They both stepped into the building and sighed. The air-conditioning felt like heaven. Josie washed her arms and hands as best she could in the bathroom sink upstairs and met Otto at the conference table.

"The fire marshal find anything new?"

Josie summarized the marshal's confirmation that the fire was set intentionally by a liquid accelerant, and the discovery of the syringe under the couch.

Otto listened to Josie's account and said, "We have two dead men, an arson, and a suicide that we're not sure we believe."

"Brenda claims Billy won't even take aspirin for a headache. She basically admitted to searching his luggage when they go on trips. She swears he didn't have any pills with him in the hotel."

"Here's another thing. While you were with the fire marshal today I tracked down the clerk at the liquor mart who was working the night Billy drank himself to death. He remembered Billy coming in at about eleven thirty and buying the whiskey."

"What did he say about Billy's demeanor that night?" she asked.

Otto shrugged. "He claimed Billy was normal. The clerk told me he was a fan of Billy's so he asked him about the recording contract. Billy told him they were getting close to a deal. He even told the guy that if they got the deal he'd bring him a signed copy of the CD when it came out."

Josie frowned. "Doesn't sound like a guy getting ready to go drink himself to death."

"I agree. Seems odd a guy would dash off a quick 'I'll be back' note, leave his wife in a hotel room, then go buy enough whiskey and prescription drugs on the street corner to kill himself."

"Who would want both Ferris and Billy dead? Brenda would want Ferris dead, but not Billy. If you go the jealousy route, other bands might want Billy dead, but couldn't care less about Ferris," Josie said.

Lou buzzed Josie on her desk phone. "Cowan's on his way up to see you."

Josie grinned at Otto. "Cross your fingers. He wouldn't drive over here without significant news."

They listened as Cowan slowly clumped his way up the wooden stairs to the office. He appeared in the doorway and took a deep breath before entering.

"Good morning. I trust I'm not disturbing you too terribly with an unannounced visit?"

"Come on in. Would you like coffee?" Josie asked.

"Yes, please. Half cup. Cream and heavy sugar."

Cowan sat down with a sigh of relief and then got straight to the point.

"First, OxyContin and Ambien both were present in Billy Nix's bloodstream. Amounts will come later."

"Good," Josie said. It was no surprise, but the confirmation was necessary.

"Now, on to Ferris Sinclair. Dental records confirmed the burn victim is indeed Ferris. I also initiated an HIV antibody test which came back positive. To confirm, I used the more reliable Western blot test, which also came back positive. Ferris Sinclair was without a doubt HIV positive."

"Can you tell how much virus was in his body?" she asked, handing him his coffee.

Cowan gave her a look like he didn't understand the question.

"I used to hear people refer to someone as having full-blown AIDS. Those people you could look at and know they had the virus. I want to know, can you tell if it would have been obvious to others that Ferris was HIV positive?"

"Ah, I see. HIV is the virus that attacks a person's immune system," Cowan said. "A person can have HIV and show no outward symptoms. AIDS occurs when your immune system is severely compromised and it can take years to develop. It's the final stage of the disease after the immune system is too weak to deal with all of the other infections. I believe what you're asking is, was Ferris Sinclair's immune system compromised to the point that others would know that he had the disease."

"That's exactly what I want to know," she said.

"With the body as severely burned as it was, there's no way at this time for me to know what kind of infections he might have been fighting. In short, I can't answer your question."

Josie nodded, frustrated with the answer.

"I'll run the same tests on Billy Nix and let you know ASAP."

Otto seemed to be mulling the conversation over. He finally said, "Maybe Ferris came right out and told Billy. Maybe he thought it would buy him some sympathy. Get him more attention."

"Would a diagnosis of HIV give Billy Nix the motive to kill Ferris?" Cowan asked.

"Maybe," Josie said. "Trouble is, Billy was two hours away when the fire was started at his home. Billy didn't kill Ferris, and neither did Brenda."

"I'll tell you what's troubling me," Otto said. "It's not the idea that Billy would commit suicide, but rather how he did it. If Brenda is right, and he didn't have the pills with him, who brought them to him? If someone brought him a deadly combination of prescription pills, knowing that he was already drunk, then did Billy Nix commit suicide, or was he murdered?"

"Ahhh." Cowan took a sip of his coffee and smiled. "The conundrum. Is the gun seller who provides a man the gun that the man uses to murder his wife culpable?"

"He is if the gun seller *tells* the guy to go home and kill his wife," Josie said.

"What about all the Internet sites that explain how to commit suicide? They provide instructions for how to end your life. If you follow those instructions and end your life, are the people on the Internet culpable in your murder?" Cowan smiled again, apparently enjoying the debate.

Otto looked annoyed. "So what are you getting at? If someone gave Billy those pills and said take these, they're culpable in his murder?"

"I'm saying no such thing. I'm simply suggesting that you have a mess on your hands."

Otto stood and said, "Okay. Thanks for bringing the information, Cowan. It was much appreciated. We're headed back to the crime scene."

Cowan took the cue and stood himself, taking several gulps to finish his coffee. Once he had left the office Josie gave Otto a look. "We're going to the crime scene?"

"I couldn't take any more theorizing. We have a murder to solve. I just said that to get him out of here."

Josie grinned and walked to the whiteboard at the front of the office. "I don't know why you have to give him such a hard time."

Otto ignored her comment. "What if we have two suicides? Ferris confesses to Billy and Brenda he's HIV positive. Billy shuns him so he stays at their house and commits suicide."

"Who used the stun gun on him then?"

"Damn."

"Susan, the deputy from Presidio County, called Ferris promiscuous. Juan called him a whore dog, and Dave agreed. Maybe someone else found out Ferris had HIV and feared he infected them. That person could have killed him too."

Otto nodded. "But it had to be somebody who knew Billy and Brenda were leaving. Their house would have been the perfect place to commit murder. The murderer would have assumed it was in the line of fire so it would cover up any evidence. They lure Ferris to Billy's place, stun him, and kill him."

"That means we've narrowed the killer down to someone who knew the Nixes. Who knew the inside of their house well enough to know there was a stun gun in a box in the bedroom." Josie pointed a finger at Otto. "Know who was in their house just a few months ago? And told me he was at the Hell-Bent during the evacuation, so he knew when the Nixes left town?"

Otto looked at her.

"Mick Sinner."

———⋅✦⋅———

Josie and Otto hit the jackpot. In calling around to track down Mick, they discovered from Vicki that he was at the Hell-Bent practicing with the band for a performance later that night. Josie drove and Otto rode passenger. She followed two other cars down the road, both of which turned down the lane for the Hell-Bent. The parking lot was packed.

"I bet there's a hundred cars," she said.

"Since when does the Hell-Bent draw a crowd at ten on a Friday morning?" Otto said.

They stepped inside and found a mass of people milling around the dance floor. Josie noticed pockets of people crying and hugging.

"Oh, hell," Josie said. "You know what this is? These people are here for Billy."

Most of the crowd was wearing blue jeans and cowboy boots but a few women wore dresses. Josie noticed Angela carrying a tray full of Budweiser over to a table surrounded by a dozen people. Grieving or not, she thought ten was a little early for a Bud.

Above the low rumble of conversation they heard raised voices coming from the stage, where they could see Slim Jim and Mick Sinner facing each other in heated conversation. Otto motioned his head that way and Josie followed him.

When they reached the stage they could see that Mick was holding a cable where he was apparently attempting to set up his sound system. Jim stood between Mick and the speaker and was yelling something that had to do with Billy. People milling around the dance floor were migrating that way to check out the argument. One of the patrons, wearing a cowboy hat and a black concert shirt that read BILLY AND THE OUTLAWS, yelled, "You tell him to get the hell off the stage, Slim. He oughta have more respect than that."

"This is bullshit!" someone else yelled.

Josie followed Otto through a door to the left of the stage and walked out to stand between Slim Jim and Mick and the people on the dance floor so they could have a semiprivate conversation.

"What's going on, fellas?" Otto said.

"This son of a bitch is up here about ready to do a sound check! These folks came out to pay respects to Billy. They're hurting right now. We all are." Slim Jim choked up and had to stop and take a deep breath. "We want a little respect."

Josie faced Mick. "We actually came out here this morning to talk with you. You mind if we go back to the dressing room for a minute?"

He threw the cable he was holding onto the floor. "I got a job to do. I'm on the schedule this morning, and this is the only time I can make it today. I got people coming to town from Nashville to watch the band tonight."

"You aren't playing tonight." Slim Jim said the words through clenched teeth.

"Like hell I won't! I got a scout coming to hear the band. You know how hard it is to get someone from Nashville to travel all the way to West Texas? You had your break and you—"

Slim Jim raised a fist and reared back. Otto raised his own hand and stepped directly in front of him. Slim kept his hand in the air for another moment and then dropped it to his side.

Josie broke in. "Otto will talk this over with Hank. He'll take into account Billy's death and the schedule and what needs to be done for the crowd. He's the owner here, not you guys. His decision stands." The men stared each other down until Mick finally turned and walked back toward the dressing room. Josie took off after Mick and figured Slim Jim would follow Otto to take up his case with Hank.

Josie entered the dressing room and was pleased to see the other two members of the Calloway Boys: bass player Craig Wells and drummer Tim Holton. She had arrested Craig for possession of marijuana about a year ago. He gave her a crooked smile and tipped his head at her, looking vaguely embarrassed. Craig was a stereotypical doper with heavy-lidded eyes, a lazy smile, and slow speech. He was also an awesome bass player who'd been asked to tour with several big-name stars, most recently Kenny Chesney. Craig had notoriously turned down the offers, claiming allegiance to the Calloway Boys.

He sat on a tattered couch in the corner of the room with a binder and what looked like sheet music spread out on a large coffee table in front of him. Josie walked over and shook his hand and said hello.

Josie knew the drummer, Tim Holton, fairly well. He was sitting on a chair next to Craig, playing his drumsticks on his thighs. She and Tim worked out at the high school gym in the evenings on roughly the same schedule. Josie had talked to him about applying for the evening dispatch job when the job opened up in a few months. He had seemed genuinely interested. In his midtwenties, Tim looked more like a clean-cut engineering student from Texas Tech than a drummer for a country band. He wore a pair of khaki pants and a shirt buttoned almost up to his neck. He smiled and said hello when Josie reached out her hand to him.

She turned to see Mick standing in what appeared to be the kitchen area. Hideous kitchen cabinets from someone's seventies kitchen remodel hung on the wall and a burnt-orange countertop ran the length of the wall and was cluttered with junk. The rest of the room appeared to be a jumbled mess of accumulated stuff from the various bands that played at the Hell-Bent.

Josie said, "I appreciate you talking with me, Mick."

"You know what bullshit this is? Do you have any idea how much more talented our band is than Billy and the Outlaws ever thought of being?"

"Dude," Craig said. "He just died, man. Lighten up."

Mick turned on him. "We got a shot this weekend. Right? We might finally catch a break, and Billy screws us over again."

"Dude, seriously."

"I'm not kidding. Only Billy could orchestrate his death so perfectly as to screw me out of my chance to leave this little corner of hell." He kicked a plastic chair and it clattered across the room as his band members exchanged looks that appeared to say, *Here we go again.*

"When was the last time you were at Billy's house?" Josie asked.

He slowly turned around and tilted his head as if he'd not heard her correctly. "What did you say?"

Josie repeated her question.

He laughed, wide-eyed and openmouthed, looking at his band members like he couldn't believe the question. Tim looked toward the door as if he was considering leaving.

"I told you." Mick said each word distinctly.

"Look, Mick. I get you're upset about your band not getting your big break, but being a smart-ass isn't going to help anybody. Two men are dead. One man was murdered, the other committed suicide. I'm going to ask as many questions as I need in order to find out who killed Ferris Sinclair and why Billy decided he needed to end his life."

She had their attention. All three band members looked shocked, presumably at the news about Ferris.

"What do you mean who killed Ferris?" Mick asked.

"Ferris Sinclair was found murdered in Billy's home."

"What the hell?" Mick said, barely whispering the words.

"Now, please answer the question. When was the last time you were at Billy's house?" she said.

Mick's glare softened somewhat and the fists at his sides unclenched. He took a deep breath and blew it out slowly before continuing. "Vicki and I delivered a couch there a while back."

"Give me a month."

He sighed as if frustrated with the question. "I don't know. February, maybe March."

"So, not too long ago. Were the Nixes home when you delivered the couch?"

He looked surprised. "I don't remember. We deliver stuff all the time, all over the place."

"Think back to that day when you took the couch inside. Was Billy there to greet you, tell you where to put it?"

"No, I don't guess so. They just left the door unlocked for us."

"Did you look around?"

"What kind of question is that?"

Josie noticed the other two band members staring intently at Mick, waiting for his answer.

"No! We just dropped the couch off."

"You're sure? Because Vicki might remember it differently."

"What the hell are you getting at?"

"Did you look around the living room? Maybe look at the pictures on the wall, open up some boxes sitting on the end tables, check things out."

Mick evidently considered what Vicki might have to say, because his expression changed. He smiled, ready to laugh it off now. "Come on. You can't help looking at somebody's pictures hanging on the wall. That's what they hang 'em up for. It's not like I went room-to-room snooping through the house though."

"Did you open any boxes? Open any drawers in the living room? Look around the house?"

He shrugged, made a face like, *Yeah, no big deal.*

"Did you find anything?"

"What the hell's that supposed to mean?"

"Did you find anything troubling? A gun or something that would make you worry about the Nixes? Maybe something in the living room that made you worry about things they're into?"

He gave her a look like he had no idea what she was talking about. "No. We were there like five minutes. You're making this into something more than it was. We delivered a couch. That's it."

"Have you been back since?"

He hesitated. "What, me? No. Why would I need to?"

Josie turned to Tim. "How well did you know Ferris Sinclair?" she asked.

Tim watched Josie pick up the plastic chair that Mick had kicked across the room and drag it over to the small area where he and Craig sat. She took a seat and stared at Tim until he answered.

"Ferris has been around . . ." He paused and seemed to consider his answer. "Maybe a year or so. He was always hanging out up front by the bands."

"You ever hear any rumors about him?"

"Like what?" he asked.

"I don't know. You tell me. What did people say about him?" Josie asked.

He narrowed his eyes and looked uncomfortable with the question. "This is a police investigation, right? So I don't know about giving you rumors. Who knows if any of it's true?"

"You tell me what you heard about Ferris, and I'll check into it. I won't hold it against you if turns out to be bogus." She smiled and he seemed to relax somewhat.

"The rumor was that Billy and Ferris had a thing going on."

"As in an affair?"

He made a face and laughed. "I don't know if that's the word I'd use."

"You mean they had a sexual relationship?"

He nodded. "That's what I heard, but like I said, who knows."

"Did Brenda know about it?"

"I don't think so."

She looked at Craig to get his reaction. Craig had lost his heavy-lidded doper expression and seemed highly engaged in the conversation now.

"The whole thing was weird," Craig said. "Billy was this massive guy, but he had this little ferret following him around. That's what everybody called him. Telling Billy how great he was all the time." Craig smiled. "One Saturday night after Billy and the Outlaws played I was sitting up at the bar. Brenda happened to be standing there ordering a drink when Billy and the ferret came up to the bar. The ferret pats Billy on the back and tells him he was brilliant." Craig laughed. "Brilliant? Even if he was brilliant, you don't call some hard-ass guy that."

Tim smiled. "I was sitting there too. The best part was, Brenda rolled her eyes and walked away. She didn't even wait around for her drink."

"You guys ever hear any rumors about Ferris having HIV?" she asked.

"No shit?" Craig said.

Josie remained quiet. She scooted her chair so that she could see Mick, who was standing next to the cabinets behind her. She raised her eyes at him as if waiting for his input.

"It's just people talking smack," Mick said.

Josie kept her attention on Mick. "I've heard Ferris was promiscuous, that he was probably bisexual. You ever hear that? Maybe who some of his other partners might be?"

"Just because you're bi doesn't mean you're promiscuous," Mick said.

"That wasn't what I said. Was Ferris promiscuous with people of either sex?"

Mick nodded. "That'd be my guess."

"He ever hit on you?"

Craig laughed. "He hit on everybody."

"There's a strong possibility that Ferris is HIV positive." Josie looked at the three guys but saw little change in their expressions.

Craig said, "Then I'd say the trauma center better stock up on HIV tests."

While Josie spoke with the band, Otto pulled Hank aside to talk to Slim Jim. Hank had obviously already been clued in to the drama and had already decided the show would go on that night.

Hank put a hand on Slim Jim's shoulder. "As much as I'd like to keep the bar open for Billy's fans tonight, I can't cancel a show last minute. We'll have a memorial service tomorrow, starting at four p.m. We can let it go as late as people want. I'll let everyone know here in a while. Mick's just gonna have to skip the practice this morning. It's a compromise."

Slim Jim put a hand in the air to acknowledge he understood and started to walk away.

Otto said, "Quick question before you go. Can you tell me what time Billy called you the night he died?"

Slim paused and his expression changed from anger to confusion. "Why?"

"I'm just clearing up some loose ends."

"It was about two in the morning."

Otto looked at Hank and he nodded his head in agreement. "That's when he called me."

Slim turned and walked toward the back of the bar.

"A lot of drama," Otto said.

Hank watched Slim Jim walk away and open the back door of the bar. White light surrounded his silhouette as he walked out of the building and into the sunlight. "I feel for him. This has hit him awful hard."

Otto nodded and pointed backstage to where Josie was meeting with the other band. "Mick's got a temper, doesn't he?"

"Mick's okay. He's got a chip on his shoulder. He's one of those guys that figures everybody else has it easier than he does. In his eyes, Mick's the only one in town that had to scrape through life to get anything good."

"You think that's true?"

Hank made a dismissive noise. "He's got a good band, a good job that pays the bills, a nice house to live in. I don't think he has it too bad."

Otto glanced around him and pointed toward a place at the end of the bar where there weren't any people standing around. "I want to ask you a question," he said.

When they reached the quieter spot Otto said, "I guess you heard that Billy died from an overdose of alcohol and pills."

Hank nodded.

"Did that surprise you, that he would take pills?"

Hank leaned back against the wall and nodded his head toward the dance floor where over a hundred people were milling about on a Friday workday. "Nothing would surprise me anymore. I think if a guy wanted to score a bag of weed, or a bag of pills, or any other kind of drug you could name, all he'd have to do is walk through that crowd and start asking some questions. I hate to say that about my own bar, but that's the truth of it."

"You aren't surprised Billy would take pills?"

Hank looked at Otto like he was crazy. "Billy? He was a bundle of nerves. All the time. I'm sure he's taken his share of pills to calm down before a big show."

"Brenda claims Billy's never taken any drugs."

Hank's mouth turned down and he looked away as if pained by the thought. "Brenda believed the best about him. She thought he could be a star. I doubt Billy ever believed it."

—— · ——

After a quick lunch with Josie at the Hot Tamale, Otto left to meet with the principal at the elementary school. Chris Conroy had called and said a teacher in his building had found a bottle of Vicodin in a fourth-grade student's backpack when she was searching for a missing permission slip. While Otto interviewed the student and the boy's mother, Josie drove to the trauma center to meet Glenda Crosley, the nurse who had been working the night Billy died in the park behind the building.

Josie entered the trauma center through the emergency room door and found a flurry of activity. A receptionist was checking in several patients, and the nurse that Josie had come to see had just entered the waiting room to retrieve a patient. She saw Josie and glanced at the clock on the wall. She put both hands in the air and mouthed the words *Ten minutes.* Josie gave her a thumbs-up and the woman disappeared.

Josie sat down in one of the dozen plastic molded chairs and pulled her cell phone out of her shirt pocket. It was 5:30. It was time to go home. Time to eat dinner. She tried to think of something that sounded good to eat. She was sick of ramen soup, canned chili, and peanut butter sandwiches. Nothing sounded good. She resigned herself to a bag of microwave popcorn and one juice glass of bourbon to settle the demons in her head.

Ten minutes stretched into thirty minutes. Josie watched a young mother come in carrying a baby in a carriage seat, holding the hand of a toddler while she tried not to let a diaper bag and a purse slip down her shoulder. The little girl hopped and then stepped, repeating "Mommy, Mommy" to get her mother to watch her walk while the baby screamed—ear-piercing wails. She gathered the kids and bags around her and sat down in front of the woman at the reception desk. Her face held a combination of worry, irritation, exhaustion, and love, all in one frazzled package, and Josie realized that the combination, that of a parent in the grips of exhausted caregiving, was one she had never experienced. An emptiness gnawed away at the pit of her stomach. One that she thought nothing could fill but her own child.

The nurse, Glenda Crosley, poked her head out of the door that led back into the examination rooms. "Josie?" she called.

Josie stood, suddenly feeling self-conscious, as if her private thoughts had been broadcast throughout the waiting room.

She followed Glenda back into the nurses' area, a wide-open space that looked a bit like a command center. The nurses' desk was half-moon-shaped and was large enough behind the counter for five or six medical staff members to work together comfortably. Across from the desk, several patient rooms and other offices and storage rooms fanned out around it.

"I hope you don't mind sitting back here to talk?" Glenda asked.

"Not at all."

"Sorry it took so long. We've been swamped today. You just never know."

"No problem. This won't take long. Before we get started, have you talked to Vie and Smokey since they found out about losing their house?"

Her shoulders slumped. "Isn't it just horrible? I talked to Vie last night. She's a mess. You know how Vie is. We call her the governor here at work. She's always in control. But with the house? It's like she's come undone." The nurse put her hand up as if to stop Josie from saying anything. "Don't get me wrong, I would be devastated too! It's just such a shock to see Vie so messed up."

"Have you talked to Smokey?"

"No. He and Donny were over at the house sifting through the mess, trying to find anything they could salvage. Vie was at the hotel when I talked to her. She said she couldn't stand to go back. She said Smokey's already talking about rebuilding but she just can't think about it."

Josie sighed. "Do they have temporary housing?"

"That's the little bit of good news. The Ferrarios have a rental. They'll start moving in tomorrow."

"Let me know when they're ready to start setting up the house. Food and furniture. We'll all want to pitch in at the police department."

"I'll do that. Thanks."

Josie opened up her notepad and took her pen out of her pocket. "I want to talk for a few minutes about your shift, night before last. The night Billy Nix passed away in the park behind the center?"

"Yeah, of course. Wednesday night. I was the only nurse on duty that night. We had a rotating ER doc on-site too. He'd driven from Fort Stockton after a ten-hour shift at their ER, so he was asleep in one of the patient rooms from about nine o'clock on. We were dead that night. I had two patients come in. One with a bad migraine wanting pain pills, and the other, a man who'd run out of insulin. Both were routine. Billy never came inside the center. I would have remembered. My husband and I watched Outlaws shows every chance we got. So sad."

"Did you go outside during your shift that night? Notice anything odd at all?"

She frowned and shook her head. "No, I brought my supper with me. I didn't go anywhere." Her expression changed slightly. "I did go outside around midnight to get my Diet Coke out of my car. I was tired and figured a shot of caffeine might get me through the last hour."

"Were you parked behind the building?" The park was just behind the parking lot.

"Yeah. It made me sad to think about it when I heard about Billy. I mean, I got off my shift at one in the morning. If I had known he was there I could have saved his life maybe. Who knows."

"Were there any other cars parked in the lot when you went outside to get your Diet Coke?"

Glenda made a humming noise as she thought. "I was parked in the back of the lot, right next to the doc's car. I drive a crappy old minivan and his is a silver Lexus. I know those were the only two in the lot." She looked at Josie carefully, her eyes squinted in concentration. "But I'm pretty sure there was a pickup truck parked along the street. Just on the other side of the park."

Josie was quiet, letting her think through the details.

"It's funny. I didn't think a thing about it at the time. But there's no houses across the street. I'm not sure what a truck would have been doing there at that time of night."

"Do you remember the color?"

"I'm pretty sure it was dark, dark blue or black. One of the big four-doors. I remember now because it crossed my mind that that's what kind of truck David, my husband, wants. I think he's crazy because the gas mileage is a killer."

EIGHTEEN

All three officers were scheduled off for the day. They rotated weekends with the sheriff's department to ensure that at least one car was on the road at all hours. But days off did not take precedence during a murder investigation. This Saturday, all three members of the police department came in to debrief about the Ferris Sinclair murder, and Billy Nix's apparent suicide. There were no homicide detectives to take the case, just an understaffed, underfunded department of three. After the debriefing, Josie would dole out the work assignments for the day.

She arrived early and started the coffee. Having skipped breakfast, she was happy to see Marta enter the office with a large baking dish.

"Coffee cake fresh from the oven," Marta said.

Otto entered directly behind her. "The woman is a saint. Delores made oatmeal this morning and got mad when I added butter and sugar. How is a man supposed to suffer through a bowl of oatmeal with no flavor? She'll kill me in the process of saving me."

Josie carried paper plates and cups to the conference table. By eight o'clock they had all enjoyed a warm breakfast and were caught up on each other's personal lives. Josie counted herself lucky to work with such good people.

Marta covered up her casserole dish with tinfoil and said, "Okay. Bring me up to speed."

"The big news yesterday was the video surveillance tape that Turner, the Nixes' attorney, provided. The surveillance tape was captured on a camera in Sonora and shows the Nixes entering the store at nine thirty the night Ferris was killed. Sonora is about three and a half hours from the Nixes' house. If they left the Hell-Bent at six, drove home to kill Ferris, and started the fire, the absolute earliest they could have left the house would have been seven fifteen. Even if they left at seven, that puts them in Sonora at ten at the earliest."

"And we have time of death as seven thirty-eight. That's when the watch stopped on Ferris's watch, and the clock in the kitchen. The timing just doesn't work," Otto said.

"So, what you're saying is that the Nixes didn't kill Ferris," Marta said.

"I don't see how," Josie said. "The other surprise we received yesterday was the report from the fire marshal out of Odessa. He came in and worked with Doug Free and me. He claims the house fire was started outside the front door that leads into the living room, most likely with kerosene."

"Isn't that what you already expected?" Marta said.

"We did, but it was good confirmation. He also found a syringe located underneath the couch where Ferris Sinclair was found."

"So Ferris was shooting up and overdosed? Committed suicide?" Marta asked. "Or someone used the syringe to kill him?"

"I can't imagine Ferris would shoot up with heroin and then tuck the needle under the couch for Brenda to find later. I think there's a good chance that whatever is in the needle killed Ferris. The fire marshal has rushed the toxicology on the syringe. I'm hoping we'll know by Monday."

Otto said, "Remember too that a Zaner was discharged. This was no suicide."

Josie stood and walked to her desk, where she retrieved a two-gallon plastic evidence bag containing an empty whiskey bottle. She set down the bag in the middle of the table for Marta to see. "Cowan has another bag that contains three pills. He's testing them, but they appear to be a combination of OxyContin and Ambien. If Billy ate a bagful of those mixed with that bottle of Jack Daniel's?"

"So it's a suicide?" Marta asked.

"Except that Brenda claims Billy never takes pills. She admitted to searching his bags while they were in the hotel room together. She says he couldn't have had anything on him when he left the hotel room the night he died."

Marta made a dismissive gesture. "It's not like a guy couldn't score a bagful of pills."

"Cowan is supposed to call today with results on the autopsy. It looked like a suicide, but I'm not convinced yet. There's one other piece. I talked to the nurse who was on duty the night Billy died behind the trauma center. She said there was a dark-colored truck parked on the side street that runs next to the park. On the east side of it. There's no houses there, so she couldn't imagine what a truck would be doing there at that time of night."

"You know how many dark-colored trucks there are in Artemis?" Otto said.

"She also said it was a four-door, one of the big gas guzzlers. She remembers because it's what her husband wants."

Marta made a face. "How do we track that down?"

"I had a brainstorm at about three o'clock this morning," Josie said. "I woke up thinking about Billy's memorial service that Hank said they would hold at the Hell-Bent tonight."

"Ah," Marta said. "Let me guess. I'm third shift. You want me in the parking lot taking license-plate numbers on any dark-colored four-door truck."

Josie grinned.

"What did I tell you?" Otto said. "She's a saint."

Marta smirked. "If Billy didn't kill Ferris, why would he commit suicide? Was he that distraught over Ferris's death?"

"That's the question of the day," Otto said. "I can't figure out if he was having an affair with Ferris, or if Ferris was a nuisance fan who was bothering Billy and screwing up his marriage. It depends on who you talk to."

Josie tilted her head. "I just wonder if Ferris provided Billy with something he didn't have in his life. We keep hearing how Brenda spent all her time trying to make Billy as good as he could be. Maybe Ferris just accepted him for who he was. Ferris thought Billy was already brilliant. Maybe Billy just needed the boost that Ferris gave his ego."

"You're changing your mind? You think it's plausible that Billy committed suicide over Ferris's death?" Otto asked.

"I suppose I do," she said. "But it bothers me that we don't know how Billy came up with the pills that he mixed with the alcohol."

"Or who wanted Ferris dead," Marta said.

"My plan is to meet Deputy Susan Spears at Ferris's house in Presidio this morning. She's got a search warrant approved. She agreed to help me search the house. Hopefully we'll find something to help us figure that out."

The drive from Artemis to Presidio took Josie down a twenty-mile stretch of tan-colored desert dotted with patches of deep green mesquite bushes. The occasional hills and curves that snugged up to the Rio Grande broke the scenic monotony with glimpses of the muddy brown water. At ten o'clock in the morning, with the temperature pushing ninety, she drove with the windows down, letting the warm air blow the dust and sand around the old jeep. Radio stations faded in and out, so she dug through the glove compartment to find a tape for the ancient cassette player. She popped in one of Dillon's old Elton John tapes and turned "Benny and the Jets" up as loud as the speakers would take. She smiled and sang, enjoying the sun and the wind and the freedom of the open road.

In a police department so remote, with so little funding, department perks were rare. Her retired-army jeep, vintage 1995, somewhat made up for the lack of modern radio and radar equipment. The four-wheel-drive could take her almost anywhere: the jeep had been built for military use, so she drove it as the job required, and occasionally as the road called to her, through rocky creeks, narrow mountain passes, and tight arroyos that an SUV or pickup truck couldn't handle.

Thirty minutes after leaving Artemis, Josie parallel parked in front of the small brick home that Junior Daggy had referred to as the Winferd station house. She wasn't sure what she had expected, maybe something cobbled together by other people's hand-me-downs, but what she found was a tastefully landscaped brick home with long narrow windows and curved limestone lintels. A cobblestone pathway led through a well-kept garden and up to a large wooden entrance door with heavy wrought-iron hardware.

Susan parked her brown and beige deputy patrol car across the street from Josie. While Susan called in her position Josie took the time to glance around the tree-lined neighborhood. The street was primarily made up of tasteful adobe homes, understated and cared for by their owners. This was not the neighborhood Josie had imagined Ferris Sinclair inhabiting.

Susan exited her car and walked over to join Josie on the sidewalk in front of the house. Not many women were able to wear a police uniform and maintain any sense of femininity, but Susan looked every bit the grandma that she bragged about being. The brown uniform fit her curvy fifty-something-year-old body well. Josie realized then that Susie wasn't wearing a bulletproof vest under her uniform, which gave the impression of a block chest, an okay look on a man, but not so flattering on most women. In the desert climate the vest was miserably hot, but Josie insisted the officers in her department wear one at all times while on duty. It surprised her to find Susan without one.

Susan approached her with her hand outstretched and a wide smile. "How are you, Josie? Long time no see!"

Josie smiled back and shook her hand. "I'm doing all right. How's life in Presidio?"

"Can't complain." She pointed up the pathway that led to Ferris Sinclair's front door. "Nice little place, huh?"

"I'll admit, this isn't what I expected. From everything I hear he was a mooch. How's a mooch afford a place like this?"

"Good question. Let's take a look. I don't know where he worked. He seemed to flit from one party to the next. I'd figure a sugar daddy." She wrinkled her nose at Josie. "Can a guy have a sugar daddy?"

Josie laughed. "I don't guess there's a rule book on sugar daddies."

"Does Billy Nix fit that description for Ferris?"

"Billy was barely scraping by. He was close to a Nashville contract, but that hadn't happened yet," Josie said. "Not to mention, his wife kept a pretty close eye on him. I can't imagine Brenda Nix allowing enough money to leave her checking account to pay for a place like this."

Susan unlocked the front door and said, "After we got the warrant approval I got a key made and came over to print the outside of the house and check for breaking and entering, vandalism, whatever. The outside of the house looked undisturbed. I haven't gone in though."

They stepped inside the house and both had the same response. "Wow."

The light in the home was magnificent, streaming in from the long windows and bouncing off ebony hardwood floors. Dark wood trim surrounded the doors and windows and contrasted beautifully with white stucco walls.

"Not your typical bachelor pad," Susan said, surveying the room from the doorway and taking in the bold artwork that hung on the walls. Leather couches and heavy wooden tables and benches gave the room a masculine feel without looking too over-the-top.

"Hard to imagine this is the home of the man I heard described as a ferret," Josie said.

Susan glanced at Josie. "I feel a little bad about that now. He was just so whiny. Played the victim like he practiced the part. You know the type?"

"I do. Any idea why he felt so victimized? Was it tied to him being gay and getting harassed?"

"I don't know much about his background. I heard he moved here from Georgia. Left his daddy's tool and die shop and came out here to pursue something."

"Stalking country music performers?" Josie asked.

"Apparently."

"What's the search warrant cover?"

"Judge gave us free rein. I told him the body had been identified. You have target areas?"

"I'd like you to start with his finances. We need to figure out who's paying for this lifestyle if he doesn't have a job," Josie said.

"Blackmail?" Susan said.

"Wouldn't be the first time." Josie pointed to a hallway across the living room, directly opposite the front door. She figured the house was only about twelve hundred square feet, with the bedroom down the only hallway. "I'll start in the bedroom. I'd like to get a sense for him on a personal level. The descriptions I've received from the locals haven't been kind. And, yet, Billy Nix appears to have committed suicide over him. Ferris obviously has something going for himself."

Josie walked around the living room furniture first, noticing the dust on the end tables and the wood floors. Aside from several days of disuse, the house was impeccably decorated and clean. There were no dollar-store knickknacks like the Nixes had accumulated on their bookshelves and end tables. Ferris collected art and knew how to display it.

The polished ebony planks of the floor led Josie past a bathroom with a marble countertop and gleaming silver hardware and fresh white towels. The bedroom, just beyond the guest bath, maintained the dark masculine feel of the living space, but the fabrics and linens were soft and textured, creamy rather than stark white. It was the kind of place a person would love to come home to at the end of the day. So why had Ferris chosen the Nix household, where he was obviously so unwanted, to spend the last day of his life? Why would he have gone to Artemis, in the middle of a wildfire evacuation, to the Nixes' home after they had already left town? Was he looking for something? Josie couldn't imagine what the Nixes could own that would be worth murder.

Josie went to the bedside table and opened the drawer. She found it filled with letters, most in envelopes, and several postmarked Artemis, Texas. Three envelopes bore no return address, but the letters began "Dear Ferris." Two of those letters were signed "Love, Billy."

Josie took the letters and sat on the edge of the bed, a sadness overcoming her for Brenda, who appeared so intent on controlling a life that she didn't understand, or at least chose not to acknowledge.

Josie put the letters in the order in which they were mailed and read each one. The first letter filled half a notebook page and simply thanked Ferris for helping set up the band at a performance in Presidio. The letter talked about details from the concert and Billy's comments about a song they tried out on the audience that night that was a big hit. The date was fourteen months prior. Josie wondered if that was when the two had met.

The second letter was dated two months later. Most of the content suggested little beyond a simple friendship; however, at the end of the letter Billy had written, "Please don't send any more letters to the house. Brenda takes things wrong. She's a good woman and wants to see the band make it. She worries about distractions. Send me a text if you need anything. Love, Billy."

The third letter's subject was more veiled.

> *Dear Ferris,*
> *I'm sorry about the misunderstanding. You know she just wants what's best for the band. And to her that means knowing all the details. She can't give you jobs to do because it keeps her from knowing everything. I know you were trying to help the band too*

and I appreciate that. You are a good friend and I hope this doesn't cause hard feelings between us. I'll try and get to Presidio this week to see you. You know this isn't easy. It takes time. Be patient with an old man.

   Love, Billy

Josie reread the three letters and set them aside. She riffled through the other letters and opened a few that weren't in envelopes. Most were personal in nature, from both men and women, many of them containing a similar theme: Sorry there was a misunderstanding, please don't give up on me.

Josie left the pile of letters on the bed and opened the door to the bottom of the bedside cabinet. Inside she found a small wooden trunk, which she pulled out and opened. It appeared to be a mess of unrelated memorabilia: an autographed first edition of a Kurt Vonnegut novel, several playbills, a model car of a Corvette with a smiley face drawn onto the hood, an autographed baseball with a signature Josie couldn't read, a coffee mug from Churchill Downs, and a six-inch-tall replica of the Eiffel Tower with the word *Unforgettable* inscribed on a silver plaque on the base. Josie wondered what qualities made a person unforgettable and decided whatever they were she evidently didn't have them, because she didn't have a box full of mementos and a drawer full of letters from admirers. Currently she had no admirers.

Josie was on her hands and knees looking through boxes she had pulled out from under the bed when Susan walked into the room carrying a black book in her hands.

"What you got there?" Susan asked.

"He has boxes of memorabilia and letters that date back five years or better. I found a stack of letters in the desk drawer, and there's more here in these boxes. I found one dated from 2010 from a jilted lover. Check this out." Josie dug back through one of the boxes, found the letter she was searching for, and handed it to Susan. "Look at the back of the envelope." Drawn on the back was an ink sketch of a young girl's face with tears dripping down her cheeks and her bottom lip stuck out in a sad-faced pout.

"The letter's pretty sappy. The girl basically says Ferris ruined her life when he left her. It's postmarked Montpellier, France."

Susan scowled. "What's the attraction with this guy?"

"I don't get it either." She pointed to the black book. "You find something?"

"I did. A leather bank ledger that Ferris writes in faithfully. Each month he records a ten-thousand-dollar deposit into the account."

Josie's eyes rose. "You find the sugar daddy?"

"We'll have to subpoena the bank records. I can't tell. The deposits started the month after he turned eighteen."

"Sounds more like a trust fund."

"He's also had larger deposits made sporadically. The most recent was a one-hundred-thousand-dollar deposit two years ago, about the time he moved to Presidio. I would assume to buy this house."

"What a life, huh?" said Josie.

They both heard banging coming from the living room and realized someone was knocking on the front door.

"Is anyone coming to meet you here?" Josie asked.

"Nope."

Josie walked through the living room and the pounding started again. When she opened the door a thin woman with small pinched features and a very angry expression stood with her hands fixed firmly to her hips.

"Could you not have let the family in first?" the woman said.

"My name is Josie Gray. I'm chief of police with the Artemis Police Department." Josie motioned behind her where Susan stood looking out at the woman. "This is Deputy Susan Spears with the Presidio County Sheriff's Department. And you are?" Josie had little doubt the woman was a close relative of Ferris's.

"I'm Ferris Sinclair's twin."

"And your name?"

"Julia."

Josie stepped outside, forcing the woman to take a step back on the front porch.

"Have you spoken with your parents about Ferris?"

Julia's chin dimpled and she puckered her lips in an attempt to keep from crying.

"I'm very sorry for your loss," Josie said.

"Why are you here?" The young woman's voice came out as a high-pitched whisper.

"We have a court-ordered search warrant, Ms. Sinclair. We're here to find out what happened to your brother. We're going to do everything we can."

"By rooting through his things?"

"That's not our intent. We're trying to understand who would want to hurt your brother. Do you know of anyone who would want to cause harm to Ferris?"

Tears fell down her cheeks. She hugged her arms around her thin chest and squeezed her eyes shut. The thin frame that gave Ferris a rakish, handsome look in photographs Josie had seen made Julia look sinewy and harsh.

She pulled her shirt up to wipe her eyes on the bottom of it and revealed a taut belly. Josie looked away toward the street until the woman had returned her shirt.

"Had Ferris told you about anyone who he was worried about? Maybe someone he'd been having a relationship with that had ended badly?"

"Relationships ending badly for Ferris?" She laughed abruptly, though it sounded more like a cough. "He is the most shallow complicated person I've ever met. He's my twin, and I still don't understand what motivated his relationships."

"What do you mean by that?" Josie asked.

Julia dug a crumpled tissue out of her purse and wiped her eyes again. She put it back and finally said, "Relationships were like a hobby to him. He played with people like dolls. When he got bored with them he'd throw them in the Dumpster and move on to someone new."

She seemed to notice Josie watching her closely, and then saw Susan standing in the doorway. "Figuratively, of course. He didn't actually get rid of people. He just never managed to keep a relationship for more than a few months. A year or two at the most."

"Did he keep letters and mementos as keepsakes?"

She smiled and dipped her head, apparently realizing Josie was trying to find out what she knew.

"You found his stash," Julia said. "He'd drag boxes of that stuff out at parties. He'd impress people with the gold box he received from some Arab prince, or the tennis bracelet he received from some young actress. People would dig through his treasure boxes and listen to his stories about hanging out with rich people. I loved Ferris but it was all a little pathetic."

"What about jilted lovers? He seems to have a fairly big collection of admirers," Josie said. "Male and female."

Julia raised her shoulders in an exaggerated shrug, as if to say, *What could I do about it.* "He's had his share, and then some."

"Anyone who would want to hurt him? Someone angry enough, or unstable enough, to want to kill him?"

She sighed heavily and her shoulders deflated. "Honestly, if he dumped me the way I've seen him dump other people I'd want to kill him too." She seemed to notice Josie's scrutiny again. "Figuratively."

Josie nodded. "I see what you're saying. He didn't let people down easy." Josie hesitated, unsure how to bring up his HIV status with his sister, who might not have known. "Were you aware of any illnesses? Any serious diseases he may have had?"

Julia looked closely at Josie, but didn't respond.

"Do you mind if I call you Julia?"

"I don't mind."

"Okay, Julia. I can't let you go through Ferris's house yet, but I'd like to move in off the street. Are you okay with sitting in the living room for a few minutes with us? I'd like to talk about his medical issues with you."

Josie noticed Julia's face tighten, her mouth draw down into a frown, but she nodded and entered the house. Josie knew she shouldn't be allowing the woman into the house at this point in the investigation, but she had several tough questions to ask, and it seemed cruel to make her stand on the front porch.

The three women sat down on the leather couches. Julia scanned the living room. "He had good taste, didn't he? He never used a decorator. And he certainly didn't get taste from our parents."

"Why do you say that?"

"My dad owned a manufacturing plant that made metal parts for car companies. My mom was his secretary. They were obsessed with the business and didn't care much for Ferris and me. We spent every summer and holiday with our grandparents, my mom's family. When my grandparents died in France a few years ago they left everything to Ferris and me. They were loaded. My parents were furious. Mom contested it, fought us for the money, but the court said the will was legal. She spent a few months trying to make nice and convince us to share the loot, but it was an act."

"Do you talk with your parents anymore?" Josie asked.

"When Dad called a few days ago to tell me about Ferris? That was the first time I'd talked to him in five years."

"Did your dad mention anything about health issues that Ferris had?"

Julia frowned. "I don't know what you're getting at."

Josie glanced at Susan, who was sitting quietly, occasionally jotting down a note in her notebook.

"Ferris tested positive for HIV."

Julia squinted her eyes at Josie and leaned forward, as if not hearing her correctly. "What? HIV?"

"The coroner confirmed with the blood test."

"Oh, Ferris." She whispered his name and gazed out the long window facing the street. The bright afternoon light made her face appear even paler. "I talked to him every week on the phone, sometimes a couple times a week. He never mentioned it. Not even a hint that he was sick." She looked back at Josie. "Why are you telling me this? You think it had something to do with his death?"

"You know his body was found at Billy and Brenda Nix's house? We found him after the fire?"

"Dad said he was burned in the wildfire. He told me about the Nixes."

"Do you think Ferris was having a relationship with Billy?"

She picked up her hands and dropped them back onto her lap, her expression helpless. "I'm sure he was. Billy seemed to be his latest obsession. Ferris only obsessed over someone until he gained their love, or their approval. Once he found love, he lost interest. I'm sure a shrink could write volumes about our family."

"I guess what I'm wondering is, could someone else have found out about the relationship with Billy and killed Ferris out of revenge? Or, maybe they found out about his HIV status and killed him because—" Josie hesitated. It was a cruel conversation to have with this woman, but Julia knew Ferris better than anyone, and Josie hoped she might have an idea of who might hold a grudge.

"You think Ferris might have passed HIV on to someone else who killed him when they found out?"

Josie said nothing.

"I can't answer that," Julia said.

"I'm sorry to bring something like this up. We're just really struggling to find out what happened."

Julia just nodded once. Her expression had turned angry and Josie knew she had offended her. Josie stood and put her hand out, stepping forward to Julia so she would stand as well.

"I want to thank you again for talking with us today. I want you to know we'll do everything we can to find out what happened to Ferris and to find justice for him. If you think of anything at all, please call me. Day or night. And I'll be in touch about the investigation."

After Julia left, Josie and Susan spent another two hours collecting letters and financial papers, and searching each of the rooms inside the house. Other than prescription medicine that Cowan confirmed by phone was used to treat HIV, they found little more in terms of new evidence. In the end, their original summation of Ferris stood firm. He was a playboy with enough funds to live comfortably on his own and enjoy the games of life as he wanted to play them. Any number of people could have had the motivation to kill Ferris Sinclair.

NINETEEN

Josie followed Otto out the police department door at six o'clock, arguing with him over her plans for the evening. He was convinced her social life needed a boost, and he couldn't accept that she didn't want to participate in the same activities as he did.

"People hear the word *polka* and they prejudge," Otto said. "If you'd give it a chance once I think you'd enjoy it. You'd like our friends too. And there aren't just old people there. There's young people, your age even."

"Seriously. I just want to go home and relax," she said. "I'm happy with a night on the couch."

"It's Saturday night! A young woman your age ought to be out socializing. Meeting people."

Josie unlocked her car door. "Tell Delores you did your best, but you just couldn't make me budge. You guys have fun tonight." She waved and got into her car. She loved Otto, but his persistence annoyed the hell out of her at times.

Before she pulled out of the parking space she checked her cell phone: a missed call and voicemail from Nick Santos. The hostage negotiator's name caused an instant spike in her heart rate and a dread of what was to come. She'd not heard from him in over three months, when he'd filed a final report on the kidnapping and provided an update on the Medrano cartel. The word on the street in Mexico was that the Medranos had recovered the millions in stolen drug money that had been tied to Dillon's kidnapping. Nick had explained this story was the Medranos' way of saving face, and ultimately, the approach had most likely saved her life. They'd had no reason to retaliate if they had recovered their money. But in reality, the money had actually been remanded to the feds the night they had recovered Dillon.

Nick had stressed that Josie should not travel to Mexico. He felt the Medranos had bigger issues at home to deal with than traveling to the United States to kill a police officer. But she also realized the cartel's leader, the Bishop, could have killed her years ago when he'd had the opportunity. On her darker days she acknowledged to herself that she was alive because he wanted her alive. She was a pawn to him in a game that she didn't fully understand.

Josie dialed Nick's number hoping for something other than disaster.

"Josie!"

She smiled at his voice. He lived in Mexico as a kidnapping negotiator but he had been born in South Texas and had spent most of his life in the U.S., including a stint in the military and eight years as a city police officer in New Jersey. He still had traces of the Jersey accent and the tough mannerisms of a street cop.

"Hey, Nick. How are you?"

"I'm okay. Listen. I'm coming through Artemis this evening. I'm staying in Marfa tonight. On my way to a job in Alpine tomorrow. Thought I'd stop in and buy you supper."

"Oh!" Her mind went blank. It wasn't at all what she had anticipated.

"Don't sound so happy about it. Bring Dillon. I'll buy you both dinner at that Tamale place. I've been craving a fat burrito."

"Well, Dillon won't be coming. He's left."

"What do you mean he left?"

"He left me. He's moved back to St. Louis to start a new life."

"Shit. I'm sorry."

"I bet you have statistics that would have predicted this," she said.

"Okay. So let me buy *you* dinner *without* Dillon."

She laughed at his inability to accept anything but yes. "Okay. Dinner would be nice."

"See you in an hour?"

"That'll work."

Josie glanced at her watch. It would give her just enough time to get home, shower, and dress.

At precisely 7:00 p.m., Nick Santos pulled into her driveway in the same black Lexus SUV that had been parked in her driveway while he lived at her house during the negotiation. Nick had moved in, commandeering her spare bedroom as his own and using her dining room table as a workstation. But he had been neat, polite, and stayed out of her way as much as the situation permitted. Josie had grown fond of Nick and valued him as a professional and as a friend.

Josie dressed in a pair of faded jeans and a white camisole top, and dried her hair and put it up in a messy bun. She never wore makeup, but she did take the time to apply lip balm. As she looked in the mirror at her shiny lips, she thought it felt a little like playing dress-up.

She realized she had butterflies in her stomach and tried to blame it on the idea of spending an evening with a man she didn't know very well. But that wasn't exactly true. She had lived with him. He had seen her at her absolute worst and probably at her best. They knew each other in the extremes, but hardly at all in everyday life: she had no idea what kind of music he liked, what he did in his spare time, whether he liked sports or art or driving fast. What she did know was that he was a hell of a negotiator, and he was committed to his work above all else.

Josie smiled as she opened her front door to greet him.

"Hi! It's good to see you!" She smiled and watched him walk up. He wore jeans, black work boots, and a white T-shirt that fit snugly around his biceps. Nick was a stocky, well-built man by nature, and he also worked out daily to stay in shape for the job. He had short black hair, reminiscent of his days in the service, and black piercing eyes: a man born for law enforcement.

He smiled back at her and she blushed as he took her in. "You look beautiful."

She laughed, unsure how to take the compliment. "Come on in."

They walked inside and Chester trotted over to him, lifting his big brown eyes as if expecting Nick to offer something more than a pat on the head.

"What, I have to bring you treats to visit?"

Chester walked away and slumped back down on his rug, his eyes closed within seconds. Josie imagined the dog had been hoping for Dillon.

"What brings you this way?" she asked. They walked into the living room and sat down next to each other on the couch.

"A kidnapping in Alpine. A retired oil executive from Exxon."

Josie felt her skin grow cold and she saw the realization in Nick's expression.

He looked away from her and pointed back to the door, trying for a quick change in conversation. "You gonna take me for a burrito? I've been craving one for months now. I have to come to Texas to find a Mexican burrito. My father would disown me if he heard that."

―――――――

When Josie and Nick arrived at the Hot Tamale, Lucy was standing at the door smiling. She opened the door and ushered them into the diner.

"You back to visit us? I missed you! So many burritos you ate! Remind me, what's your name?"

He grinned. "Nick. I'm Burrito Nick."

"Yes, yes!" She looked at Josie. "And my favorite cop too. Come in and sit down anywhere. I'll get you menus and two Dos Equis. Yes?"

Josie nodded. "Perfect. Thanks, Lucy."

They sat at Josie's spot by the front window.

"You're still her favorite, huh?"

"Until another cop walks in and takes my place."

Lucy set two opened Dos Equises on the table, sweat already dripping down the labels. "You want me to order for you? I know what you want already."

Nick grinned again. "You are the ultimate waitress. You take all the work out of being a customer. Whatever you bring me will be outstanding."

Josie gave Lucy a thumbs-up and she disappeared. Twenty minutes later she returned with plates with massive chicken burritos piled high with lime rice, salsa, and pico de gallo so hot it made Josie's tongue ache.

Josie caught Nick up on the local politics and Mayor Moss's latest antics. She discussed the murder of Ferris Sinclair and Billy's suicide. Nick avoided talk of the Medranos, saying he didn't want to ruin a nice evening. Instead he talked about the vacation he took to Belize after he finished with Dillon's case. He'd spent two weeks there with his younger brother hanging out on the beach, reading and sleeping.

Josie was surprised at how comfortable the evening was. Even the ride back to her house was filled with easy conversation. She realized she wasn't nervous at all—until they pulled into her driveway, and things suddenly became more complicated.

Nick turned off the car and got out when Josie did. He didn't ask if he should come in, and she wasn't sure how to respond. While she wanted Nick to follow her into the house, she had no idea what to do once they entered.

Standing in front of the door, Nick grabbed her wrist as she started to press her code into the security pad. Surprised, she turned slightly and found Nick behind her, his chest pressing into her back.

"Let's see how good of a cop you are," he said.

He reached around her and pressed the first number of a six-digit code. She had given him the number when he was staying at her home during the negotiation. She smiled. The day he moved out he had told her to change her security codes. He pressed the remaining five numbers and the tumblers clicked and whisked and the door opened just an inch, allowing him access into her home.

His head was just behind hers. He whispered into her neck. "Josie. You don't follow directions very well."

She pushed the door open, grinning.

The light from the table lamp in the living room cast a soft white glow across the room. She laid her purse on the coffee table and offered him a drink.

"You don't want to deaden your senses."

She turned from the coffee table to face him, smiling still. "What does that mean?"

"It means you need a clear head tonight."

"I always heard, a cop should never hook up with another cop."

"I'm not asking you to marry me."

"What are you asking for then?"

"I'm asking you to kiss me."

She hesitated. "Dillon hasn't been gone that long. It's too soon. It's—"

"Too soon for what? To feel happy? To enjoy life for an evening?"

Josie felt her face turn hot. "I'm no good at this."

He put his hand out and she took it. He turned and led her down the hallway and into her bedroom, where he unlocked and opened the window. She stood at the end of her bed feeling like a high school girl.

A breeze fluttered the curtains. The moonlight cast long shadows across the white blanket and sheets. The smell of the night desert filled her bedroom and she took in the scent. He stood in front of her but didn't touch her.

"I've thought about you almost every day since I left here," he said.

Josie didn't know what to say. She'd thought of Nick, but mostly in terms of the job he had performed. She had been so caught up in her own drama that any other feelings were silenced.

"I know this room like it's a room in my own home. I imagined any number of people coming in here. I imagined saving you a hundred different ways. I would have laid down my life for you in a heartbeat."

She breathed in suddenly, his words catching her off guard.

Nick ran his hands up her arms and stepped closer, the heat of his body on her skin.

"I'm no good at this," she said again. "The romance and all of this just eludes me." As the words came out she felt ridiculous. He made her nervous. He was out of her league on so many different levels. With his back to the window his face was in shadow, but she could sense the smile on his face.

"Do you trust me?"

She thought for a moment and had no other answer but "Yes."

"We all have talents, right?"

She nodded, smiling again.

"Romance is a talent of mine. Let me show you how it works."

"You're going to school me in the ways of romance?"

He laughed. "That's exactly what I'm going to do."

"Tell me what the first lesson is, and I'll consider it."

"Okay. Number one, stop thinking about romance like a cop."

"What's that supposed to mean?"

"Think about your words. Eludes? School? Lesson? These are not words that a man associates with lovemaking."

She laughed and felt his hands pulling her shirt out of her jeans, slowly, the fabric sliding against her skin like silk.

"Here's the problem. You're asking me to be unanalytical. I should be free to think any way I want."

"Josie." He ran his fingertips up her arms. "This doesn't have anything to do with thinking. It's all here." He touched a fingertip to her chest. "You feel it, you don't think it."

He placed his hands on her shoulders and gently turned her around. "You said you trust me."

She nodded once.

He lifted her shirt up over her head and dropped it to the floor. He pressed his thumbs into the sides of her spine, slowly working down her back, whispering her name and kissing her neck until her thoughts faded away.

TWENTY

At seven o'clock that evening, Marta stumbled out of bed to stop the buzzing alarm clock going off on her dresser across the room. Following the debriefing meeting with Josie and Otto that morning, she had gone back home to putter around in her cactus garden behind her house. She had finally lain down at noon to get a restless seven hours' sleep before her shift that night. Marta loved her job, but the shift work kept her from ever feeling truly rested.

By the time she arrived at the Hell-Bent, at eight o'clock, she found a sea of pickup trucks parked helter-skelter in the field behind the parking lot. Marta had never seen it so packed. Hank needed someone directing traffic or she would end up with a half dozen accident reports to write up before the night was over. She went inside and offered to park cars for Hank, who seemed beyond overwhelmed and appreciative of any help he could get.

"This is insane, Marta. I've never seen so many people, and it's still early. I hate to do it, but I may have to turn people away before it's over. The fire chief will shut me down if I get too many more people in here."

They both looked out across the dance floor, which was filled with people milling around in groups, laughing and crying and drinking beer. "I'll call the sheriff's department and see if we can get some deputies over here tonight," Marta said. "You're going to need it."

After calling the sheriff's department for backup, Marta walked the parking lot with her clipboard and paper. Parking cars was a good excuse to get the information Josie had requested. Marta wrote down the make, model, and license-plate number of every dark-colored, four-door truck in the lot. By ten o'clock she was caught up with the list of plates and was helping the deputies park the vehicles in the field in rows.

By one in the morning, Marta had a list of twenty-four trucks that fit the description, and she'd arrested two drunks for disorderly conduct: a productive night. Two deputies agreed to continue working the parking lot and taking names. Marta dropped the list off at the police department and clocked off at 2:00 a.m.

———•———

At seven o'clock on Sunday morning, Josie received a text from Mitchell Cowan asking her to come by the coroner's office. He had results. She rolled over, her phone still in her hand, and looked at Nick, who was facing her with his eyes open.

"I like you, Josie."

She laughed. "I like you too, Nick."

He propped up on his arm so he could study her better. "This isn't a normal thing for me. You asked me last night what I wanted from you. I want more than a kiss. But my life is seriously screwed up. You know that. And yours isn't much better."

She didn't say anything for a moment. "Have I told you I'm not very good at this?"

He smiled then, and lay back down. "This is a good situation. If we're both screwed up, and neither one of us knows what we're doing, then there's no expectations. Right?"

Josie lay on her side with her head now tucked into his arm. "I'm not sure this makes sense right now. Dillon just left. I was with Dillon for years. Aren't there rules about rushing into relationships? Re-bounds and whatever?"

"That's basketball. You're okay."

She smiled again and decided he was right. There were no rule books in life, and even if there were, she was pretty sure her life would be indexed in the appendix under "abnormal."

Still holding her cell phone she lifted it up for him to see. "The coroner texted. I need to get to his office."

"No waffles and coffee in bed?"

"You lived here long enough to know me better than that."

At a little after nine on Sunday morning, Josie pulled into the park-ing lot at the Arroyo County Jail, where Mitchell Cowan's office was located. The jail was a brown cinder-block and brick building with a brown awning over the entrance door. Josie entered a vesti-bule furnished with two chairs and a framed picture of the Pledge of Allegiance. She pressed a buzzer and stated her name and a second set of doors opened into a central hub where Maria Santiago, intake officer, was sitting. The room was octagonal, with Maria located be-hind a desk in the center. Several doors led to different areas of the jail such as the booking room, the interrogation room, and the pris-oner pods.

Josie chatted with Maria for a few minutes and was then buzzed through another set of doors, with the words COUNTY CORONER painted in black on them. She pressed an intercom button and announced her name. A moment later the door clicked and she pushed it open. The state-of-the-art jail was paid for by a Homeland Security grant that the mayor received shortly after 9/11, as was the trauma center. For such a small town, the facilities were first-rate.

Mitchell Cowan was wearing a white lab coat, a mask, and a blue surgical cap. He leaned over a body on a stainless-steel gurney, his hands pushing and pulling at something in the open abdominal cavity. Josie turned her head and stared at the wall of cabinets across the room, avoiding the body on the table.

"Chief," he said by way of a greeting.

"Morning."

"One moment here while I fit all this back inside. It's a bit like trying to repack a box. Sometimes you wonder how all the pieces in the package could possibly have fit inside such a small space."

Cowan finally covered the body and went over to the sink to wash up. Josie could smell the medicinal soap and wondered if that scent ever left his skin.

As he was drying his arms and hands he said, "I hear the negotiator's back in town. Paying you a visit."

Josie raised her eyebrows in response.

"You be careful with that one. He strikes me as a little on the dangerous side. You've got enough of that to contend with on your own."

"How on earth did you find out about Nick being in town?"

Cowan grinned. "I had breakfast at the Hot Tamale this morning. There was a fair amount of speculation going on amongst the regulars."

"Unbelievable." Josie shook her head and saw that Cowan was enjoying her discomfort. "I hope you texted me about something case-related."

Cowan lumbered across the room to pick up a stack of file folders. He motioned with his head for Josie to join him at the end of the counter where he stood.

"I received a call from the toxicology lab." He turned and looked at her to make sure she knew what he was referring to. "The lab that the fire marshal used for the syringe?"

"Sure. What did you find out?"

"The marshal must have some pull. I've never had results that quick."

"What were the results?" she asked, becoming impatient.

"The syringe was empty."

"No trace amounts of anything?"

"Empty. The syringe has never been used."

"Damn. The murderer planted it at the scene to make Ferris look like a drug user?"

"Maybe Ferris intended to use it and ran out of time," Cowan said.

"But we didn't find any drugs on the premises. And why put it under the couch?"

"To hide it?"

"Hmm." Josie tried to imagine Ferris being stunned in the hallway and then somehow slipping the syringe under the couch. It was hard for her to imagine a scenario where that worked, unless he hid the syringe and then tangled with the murderer. But if he hid the syringe, surely he would have hid drugs along with it. "What about the bloodwork you sent off for Ferris?"

"It'll be at least another week before we hear back from them. It's a different lab, different test than what the fire marshal was looking for."

"So we still have no idea on the cause of death for Ferris?"

"No," Cowan said. "But I have confirmed the pills in the baggie you gave me from Billy Nix. One pill was Ambien. Two pills were OxyContin. Official cause of death is asphyxiation. His heart slowed to the point where he wasn't getting enough oxygen pumped through his lungs to breathe. My guess is, he bought a baggie full of pills and swallowed as many as he could along with the alcohol until he passed out. It was a deadly combination of the pills and the alcohol. For a man his size, with a propensity to drink, he had to work at it. His blood alcohol level was point four five two, enough to put him in a coma even without the pills."

"The idea of someone forcing pills down his throat and getting him to swallow is—"

Cowan cut her off. "Is ridiculous. He was probably so drunk by the time he finished the pills he could barely swallow. And, there were no abrasions, no bruising around his mouth or cheeks that would indicate someone was forcing pills down his throat. There were also no pills caught in his esophagus."

"Meaning?"

"If someone had been forcing pills down his throat, I would expect to find some caught in the esophagus."

Josie nodded her understanding. "It's hard to imagine homicide at this point."

"Any thoughts on where a person could get those pills on a Saturday night?" she asked.

"That's your bailiwick, Chief. Can't help you there." He pulled out another piece of paper in his stack. "One more bit of news. I ran the Western blot test on Billy Nix. He tested negative for HIV."

Josie arrived back at the department and found Otto in the office. She gave him a quick rundown of her conversation with Cowan.

"So you're ready to concede it was suicide as cause of death?" Otto asked.

Josie nodded, her expression troubled. "It bothers me. Someone helped Billy along, but I don't know what else you would call it. Billy's the one that swallowed the pills." Josie grabbed a bottle of water and sat down at her desk to cool off. The day was already heating up to be a scorcher. "What else do you have?"

Otto said he had already run half of the license-plate numbers that Marta had left for them the night before.

"Any surprises?"

"Mick Sinner's on here. Thought that was odd, that he'd show up at the memorial service after he pitched such a fit about his band performing the night after Billy died."

Otto handed Josie what he had compiled so far.

She scanned the list and noticed Hank's name. "Hank drives a four-door truck too?"

"Yeah. I know his truck. It's a beauty. Big black truck. He ordered it brand-new out of Odessa."

"Remember what Brenda told us? She said Billy called two people the night he died."

Otto nodded. "Just what I was thinking. Slim Jim and Hank. And she said both of them told Billy to go back to the hotel and sleep it off."

"What if Hank learned Billy was drunk and took the pills to him?"

"I asked Hank if he thought Billy would take pills and he said he was sure of it. He talked about Billy's nerves before a show. Said Billy could have gotten pills from any number of people."

"What possible motive could Hank have for helping Billy commit suicide?"

"I don't know," Otto said. "Billy made the Hell-Bent a heap of money."

"We should talk to both Hank and Mick, but I'd like to start with Brenda. I'd like for her to come clean on Billy and Ferris and how those two deaths may be related. She has to be a link in this somehow."

Otto glanced at his watch. "It's almost eleven. You talk to Brenda and I'll finish running the license plates. Then we can grab a bite to eat and go talk with Hank."

Josie walked outside and the oppressive heat made her feel like turning back around for the air-conditioned office: ten straight days of temperatures above one hundred. Blue sky stretched out in all directions, promising nothing but sun. Sweat dripped down her temples by the time Josie reached Manny's office, just a block away. She opened the office door and found him sitting in his chair behind the counter watching TV. He pushed himself up and stepped to the counter.

"How are you, Manny?"

"Fat and happy, like my daddy used to say. A glass of iced tea in one hand, the remote in the other. All in all, a good morning."

"You got life figured out."

He chuckled. "I'm just a lazy old man. What can I do for you?"

"Remind me what room number Brenda Nix is in."

He pointed off to his left. "Room Five. I just delivered fresh towels. I know she's home."

"No problems here?" she asked.

"It's all good. I appreciate you checking on me."

Brenda answered the door and stepped back for Josie to enter. Her face was drawn, her eyes tired and red-rimmed. With no makeup and dressed in jeans and a T-shirt, Brenda had lost the playmaker image that Josie associated with her. She looked like a tired, grieving widow. Josie stepped inside and a woman with Brenda's auburn hair and wide green eyes stood up from a reading chair by the window and offered her hand.

"Hi. I'm Patty Netham. We spoke on the phone a few days ago."

"It's good to meet you."

"I appreciate you calling the way you did. Brenda needed family here to support her." She glanced at her sister and the two women smiled slightly. "I'm going to go fill the tank up and grab us some lunch. We're going to Alpine for the day, unless you think this will take a while?"

"No, this won't take too long. I just have some follow-up questions."

Patty hesitated and looked at her sister again. "Do you want me to call your lawyer? To let her know you're speaking with the police?" Patty glanced at Josie apologetically, but Josie shrugged it off.

Brenda waved a hand in the air. "I'm too tired for lawyers. I just want this over with."

After Patty left Josie took her place in the reading chair and Brenda sat in a matching chair at the writing desk across from the bed.

"Brenda, I've come to ask you some tough questions today. I want you to understand, I'm not asking them because I think you're a suspect. I'm asking because I believe that Billy's death and Ferris's death are connected in some way. I need to understand their relationship."

"I wouldn't know where to begin." She seemed lost and overwhelmed and Josie wondered if she would be able to provide the honest answers needed.

"I want to understand why Ferris was attracted to Billy. I need to understand what Billy thought of Ferris. I need to know if their relationship was causing problems for other people, maybe other band members. I'd like for you to tell me their story so I can pull out the details that may help us make sense of their deaths."

Brenda stood and walked to the coffeemaker by the TV. She took the carafe, filled it with water in the bathroom, and came back, busying herself as she began to talk.

"In a matter of days I've discovered that almost everything I think about myself and my family, everything that I believed in, was wrong," she said. "It's not just Billy, either. It's my own family. Patty and I spent the last two days sitting in this hotel room telling the truth. Not what we thought needed to be said. Just the truth. It was the most revealing conversation of my life."

Brenda took a deep breath and sat back down in her seat, looking at Josie now. "I left my family because I didn't think they wanted me. I was twenty years old. I knew I couldn't sing or play an instrument like the rest of them. I always felt like a misfit. Like they were ashamed of me, and they didn't know what to do with me. Patty said she thought it was jealousy on my part. My sisters thought I was jealous of the rest of the family, and I put such a distance between us that they didn't know how to talk to me." She was quiet for a moment. "Looking back on it, I think she's right about the jealousy. I miss my family. I miss my sisters. And I think they miss me too." Brenda shut her eyes as if she might cry again but no tears came. "All these years without my family."

"What did your family think about Billy? Were they fans?" Josie asked.

She smiled a little. "Patty said the family used to joke about me coming back to manage them. They claimed if I could make Billy a star that I could manage anyone."

Josie was taken aback that Brenda didn't appear angry at the harsh opinion of Billy.

Brenda waved off Josie's surprised expression. "Here's what I've known for a long time, but never allowed myself to really acknowledge. I worked a lot harder at Billy's career than he did. He was a country musician because it was a job. He had someone making his decisions for him: telling him when to show up, what to wear, where to be, and what songs to sing when he got there." She was quiet a moment, her expression grim, as if she wasn't sure if she should go on. "Billy wasn't a thinker. He needed someone to do that for him. I don't know if he really wanted a wife, but he needed a manager. And I came as a package deal."

"The rumors about Billy and Ferris. Had you heard them?"

"Please." She made a dismissive face. "People are so cruel. They love to humiliate. Better yet, they love to knock you down a notch. One of the waitresses at the Hell-Bent pulled me aside one night when the band was onstage. She actually had me follow her outside behind the kitchen. It was dark out. I could hear the band pounding out a Waylon Jennings song inside. The crowd was crazy—it was a good night. And she stands right next to me and puts her hand on my shoulder and says, 'Honey, I'm telling you this as a friend. For your own good.'" Brenda tipped her head down and looked at Josie to make sure she knew the truth.

"She was no friend," Josie said.

"Exactly. She tells me that Billy and Ferris are lovers. That was the term she used. I could have thrown up right there. Until that moment I had known Ferris had a thing for Billy, like a fan thing, but nothing more. I knocked the woman's hand off my shoulder and went back inside."

"Do you think there was any truth to the rumors?"

Brenda shrugged, almost imperceptibly, and took a moment to

continue. "I don't know if they actually were lovers, like she suggested. But I know Billy went to Presidio to visit Ferris on several occasions, and then lied to me about it. He called Ferris daily when he wasn't around. I honestly couldn't tell you what the attraction was. I found Ferris to be obnoxious and not terribly good-looking."

"I've heard Ferris stroked Billy's ego, told him how wonderful he was. Did you see that?"

She choked out a laugh. "It was disgusting. All the time. Billy was so gifted. An incredible performer. Ferris would tell him he was going to be a megastar. He'd be top ten on CMT." Brenda shook her head. "You know what pissed me off? Ferris and I both knew Billy wasn't gifted. He was good. And he looked the part. And he had a good band to back him up. With the right set of circumstances Billy could have made it in Nashville. But Ferris's fawning all over him was not helpful."

"Do you have any idea who could have killed Ferris?"

Brenda looked at her for a long moment. "I could have killed him, but I didn't. As far as who else hated him as much as I did? I can't answer that."

"Do you have any idea why he would have been at your home the night of the evacuation?"

"I don't know. He knew we were leaving. Billy told him. I honestly don't know why he would have come to our home."

Josie noted that this was new information—she hadn't known that Billy had told Ferris they were leaving—but she saw no benefit to questioning Brenda about the omission at this point. "Could he have been looking for something?"

Brenda made a face as if the question was ridiculous. "We don't have anything worth looking for! The guitars and amps were headed with us to Austin."

Josie paused, dreading the rest of the conversation. "I received some troubling news from the coroner. Are you aware that Ferris was HIV positive?"

Her eyes widened and she put a hand to her chest. "What?"

"The coroner tested him. He confirmed the results with a second test."

Brenda's hand moved up to her mouth, her expression filled with dread. "Billy?"

"His test came back negative. Just to be sure though, the coroner said you'll still want to test now and then test again in a few months."

"I don't know what to say."

"You weren't aware of this?" asked Josie, keeping her voice kind in light of the harsh questions.

"No. Did Billy know?" Brenda whispered the words, her expression bereft. "Is that why he committed suicide? Because he was afraid he had AIDS too?"

"I can't answer those questions," Josie said. "There were rumors about the relationship, but no one I've talked with knew that Ferris was HIV positive."

"The humiliation just never ends."

"I know this is hard on you, and I'm sorry to bring all of this up again. I just have a few more questions. Are you okay to keep going?"

She sighed and nodded. "How could it get much worse?"

"You mentioned that Billy called both Hank and Slim Jim the night he died. Can you remind me how you knew that?"

She frowned then, and seemed to be thinking back. "I know because Hank called the next morning to check on Billy. That's when I discovered Billy hadn't come home. Hank told me that Billy had been really drunk and he wanted to check on him. He also said Billy told him he'd talked to Slim, and that he'd told Billy to go back to the hotel too."

Josie nodded and they listened as the coffeemaker popped and sputtered as the last of the water dripped into the pot. Brenda stood to pour coffee and Josie decided to change her line of questioning somewhat.

"As far as I know, Billy never left the area downtown where he bought the liquor and ended up at the little park behind the trauma center," Josie said. "You told me that Billy didn't have any pills in the hotel room with him."

"That's right."

"Do you think Hank or Slim Jim could have taken the pills to Billy that night? Because I'm not sure who else would have known where he was."

Brenda looked worried, as if she'd not thought about that possibility before then. "Why would Hank or Slim Jim do that? They loved Billy. Both of them. Neither one of them would have helped him end his life. I'm sure of that."

Josie nodded slowly, trying to make the pieces fit.

"Besides, he could have bought pills off of someone downtown."

Josie tilted her head, acknowledging the idea. "This is what I'm trying to understand. I'm no mental health expert, but Billy didn't strike me as a man who was suffering from severe depression. The only reason I can imagine him committing suicide is that he had a terrible sense of guilt or shame over Ferris's death."

Brenda's shoulders were slumped forward and her hands were clasped loosely in her lap, as if she no longer had the strength to move.

"When Billy found out that it was Ferris who died in your home, did he give you any indication that he knew what happened? Can you talk about his reaction?"

"He was inconsolable." She barely whispered the words. "That's when I knew how much Ferris meant to Billy." She shut her eyes for a moment and when she opened them, Josie could see they were glassy with tears. "When we found out my stun gun had been discharged? Billy actually asked me if I had used it on Ferris. He thought I was capable of killing Ferris. I could see it in his face. Even if it was only for an instant, he still thought it."

Josie asked a few additional questions about the band members so that she didn't leave Brenda in such a devastated frame of mind. When her sister returned from her errands Josie thanked Brenda for her time and left.

She walked back to the department thinking about the change in Brenda's appearance from the day Josie had met her and Billy at the police department until just now. Brenda looked raw, as if the realizations that she had come to over the last few days had stripped away everything, leaving her completely vulnerable, waiting for the next battering. In a way, Josie was relieved for this sad woman. Maybe she would reconnect with her family and begin a new life based on honesty.

Josie's mind strayed to her own relationship with Dillon, and their inability to talk honestly with each other before he left her. Their conversations were little more than polite exchanges. Then she thought about Nick, a man completely the opposite of Dillon in every way, from his career to his abrupt manner and sense of humor. *"I like you, Josie."* She heard the words in her head and the thought of him made her smile. Two screwed-up people with no expectations.

TWENTY-ONE

When Josie arrived back at the police department Otto told her he'd arranged for the two of them to speak with Hank at his home at 1:00. They stopped at the gas station for a quick lunch and ordered chicken strips and fried mushrooms. They ate in one of the two booths located on the restaurant side of the building and agreed that the food was greasy and satisfying. On their way to Hank's house, as Otto drove Josie filled him in on Brenda's summation of her husband and his relationship with Ferris.

"I'm stuck on the idea that Hank and Slim Jim were the only two that talked to Billy the night he committed suicide," she said.

"What's your issue?"

"Somebody provided Billy the pills he used to commit suicide. Who else makes sense but Hank or Slim Jim?"

"He could have bought it from someone else," he said.

"It's not like drug dealers hang out by the trauma center selling prescription pills by the baggie. There's no one around that area late at night."

"But he could have called someone easy enough. Someone could have delivered pills to him," he said. "I just filed the subpoena on

Friday. We should get the court approval for Billy's phone records tomorrow."

Josie nodded. "The phone records are key. From the various people we've talked to, no one has mentioned Billy taking drugs. Alcohol yes, but not drugs. I'll be surprised if we find he called someone for pills. Assuming Brenda's not lying, Slim Jim and Hank were the only people who knew Billy was on the path to self-destruction that night. I feel like one of them provided the pills."

Josie drove in silence for a while, thinking about the questions she wanted to ask Hank. "You know what else sticks in my mind? The day after the evacuation, when I went to the Hell-Bent to see if I could track down Billy and Brenda?"

"Yeah?"

"What's the first thing people asked you the day after the evacuation?"

"They asked if family members or friends were safe," Otto said.

"And?"

"And did their house make it through the fire."

Josie pointed at Otto. "Exactly! That was usually the *first* question. Most people already knew their friends had left in the evacuation, so they wanted to know if their homes were spared."

"Okay, what's that have to do with anything?"

"When I talked to Hank that day, I said that we had stopped by the Nixes' house. I said we were looking for them. That we needed to talk to them. Wouldn't you think he would assume that if the police were looking for them, that their home had burned up in the fire?"

Otto drummed his fingers on the steering wheel as if considering this. "He never asked about their house? You're sure of that?"

"Positive. I thought it was odd, but in all the drama it didn't stand out."

Hank lived in a small ranch home just beyond the Hell-Bent. It was a simple one-story brick building with straggly clumps of cactus in the yard. Hank opened the front door and invited them in to a sparsely furnished living room. The walls were white and the room contained a brown corduroy couch, a love seat, and a banged-up coffee table that appeared to serve as a footrest. The couch faced a large-screen TV that hung on the wall, and two recliners faced the front window. The room looked like a typical bachelor's living quarters with few decorations or personal touches. Hank motioned for them to sit down on the couch. He picked up the remote on the coffee table, turned down the volume on a baseball game, and sat down on the love seat.

"What can I do for you?"

"We're struggling, Hank. We're hoping you can help us sort some things out," she said.

"You bet. Anything I can do, you name it."

"We have two men who are dead, and an investigation that's stalled. You know the country music scene better than anyone in the area. Help us understand how Billy Nix, a man with a bright future, could have ended up committing suicide."

Hank considered Josie for a moment and stood. "Let me get you something."

Hank returned a minute later holding a photo album, which he laid on the coffee table in front of Josie and Otto. He flipped a few pages in and pointed to a photo of Billy, standing by himself onstage at the Hell-Bent, holding a mic with his eyes closed, his head thrown back, obviously belting out a song.

Hank sat down again. He smiled, but his expression was sad. "That was the first time Billy sang in front of an audience. I've been friends with him and Brenda since before they got married. They used to hang out at the Hell-Bent and Brenda was always telling me how Billy could sing. Billy would give me this aw-shucks grin, and I never thought much about it. You can imagine, people tell me they can sing all the time, and they can barely carry a tune."

Josie nodded. She'd seen enough bad TV to know lots of people thought they had a gift that just wasn't there.

"Finally, one morning, just as we're opening up the bar, Brenda brings Billy in and says, 'Give him ten minutes onstage.' Brenda set a boom box onstage and cued up the music. Then Billy got up there and sang, 'I Think I'll Just Stay Here and Drink.'" Hank smiled. "It was rough, but the guy had a stage presence that blew me away. He wasn't polished. But that's good. That's the death knell for outlaw country. Billy was honest country. There were a couple waitresses in there that day and by the time he was done they were all moved up on the edge of the dance floor, smiling, bobbing their heads. Those waitresses knew they'd heard something special."

"You were convinced, the first time you heard Billy sing?"

"If you saw as many bands come through here as I do, you'd get it. To have the complete package is rare. That's what Mick Sinner doesn't get. It's the raw simplicity of what Billy had that was magic. He wasn't out to impress anyone. He was just out there to sing his song. People loved that about Billy. That's not something you can learn. Mick tries too hard. And that made it all the harder for him to watch Billy rise to the top."

"After Billy sang for you that day, how long did it take before the band formed?" Josie asked.

"Billy knew Slim Jim and the guys. They'd messed around with the idea of starting a band. When they got my blessing it helped. But it was Brenda that got the band going, and Slim Jim and the others forget that now. They knew Brenda was part of the Netham Sisters, and that she had Nashville connections. They were willing to use her to get them a contract." Hank grinned. "Those boys just didn't like Brenda telling them what to do. And Brenda didn't have any problem being boss."

"Billy didn't mind her being his boss?"

Hank smiled. "He *needed* Brenda to tell him what to do."

Josie narrowed his eyes at Hank, trying to sort out the chain of events. "So why would a guy who'd worked so hard, and come so far, commit suicide? He left a lot of people who cared about him."

Hank said nothing. His expression changed from a man remembering the good old days to someone who didn't want to think about the present.

Josie unbuttoned her shirt pocket and pulled out a baggie containing the remaining three pills. "What can you tell me about these?"

Hank jerked his head back as if she'd asked a shocking question. "How would I know anything about a bag of pills?"

"Pills from this plastic bag killed Billy. He called two people the night he ate a baggieful of pills and drank himself to death. Somebody had to give him these pills and you were one of only two people that talked to him that night."

He raised his eyebrows and shrugged. "Yeah, I talked to him. I also told him to go back to the hotel and go to bed."

"A truck that fits the description of yours was seen parked next to the park where Billy died that night."

"You're kidding, right?" Hank smiled for a moment, as if doubting they were serious. His smile faded as he noted their stony expressions and the lack of friendly banter. He sat up then, his look now defensive.

Josie and Otto both sat quietly watching him.

"Do you know how many big black pickup trucks there are in this county?"

"Who gave him these pills?" Josie asked. She held them up in her hand and watched Hank stare at them.

Hank pointed a finger at Otto, but kept his eyes on Josie. "Otto asked me the other day. He asked if I was surprised that Billy took pills." He turned his attention to Otto. "And what did I tell you? I said, no. I never saw him popping pills, but he was a nervous guy. He drank whiskey before each show. It wouldn't have surprised me to see him taking Oxy before a show to calm down."

Josie glanced at Otto, and then back at Hank. "How did you know Billy took Oxy?"

Hank laughed, nervous now. "Come on! It was a guess! I told you, Otto, a guy could pick up a bag of Oxy from any number of people."

"Did you give Billy pills?" Josie asked.

"No." He made eye contact, his expression rigid.

"Did you see Billy the night he died?"

"I told you I talked to him on the phone."

"Did you see him in person?" Josie asked.

"No."

"Do you know why Billy committed suicide? What would have driven him to that point?" Otto asked. His tone was gentler now, his voice softer.

"I don't know. He had everything going for him. He had a wife who loved him, and a career that was ready to take off." Hank shrugged. "Who knows what drives any of us to do the things we do."

"What can you tell us about Billy and Ferris?" Josie asked.

"What do you mean?"

"We've heard rumors that Billy and Ferris were having a sexual relationship. Do you believe that to be true?"

Hank turned his head away and cursed under his breath. "You think Billy committed suicide over Ferris?"

Josie waited for him to answer her question.

"I think Ferris was obsessed with fame and fortune and he saw Billy as a sure bet." Hank stared at Josie for a long while, his jaw rigid. "I'm not going to sit here and guess about what kind of relations they might have had."

"What about Billy?" Otto asked.

"Billy was one of the most insecure people I know, and Ferris took advantage of that."

"What about Brenda? Did she know the two men were having a relationship?" she asked.

Hank hesitated. "I sure as hell hope not."

⸺·⸺

When Otto and Josie got into the jeep Josie asked, "What do you think?"

"The pills bother me. I think he knows something."

Josie took the list of names Otto had printed off from her shirt pocket and unfolded it.

"Everyone on this list drives a dark-colored four-door truck that matches the description of the truck that was next to the park the night Billy committed suicide. All of these trucks were at the Hell-Bent for Billy's memorial service."

"Let's go over the list again," Otto said. "Who on this list is a known drug dealer? Who had the means to deliver pills to Billy?"

They scanned the list together and Otto pointed to a name at the bottom of the list. "Paula Muñoz."

Josie groaned. "Damn. She drives me crazy."

Otto glanced at his watch as he pulled out of the lane and headed toward the police station. "Josie, it's six o'clock. We've been at this seven days straight. I need a few hours tonight. Delores is making noise about the long hours and me retiring again."

Josie looked at him, surprised that Otto was worn out by the case. "Absolutely. Let's call it a night."

"You'll take off too? Go home and call the negotiator maybe? Have a nice dinner?"

"Are you kidding me?" She laughed in spite of her irritation. "Who told you?"

He ignored her question. "Nick's a good guy. He's a hell of a negotiator. But two cops in a relationship together doesn't make for an easy life."

"Otto. I'm not marrying him. He stopped by to say hi."

"He stopped by to check in on you. And, I'm okay with that."

"Oh, really? Well as long as you're okay with it, then I feel much better about things now. Thank you."

"You're welcome."

After Josie dropped Otto off at the station so he could have a nice meal with Delores, Josie checked around town and discovered that

Paula was hanging out at Tiny's Gun Club, just down the street from the PD.

Tiny was a three-hundred-pound man who wore a feather boa around his massive neck. Aside from the boa, he wore standard gunsalesman garb: jeans, T-shirt, cowboy boots. He claimed the boa was his calling card at gun shows. Everybody knew the guy with the boa. He once told Josie that he used to be the "big gun guy." It was how people distinguished him from other gun sellers. "Hellfire! Everybody's big now. Ain't nothing special about me. I blend in with the next guy. But a boa? Nobody's got that."

What Tiny really had going for him was an amazing knowledge of every gun manufactured in the U.S., and many worldwide. It wasn't the boa that drew people from all over the Southwest to his shop; it was his knowledge of guns that allowed his eccentricities to exist in an environment not always known for tolerance.

Josie entered the shop and found Tiny perched on a stool at the end of a twenty-foot glass counter that ran down one side of the store. Behind him was a display rack that progressed in size from rifles to shotguns. Inside the glass cases was an amazing array of handguns, from miniatures that would fit into a woman's palm to pistols that would need two hands to aim and fire. And Tiny knew the provenance of every gun he sold. The rest of the shop was filled with neatly stacked shelves of ammo and gun paraphernalia that hunters, gun enthusiasts, and law enforcement used.

Paula Muñoz stood on the other side of the counter, bent over the glass with her arms perched on top, laughing her way through some story or another. Tiny, being a goodhearted man, sat on his stool patiently listening to the story and nodding at the appropriate moments, laughing when the time came. He seemed to perk up when Josie walked in and she realized he had probably been held hostage for quite some time.

"Josie! What brings you here?" he asked, and slid off his stool. He flung the boa trailing down the front of his body around to the back of his neck and walked toward her, his eyes pointed toward the ceiling. *There is a God*, he mouthed.

"What can I do for you, dear heart?" he said.

"Actually, I was hoping to have a word with Paula. You think we could have a minute to talk?"

Tiny leaned across the counter and whispered, "Honey, you can have all the minutes you want. That girl never shuts up."

He headed toward the back of the store and in a voice loud enough for both women to hear, he said, "I'll be back in a few minutes. I need to check on some inventory."

Paula smiled, her whole face involved in the act—her eyes wide, her mouth open, her cheeks round and flushed with happiness. Paula was in her midtwenties with a complexion like cream and long blond waves that gave her the look of pure innocence. Paula was also a convicted drug dealer who, to her attorney's horror, had explained to the sentencing judge, "I provide a service for people. One person with insurance gets a prescription from their doctor. They don't need it all. I connect that person with someone else who doesn't have insurance but who still needs the medication. The medicine doesn't get wasted. Everyone feels better."

"Ms. Muñoz, we're not talking about medicine here," the judge had explained. "We're talking about people buying OxyContin who aren't sick. It's called prescription drug abuse."

"No! These are my friends. They *are* sick. They're in *pain*. They just don't have the money to go see a doctor, and I'm just helping them feel better. What's so wrong with that?"

The story Josie had heard was that Paula and the judge debated prescription drug abuse until he finally sentenced her to time served and let her off on probation with her promise to let the doctors prescribe the medicine. This had been a year ago, and word on the street was that she hadn't kept her promise.

Josie stood next to her at the counter. "Hi, Paula. How are you?"

"I'm so good. How are you?" She spoke in a singsong, her voice high and airy.

"I'm okay. I think I saw you the other night at Billy's memorial service at the Hell-Bent. That was pretty horrible, wasn't it?"

"It's sooo horrible. I just feel so bad for Billy. He had sooo much talent and everything. It's just so bad for everyone in the community."

"It was nice though, everyone coming together like that to remember Billy."

"Oh, yes, very nice. Hank did such a wonderful job."

It crossed Josie's mind that all Hank had done was sell alcohol to his customers, but she let it go. "What do you think about the rumors about Billy?"

Her eyebrows wrinkled up and she looked as if she didn't understand.

"About him taking pills to commit suicide?"

A conflicted mix of emotions crossed Paula's face and Josie suspected that Paula was trying to gauge which one would be most appropriate in her current predicament. She finally said, "I think it's sooo sad."

"Where do you think Billy got the pills?"

"I don't know."

"Maybe someone gave the pills to him?" Josie didn't want to mention buying or selling drugs, or anything associated with breaking the law, for fear that Paula would clam up.

"I don't know." Her voice had become so high and airy it was hard to hear her.

"Okay. Tell me again. You said you liked Billy?"

"Yes! I loved Billy."

"And you think it's sad that he committed suicide?"

"Of course I do!"

"Then help me figure out who gave Billy the pills that he mixed with his whiskey. I won't be mad. I'm not here to bother anyone. I just need to talk to that person."

"Why?"

"I need to see what Billy said before he died. It's important. It could save someone's life." Josie was grasping for something that would trigger Paula's conscience. Behind the spacey dingbat image, Josie thought Paula had a conscience.

"Well, I don't really know."

Josie decided on a different route. "Look, Paula, I get where you're coming from. I understand that you like to connect people with what they need. You're like a nurse almost. You find out what someone needs, and then you go and find the medication that they need to help them. Is that about right?"

She beamed in recognition. "Yes! That's exactly what I try to do. I'm like a shaman. I totally help people."

"Okay. I see that. I see you're trying to help people. Can you just tell me about the night Billy died? I need to know who you helped out that night?"

"I don't understand."

"Maybe there were some people at the Hell-Bent that needed some help."

Paula shook her head no, but said nothing.

"Maybe even Billy did and you met him at the park. I'm not judging you. I just need to know who got a baggie of Oxy and Ambien that night. You tell me that, and I promise, you won't get in trouble for it." Josie watched her thinking for quite some time.

"I don't want to get anyone in trouble. I only want to help people."

Josie could see she was ready to break. "You could save someone's life by telling me what you know."

Her eyes widened, the pressure weighing on her.

"Come on, Paula. You say you want to help people. This is your chance."

"The only person who asked for an Oxy mix that night was Hank. He said he was worn out from the fire and the evacuation. He just needed a combo pack to sleep. I was surprised because he'd never asked before."

Josie smiled and patted Paula on the back. "You did the right thing," she said. She yelled toward the back of the store, where a curtain led to a storage room. "See you later, Tiny."

Josie walked out of the Gun Club smiling. These were the breakthroughs that made her happiest as a cop, not when something fell into her lap, but when dogged police work paid off. She glanced at her watch. It was 7:00, and her stomach was growling, but she wasn't ready to give up just yet. She had a package of cheese crackers and one of Otto's Cokes in the fridge at the department. She had driven by the trauma center on her way into town and seen the night nurse's "crappy" minivan parked outside. It would be a good time to catch her.

Josie first went to the PD and logged into her computer. She ate cheese crackers while she searched the Internet for an image of a 2015 Ford F-350 diesel, platinum package with a lift. Otto had scoped out the truck and provided her the specifics. He figured the package had to have been close to $60,000. There might be a lot of trucks driving around Artemis, but very few of them had premium lift packages that matched Hank's truck. He made a boatload of money at the Hell-Bent. He didn't spend his cash on a home or travel or a wife, so why not a truck? Josie printed a photo of a truck that matched Hank's. The photo showed the truck at the same angle that the nurse would have seen it the night Billy died.

Josie drove over to the trauma center and found Glenda Crosley bent over paperwork at the nurse's station. There was no receptionist. An elderly couple sat in the waiting room, holding hands, watching the TV on the wall in silence.

Glenda looked up and smiled when Josie approached.

"It's a little more normal in here compared to last time you stopped in."

"You look a bit less frazzled," Josie said, smiling. "I have one quick question for you."

"Sure."

Josie took the color photo she had printed out of a manila folder and handed it to Glenda. She started smiling and nodding as Josie talked. "Can you tell me if that's the truck you saw the night Billy died?"

"That's it." Glenda pointed to the wheels. "I remember because it was lifted. I hate those trucks. I think they look ridiculous. I told my husband he'd have to buy me a step stool to get up into the thing." She handed the photo back. "I can't imagine there's too many of those trucks around. The gas would kill you."

TWENTY-TWO

Josie pulled into her parking place at the police department on Monday morning and felt her cell phone buzz. She opened her phone and found a text from Nick. It read: *Staying in Marfa again tomorrow night. How about dinner? You cook. I'll clean up. Or the other way around.*

Josie grinned and texted back: *Other way around. See you at 6.* It was a great feeling, the flutter in her stomach at the thought of seeing Nick again. She thought about Dillon, and she hoped he would find that same sensation of excitement and anticipation again too. She sighed at her own realization. She was making progress.

Once in the office, Josie filled Otto in on her visit to the trauma center the night before and her conversation with Paula.

"You realize, even if Hank did help Billy commit suicide, we're still a long way from Ferris," Otto said.

"Those two deaths have to be connected."

"Yeah, well, we're missing the connection," he said. "How do you want to do this?"

"Let's shake Hank up. Confront him with lying. Tell him we've got him cold on the pills and we've confirmed he was at the scene of Billy's death. Make it clear we think he's connected to Ferris's death, and see what shakes out. Let's question him at the jail in the interrogation room rather than here. You take the observation room. I'll be the hard-ass."

He nodded.

"And let's call Brenda and ask if she'll come by for follow-up. I'd like to have them both there to clarify their stories."

Otto sat down at his desk and picked up his phone. "I'll call the jail to find out when they have a room open."

———

At 3:00 p.m., Turner bustled into the jail with Brenda, already irritated that she'd had to cancel a meeting that afternoon to be there. Brenda looked stressed, as if she had no idea what might be coming next. Otto set them up in the conference room and assured them that he and Josie would meet with them as soon as possible.

"This isn't a doctor's office," Turner said. "You've got fifteen minutes before I walk."

Hank arrived a few minutes later wearing blue jeans, cowboy boots, and a Western shirt that stretched tight over his beer belly. His hair looked unkempt and his bloodshot eyes gave the appearance that he hadn't slept well. Josie made small talk as they walked down the hallway and into the interrogation room. He sat down in the chair across from Josie and asked if he needed an attorney.

"You're the only one that can answer that. I'm not filing charges, but I have some tough questions. If you think you need an attorney, go ahead and make the call."

"I haven't done anything!"

"Then why did you lie to Brenda?"

"What are you talking about? I didn't lie to anybody." Hank looked offended at the question.

"Why did you call and check on Billy the morning after his suicide when you knew he was dead?"

Hank clenched his teeth, his jaw muscles flexing, and he said nothing.

"You did it because you were there when he died. You knew you'd helped kill Billy Nix and you felt guilty."

"That's not true."

"We know you bought a baggie full of Oxy and Ambien. And that you delivered them to Billy. Your truck has been positively identified at the scene," Josie said.

Hank stared at her in silence.

"How could you call yourself Billy's friend, and then help him commit suicide?"

"Billy did this to himself."

"Tell me the truth, Hank."

Hank stared at his hand as he rubbed the edge of the table with his thumbnail.

"You know what happened to Ferris Sinclair, don't you?"

Hank said nothing.

"Billy asked you to buy him the pills and meet him at the park to end his life. Why?"

Hank continued staring down at the table, refusing to make eye contact.

After several minutes of silence, Otto entered the room carrying two Styrofoam cups of coffee and set them on the table.

"Can I get you some cream or sugar?" Otto asked.

Hank held a hand up to indicate he didn't want either, and Otto sat down at the table with them. Sometimes a brief interruption was all that was needed to change the thought process of the person being interrogated.

"Tell us what happened, Hank. Help us put this to rest. Too many people are suffering." Her voice was quiet. They sat for a long while, waiting him out.

He finally scooted his chair back and crossed his arms over his chest. He sighed heavily and said, "Ferris was at their house. Billy and Brenda's. He'd been staying there off and on for a while. They'd fought over him staying there. Brenda suspected Ferris and Billy were screwing around. Billy denied it, but not very convincingly. Brenda finally gave Billy an ultimatum. He had to choose: Brenda or Ferris."

"And he chose his wife," Josie said.

Hank nodded. "Brenda knew Billy didn't care about Ferris, not really. Ferris was a distraction. Somebody to stroke his ego, to make him feel like he was something special."

"How did Billy take the ultimatum?"

"Billy knew Brenda was serious. It was the day of the evacuation and Ferris was at their house. Billy sent Brenda to town so he could end things. He said he needed to explain things to Ferris. To end it for good. Brenda left with the car packed, ready to leave for Austin as soon as Billy was done. He said he needed an hour. He planned to give Ferris their old truck to drive back to Presidio for the evacuation."

"Where did Brenda go?"

"Billy said she drove to town and went to the bank and stopped at the Hot Tamale for a drink before she went back home and picked him up."

"And when she left the house, what happened?" Josie asked.

Hank frowned. "They got into a fight. Billy told Ferris he couldn't stay at the house anymore. He said they were through, that Ferris needed to stop coming to hear the band play. Billy said Ferris started yelling at him, calling him names and throwing punches. Ferris told Billy he was going to tell everyone that he was gay." Hank stopped, as if the rest of the story was too hard.

"What happened?" Josie asked.

Hank absently rubbed a hand across his forehead. Josie could smell the sweat coming from his body. "Ferris showed Billy a video off his phone that he had taken of the two of them together at Ferris's house. Ferris threatened to send the video to Gennett Records, to the band members, and to Brenda."

Josie stopped him. "A compromising video?"

Hank nodded but didn't elaborate. "Ferris said he was going to the Hell-Bent to tell everyone what a fake Billy was. They were in the bedroom, fighting at that point. Ferris walked down the hallway to leave, and Billy grabbed a stun gun Brenda kept in the bedroom. He stunned Ferris with it, and then—" Hank stared at Josie, as if he couldn't continue.

"Tell us what happened," said Josie.

Hank took a moment and then struggled through the explanation as if the thought of it made him ill. "Billy said he sat on Ferris's chest and pinned his arms down. Then he covered his mouth and nose and suffocated him."

"You're telling me that Billy admitted to you that he killed Ferris?" Josie asked.

"You have to understand that Ferris had ruined Billy's life. He never wanted any of this to happen."

Josie and Otto both sat quietly, waiting for him to continue.

Hank sighed and finally went on. "About three months ago Ferris tested positive for HIV. Billy got totally unstrung. He got himself tested and was negative, but they told him he needed to test again, that he could still have it. In his own mind, he was convinced he had HIV and that he'd passed it on to Brenda. He claimed he was showing signs. And, for a country star with a reputation like Billy's? The band name is Billy and the Outlaws. You know what I'm saying?"

"You're saying Billy couldn't be an outlaw country singer with HIV."

"That's exactly right. Keep in mind, Billy hadn't made it big yet. It'd be one thing if he was Magic Johnson making an announcement, but he didn't even have a signed contract yet."

"Nobody's going to sign an unknown country singer if the word gets out he has HIV," Josie said.

Hank nodded. "Billy knew Brenda would be devastated. Not only would Brenda's dream of making it in Nashville be destroyed, but her fears about Billy having an affair with Ferris would take on a whole new meaning. He was just coming apart at the seams."

"Did he tell Brenda about Ferris having HIV?"

"I don't know." Hank gave Josie an imploring look, as if she wasn't understanding him. "It was even bigger than that. Ferris was ready to tell the world everything! Send out videos that showed who knows what. You think he wouldn't work Billy and Brenda over? You think Ferris wouldn't out Billy in a heartbeat if he thought he could benefit from it? Extort money?"

Josie thought about Hank's assessment of Ferris compared to his sister Julia's kinder description. Did Hank just dislike him, or had sibling love clouded Julia's view of him?

"Do you think Billy saw that side of Ferris?" Josie asked.

"By this point, Billy had figured Ferris out. He knew Ferris was a time bomb. Billy had wanted to end things for a while, but he knew Ferris would go off the deep end. Then Brenda got in the middle of it and forced him to end it. And Ferris took it just like Billy figured he would."

Josie shook her head. "So Billy killed Ferris and laid him on the couch. When Brenda came home and picked Billy up, didn't she see the dead body?"

Hank's expression hardened. "No. Billy made it clear—Brenda had no idea what happened. When she came back from town, Billy met her at the door with the rest of their bags and they drove to the Hell-Bent to get Billy's guitars."

"But the fire wasn't set until seven. They got to the Hell-Bent at five thirty, left at six. The timing doesn't work."

"Billy told Brenda he needed to run back to the house and pick up something. He said he left her at the Hell-Bent and went back with kerosene and doused the house to make sure it burned. He drove back to the Hell-Bent at six thirty and they left town."

Josie thought through the timing with what Turner had given her from the surveillance tapes. The tape showed them entering the convenience store at nine thirty that night. If they left from the Hell-Bent at six thirty, they could have made the drive in three hours. Then she remembered the watch face that established his time of death.

"It still doesn't work," she said. "Ferris Sinclair's body was burned at seven thirty-eight. It wouldn't take that long for the house to burn if Billy started the fire at six."

Hank shut his eyes briefly, as if not wanting to go on. "Billy said he moved the clocks forward in the house, as well as the watch on Ferris. He got the idea from some cop show he saw on TV."

Josie tried to keep the shock from her expression. It was a side of Billy she would never have expected.

Otto continued the questioning. "Why did he go back if Ferris was already dead?"

"He told me he wanted to make it look like Ferris overdosed on heroin and died in the fire. He wanted to make sure the house burned from the wildfire. He wanted Ferris's death to look accidental, and in his mind, the fire was the solution." Hank considered Josie for a minute. "You have to know Billy. People have this image of him as a tough guy, but he wasn't. He was sad and confused. He told me once that every time he got on stage he worried somebody in the crowd would point him out as a fake. Bands like the Calloway Boys unstrung Billy. He knew that musically they were better than him, and it ate him up inside. Then Ferris came along and really screwed him over. His life just got all out of whack."

"So when Billy called you drunk the other night and asked you to bring pills?"

"I did what he asked me to do. He wanted to end the mess he'd made of his life. I did what a true friend would do. I helped him end his misery." Hank paused and stared at Josie. His expression was frustrated, as if he wanted her to understand his reasoning. When Josie didn't respond he continued.

"Billy's whole life was unraveling. He called me earlier that night when I was working at the bar. Check his phone records. He said he needed something to get him through the next few days. I bought a bag of pills from a girl at the bar. I wasn't even planning on giving them to him unless he called again. When he called from the park I went over there to talk to him and he told me everything. He'd screwed up Brenda's life, Ferris was dead, he was convinced he had HIV and he would destroy his band's chance of making it to Nashville. He'd be back working at the sewage-treatment plant as a pariah. The hometown hero who exploded into pieces and hurt everyone else around him."

"Why didn't you stop Billy? Try to get him some help?"

Hank put a hand to his forehead and laughed. He finally looked at Josie, his expression incredulous. "Are you not listening to me? He wasn't worried about helping himself. He was worried about cleaning up the mess he'd made of everyone else's life. This was the only way he could make things right for Brenda. The only way that he could show her that he still loved her and cared about her. With him and Ferris gone from her life, Brenda could reconnect with her family and move back to Nashville. Manage some other country singer. Hopefully find happiness again someday."

Josie listened to Hank's explanation and wondered if Hank truly bought into Billy's delusional reasoning.

"Why didn't you tell us this before?" Otto asked.

"What, so you could call me a murderer? Look. Billy was a friend. He asked me for the ultimate act of friendship, and I gave it. I don't expect you to understand that, but that's how I see it."

Josie told Hank that they needed to make a phone call, and she and Otto left the interrogation room. She opened the door that led into the observation room so she and Otto could talk.

Josie took the seat across from him and saw his angry expression. He'd disguised it well in front of Hank.

"We have two dead bodies and no charges to file," he said.

"Withholding information. Buying prescription pills. That's about it."

Otto's face was flushed red in anger. "It's manslaughter in my book. Or at least assisted suicide, and that's illegal in the state of Texas."

"We don't prosecute the guy who sells the gun or a knife to the person who shoots himself or slashes his wrist. No prosecutor would take this on. Billy drank the whiskey and popped the pills. Cowan stated suicide in the autopsy."

Otto muttered something and looked down at the floor. He seemed ready to let it drop, so Josie changed subjects.

"Is Brenda here?" she asked.

Otto nodded. "She's in the sheriff's conference room. Turner may have left. She said she'd give us fifteen minutes and then she was leaving. We better get in there before we lose her for sure."

"You ready?" she asked.

"Let's do it."

———✦———

They found Brenda and Turner sitting next to each other at the conference table. The nondescript room had bright white walls and a dozen chairs around a large conference table. The room was used by the sheriff for department trainings and for interrogations when the other rooms at the jail were full. When Josie and Otto entered, Brenda and Turner both became quiet.

"A little courtesy with the scheduling would have been nice, Chief. Next time, call me when you're ready," Turner said.

Josie ignored her comment and thanked the women for coming. She started her digital recorder with no additional complaints from Turner.

"We've gathered quite a bit of information over the past twenty-four hours," Josie said. "Hank Wild admitted to giving Billy the pills that he combined with the whiskey to commit suicide."

Brenda's expression changed from anticipation to confusion. "I don't believe that."

"He admitted it. We know who he bought the pills from. And a witness identified his truck at the park the night Billy died."

Her mouth fell open and she appeared unable to speak.

Josie chose a soft tone for the harsh words she was about to deliver. "I think you know why Billy committed suicide."

"What?"

Josie glanced at Turner, who was intently watching her client's expressions.

"The day of the evacuation, you went to town so that Billy could end his relationship with Ferris at your house. When Ferris started throwing threats around about ending Billy's career, Billy killed Ferris. Used your stun gun and then suffocated him to death. Staged his body on the couch."

Brenda broke in, her face horrified. "No!"

"You came home to pick Billy up so you could leave for Austin."

Brenda shook her head, her eyes frantic.

"Billy made a public appearance, talked to Angela, and established a time frame. Then he drove home, dumped kerosene on the front of the house, and set fire to your home. He moved the clocks forward an hour to give you time to get out of town. He drove back to the Hell-Bent to pick you up and leave for Austin."

"No! Why are you saying this?"

"Billy confessed all of this to Hank before he drank himself to death."

Turner's jaw clenched so tight Josie thought she might break teeth. She stared at Brenda, who obviously hadn't told any of this to her attorney. It was a bombshell, and Josie was surprised Turner hadn't called a halt to the questioning.

Brenda began crying and placed her face in her hands. Turner glanced at Josie without a word. She stood, grabbed a handful of tissues out of her purse, and laid them in front of her client.

Josie had brought a bottle of water into the room with her. She opened the top and slid it across the table toward Brenda. "You had to have known something, Brenda. Your husband killed a man he supposedly cared a great deal about. He set your house on fire, then an hour later rode all the way to Austin with you. You had to know something had happened."

Brenda finally got herself in control and blew her nose. She drank water and poured some of it on a tissue and dabbed the cold water against her swollen eyes. "I swear I didn't know any of this. I knew something was wrong. Billy was acting strange. He hadn't slept in days. He was a nervous wreck." She took a ragged breath and looked from Turner to Josie, her expression filled with shame. "I thought he was having an affair with Ferris. I thought he was sneaking off at night to meet him. The night Billy got up and left me the note, the night he died?" She clenched her hands into fists in her lap, her face in anguish. "I thought he left the hotel to meet Ferris somewhere. I never dreamt he would kill himself." She broke down into sobs again.

While Josie and Otto waited for Brenda to regain control, the head of intake officer Maria Santiago appeared at the window in the door. She motioned them out into the hallway. Turner was bent over Brenda, talking into her ear, and didn't seem to notice as they walked out.

Maria said, "I'm sorry to interrupt you. Cowan asked me to call you out. He'd like for you to go down to his office."

"It can't wait?"

"He just said he has information you'll want."

Josie thanked Maria and opened the door to the conference room. She looked at Turner and said, "I need ten minutes."

Turner frowned and nodded once, and Josie shut the door.

Josie and Otto walked back through the central hub and Maria buzzed them into the hallway that led to the coroner's office. Cowan opened the door and apologized for pulling them away from the interrogation.

"I don't know that this is relevant to your questioning, but I felt I would be remiss by not telling you right away."

"We'll take anything you can give us. What do you have?" Josie asked.

"I received a package today, airmail." He held up the FedEx

envelope. "It's from the lab that processed the syringe that the fire marshal found under the Nixes' couch."

Josie nodded.

"If you'll remember, I wasn't there when they found the syringe, so I had no idea what they were shipping off."

Josie nodded. Once the autopsy was complete, there had been no reason to consult with Cowan before sending the syringe off to the lab.

"As you know, the results from toxicology came up with nothing. When I opened the package that contained the actual syringe I realized this type needle isn't for IV drug use. It's a blunt-tip needle. It's a specialized needle used for surgeries."

Cowan motioned for Josie and Otto to approach the counter where he had a large lighted magnifier on a stand. He held two similar-looking syringes under the magnifier, and Josie and Otto both leaned in to examine the ends of the needles. The ends were slightly different, with one obviously sharper, the other rounded.

"A needle typically has a beveled tip to make the sharp ending that allows it to penetrate skin without causing a hole and excessive bleeding. This blunt tip is something a surgeon might use for sutures. It helps prevent needle-stick injuries to blood vessels, so it's a pretty specialized needle. It's not something somebody shooting up heroin would use."

Josie raised her eyebrows to Cowan. "Nice work."

He tipped his head at her. "Thank you."

"Would it be possible to track down a syringe like this? As in, would a local vet use it, or a medical doctor at the trauma center? We could search it on the Internet by brand?" Otto asked.

"I suspect this is used by a vet, but I'm not sure. I'd try Doc Hammond first. He'll be able to tell you if it's associated with animals or humans."

"Thanks, Cowan. We owe you one."

He placed his hands in the pockets of his lab coat and leaned back to study Josie. "And what exactly is the 'one' that you keep owing me? At some point I'd like to cash in."

"She stockpiles her ones," Otto said. "I wouldn't hold your breath."

As Josie and Otto made their way back to the interrogation room, she asked, "What's the syringe mean for the case? For Brenda and Hank?"

"It confirms Hank's comment that Billy went back to the house to set it on fire and make it look like Ferris died of an overdose."

Josie nodded. "The Nixes didn't have animals. I wonder what Billy was doing with a blunt-tip needle?"

After Maria had buzzed them back through to the interrogation rooms they stopped before entering. Otto said, "What now? We let both of them go? Hank and Brenda both?"

"Let's watch Hank for the next couple days. There's pieces to this that don't feel right."

"Like what?" he said.

"Like spinning back the clocks based on some cop show. That sounded pretty lame to me. And the inconsistencies between Hank's version and Brenda's. I want to know why Hank made it sound like Ferris has been at their house off and on for quite a while. Brenda has made a big deal about Ferris never staying at their house. Remember she said they didn't run a flophouse?"

"All right. I'll cut Hank free and you finish up with her."

———•———

When Josie entered the conference room the vibe was considerably different. Turner had lost her hard edge and had taken on a thoughtful look. Josie wondered what secrets Brenda had confided to her attorney.

Josie sat down across from Brenda and said, "Let's go back to the drive to Austin."

"What about it?"

"Tell me about your trip back to the house to pick up Billy before you went to the Hell-Bent."

"There's nothing really to tell. I pulled up in the driveway and Billy came outside and we left."

"You didn't walk into the house?" Josie asked. *And see a dead man lying on your couch,* Josie thought.

"No."

"What did Billy tell you when he got into the car?"

She looked confused. "About what?"

"He'd just killed a man. He didn't explain anything to you?"

"Of course not! I didn't know anything about it. He was a mess. I drove. He just laid down in the backseat and slept."

Josie narrowed her eyes. "You say things like that, Brenda, and it makes me not believe you. If you'd just tell the truth, you'd be so much better off in the end."

"I don't know what you're implying, but I don't like your tone of voice."

Josie nodded. "Okay. Here's the problem. Hank explained to us that you went into town so Billy could end the relationship with Ferris. The same man who had basically destroyed your life. Billy ends the relationship, and he gets in the car and doesn't explain anything to you? He just lays down in the backseat and takes a thirty-minute nap on the drive to the Hell-Bent? You didn't ask him how the conversation went? You didn't ask him how Ferris took the news? Because I'm sure you were worried that Ferris would tell the world Billy was gay. That he would blackmail you and your husband. I think you had a lot to discuss on the drive to the Hell-Bent."

Brenda looked like a cat trapped in the corner of a room, with her eyes wide and her body tense. "He may have ended things with Ferris, but he never said anything to me."

Turner raised both her hands in the air to indicate that her response made perfect sense.

"Come on, Brenda. He's your husband. You got no sense that something went bad?"

Brenda glared at Josie. "None."

Turner held a hand up. "Okay, Chief, I think we're done here. You've put this woman through enough hell for one day. Don't bother calling us again until you have something worth coming in for."

Josie said nothing. *Worth coming in for,* she thought. Brenda had just discovered that one of her closest friends helped her husband commit suicide *after* her husband killed his lover. If that wasn't worth coming in for, Josie couldn't imagine what would be.

TWENTY-THREE

Tuesday morning, before leaving for work, Josie opened her freezer to scout out the contents. She found one package of freezer-burnt chicken, and hamburger patties that were an odd shade of purple. If Nick was going to cook supper that night he'd have to bring something with him. She sent a quick text that read: *Looking forward to dinner! Please bring meat or we'll have to eat canned corn*. It wasn't very accommodating, but she hoped things were about to break open on the case, and grocery shopping wasn't on her to-do list for the afternoon.

Josie and Otto started the day at their office conference table to talk through the details of the investigation one more time. She felt like the key players were in place, but they hadn't made the right connections yet.

"What bothers you the most about the case?" she asked.

"Why would Billy confess all of those details to Hank?" Otto said.

"Because he felt guilty. Because he was drunk."

Otto looked skeptical. "Billy was beyond drunk. Comatose comes to mind. Does someone that drunk have the mental capacity to remember the kind of details Hank told us about? Turning the clocks forward? Why would Billy share that?"

Josie nodded. "That one got me too. Especially if it was a crime of passion."

"And I just don't see Billy as that calculating. He supposedly cared for Ferris to the point he put his marriage and career in serious jeopardy," he said.

"The story Hank told us was of a person who had decided to end a longtime affair, and then got into a fight that turned deadly."

"But planting a syringe, turning the clocks ahead, setting his house on fire, getting the timeline just right? Those are calculated moves," Otto said. "Those aren't the actions of someone caught up in an argument that turns deadly."

"Agreed. And I still have a problem with the inconsistencies between Hank's story and Brenda's. In the beginning, Brenda told us Ferris wasn't staying at their house. Then she changed her story somewhat. She said Billy had told Ferris they were leaving because of the evacuation. She knew Ferris was at their home and Billy was talking to him."

"How did Ferris get there?"

"Hank said Ferris was going to take the Nixes' pickup truck. My guess is, he'd been staying there, maybe a few days. Why did she keep saying he never stayed at their house?"

Otto frowned and nodded. "She was embarrassed. She didn't want to admit the relationship."

"But why did Brenda lie to us?"

"Because she knew Billy killed Ferris, and she was trying to protect him," Otto said.

Josie was quiet. There was a detail she was missing, a connection that was right in front of her. "Let's go back to what we know about the day of the evacuation. Once more on the time frame."

Otto went to the back of the office to pour them each a cup of coffee. He walked back slowly, piecing together the puzzle out loud for his own benefit as much as for hers. "We're assuming Ferris was staying at their house. According to Hank, after Billy killed Ferris, Brenda drove home and picked Billy up and they went to the Hell-Bent to get his guitar. He said she knew nothing about Ferris's death. She said the same. Their plan was to drive to Austin and book a few gigs." Otto paused and Josie watched him arranging his thoughts in his head.

She picked it up. "At some point, after Billy talked to Angela at the Hell-Bent, he drove back to his home and set it on fire, staging the scene to make it look like Ferris OD'd on their couch and burnt up in the fire."

Then it clicked. Josie felt like she'd been sucker punched. She flipped through her steno pad with her interview notes. She went back to her interview with the bartender, Angela Stamos.

"Angela said she talked to Billy for a while in the dressing room. He was torn up over leaving. He got his guitar and then couldn't find Brenda." Josie thumbed through her notes and found what she was looking for. "Angela said, 'I think he ended up talking to John Lummin for a while.'"

Josie looked up at Otto. "No one could remember who Brenda sat with. Hank even mentioned that he didn't know who she talked to. He remembered Billy getting his guitar, but not who Brenda sat with. That's because she wasn't there. I don't think Ferris was dead. I think she drove to the house and killed Ferris while Billy chatted with Lummin."

"Hang on. Remember at the first interview with the Nixes, Brenda said she talked with Yvonne Ferrario. Did you ever get ahold of her?"

"I tried once and couldn't get through," Josie said. She flipped back through her notes and found the phone number she'd jotted on her notes. Josie dialed the number on her cell phone, and it went directly to voicemail.

"Yvonne. This is Josie Gray. I need you to call me as soon as possible. I have an urgent question to ask you in regard to a current investigation." Josie provided her phone number at the PD and her cell phone number and hung up.

Otto resumed their conversation. "You think the story about Brenda leaving and Billy fighting with Ferris and killing him is bogus?"

She nodded. "I think something happened that afternoon between Billy, Ferris, and Brenda at the house. I think Brenda and Billy left to get his guitar, planning on leaving town. Something happened on the car ride to the Hell-Bent, and Brenda drove back to the house and killed Ferris."

"You think Billy knew?"

Josie shook her head. "After all the interviews, 'sad and confused' seems to be about the best description of him. I can buy the suicide a lot easier than I can him murdering Ferris," she said.

"Would he have let Brenda kill Ferris?" he said.

"Maybe he didn't know until it was too late."

"So why would he tell Hank a monstrous lie as he's committing suicide?" he asked.

"Maybe he was trying to protect Brenda. He'd driven his own wife to murder, so he tried to pin it on himself and then he committed suicide."

Otto nodded, conceding the point. "Brenda had plenty of motive. Not only was Ferris destroying her marriage, but he was destroying Billy's career. Her 'meal ticket.' Who called him that?"

"Angela said that."

"What about timing?" Otto asked. "Could Brenda have pulled this off?"

"In all the commotion with the evacuation, she could have easily left the bar and drove back to the house to deal with Ferris. Afterwards, she could have convinced Billy they didn't need to go back home after all. They had supposedly already given Ferris the keys to the truck so he could leave."

Otto nodded. "I like it. She could have called Ferris. Told him that she needed to talk to him before he left town. Maybe she said she wanted to make things right between them. Mend fences."

"The Zaner was another detail that bothered me," said Josie. "Billy's a big guy. If he wanted to stop Ferris from walking down the hallway, he hardly needed to stun the kid. But Brenda would have needed it."

"After it was all over with, Billy couldn't take the guilt. He found out his wife killed Ferris and allowed him to burn in a fire. Not only had he lost his lover, but he'd driven his own wife to murder. Billy's life was over so he asked Hank to help him end it for good." Otto banged his fist on the table. "We got this."

"Let's talk to Hank one more time. See if we can cement a few details before we go to the prosecutor," Josie said.

They arrived at the Hell-Bent at a little after nine that morning but it wasn't yet open for business. They drove a quarter of a mile down the lane and found Hank at home, watching ESPN, eating a bowl of cereal in the living room. He invited them inside and they sat down in the living room as they had done the last time they visited his home. While Hank carried his bowl into the kitchen Josie noticed a pair of women's beige dress shoes lying on the floor, underneath a chair that was pushed against the wall in the kitchen. She hadn't noticed them the last time they visited. The shoes looked as if they might have been shoved under the chair and forgotten about. Josie averted her eyes as he returned so that Hank wouldn't realize she had seen them.

"Hank, we have some follow-up questions to ask you about Billy. You're free to call an attorney, but we're just here to follow up."

Given their last conversation, Josie expected the guarded look he gave her. He studied her a moment and finally said, "Okay, go ahead."

"We're still struggling with the story Billy told you. It doesn't make sense for several reasons."

He gave her a puzzled look. "Why would Billy lie to me before ending his life?"

Josie wondered at his choice of words. She hadn't said Billy had lied, just that his story didn't make sense.

"I think Billy lied because he was trying to protect his wife," she said.

"Protect her from what?"

"The day after the evacuations, do you remember me coming into the Hell-Bent to talk to you about the Nixes leaving town?"

"Sure."

"Do you remember me asking you about the timing? What time they arrived, what time Billy got into the dressing room?"

"Yeah, I told you to talk to Angela. She said you talked to her and she told you he got the guitar at five thirty."

"Where was Brenda during that time?" Josie asked.

He frowned. "I don't know. She was in the bar."

"Did you see her sitting with someone?"

His eyes darted from Josie to Otto. "Sure. Everybody was talking in groups, walking around."

"Specifically, who did you see her sitting with?" she asked.

"I can't name a specific person."

"That's funny. Because people gave us the names of people Billy talked to. Angela said that when they were done in the dressing room Billy looked for his wife and couldn't find her. He sat down and talked to John Lummin because he couldn't find Brenda."

Hank wrinkled his forehead. "What are you getting at?"

"I think Billy made up that big story because he was covering for his wife. He drove his wife to murder and couldn't handle the guilt."

"That's ridiculous! She's not a killer! Look at the hell that woman's been through, and now you're calling her a murderer on top of it all?"

"Think back to that day in the bar, Hank. Who did she talk to? Who did you see her with?"

He frowned and looked exasperated with the questions. "I told you. The bar was chaos that day. I can't remember all the people I talked to, let alone somebody else."

Josie put a hand up in a gesture meant to calm the tension. "I'm not trying to be confrontational. We have to make sure we have the right person before we close the case. We're just sorting through the specifics."

He nodded. "Sure. I get that. I just know you're barking up the wrong tree with Brenda."

Josie gave Hank an embarrassed look. "I hate to do this, but we've been out of the office all morning. Would you mind if I used your restroom before we take off?" Josie asked.

He pointed behind him down a dark hallway. "First door on your right."

Josie walked by Otto, knowing he would keep up the conversation for a few minutes. She decided to follow up on a hunch.

She shut the door to the bathroom and scanned the room for anything that would indicate who the female was that wore the beige shoes lying in his kitchen. Sensible heels, not the shoes of one of the waitresses he supposedly chased after. She opened the medicine cabinet that hung over the single basin and found the typical bottles and tubes. She flushed the toilet and scanned the medicine bottles, and she found one prescribed to Brenda Nix. Xanax. Her pill of choice for sleeping while she and Billy traveled: apparently also her pill of choice while sleeping with Hank.

Josie took her cell phone out of her pocket and took a picture of the bathroom, the cabinet, and then the pill bottle that clearly stated Brenda's name. Hank had invited them freely into his home, and he had given her permission to enter his bathroom. She wasn't sure the photograph of Brenda's pills would be admissible in court, but it was worth the effort. It might be enough to coerce something out of Hank.

Josie quickly washed her hands and then appeared back in the living room, indicating to Otto that she was ready to leave.

"Hank, we appreciate you talking with us again. I'd like you to keep this conversation quiet. Don't mention this to Brenda. She's not a suspect. We just wanted to clear her name, get through one final set of questions before we put this case to bed." She put her hand out and Hank stood to shake it.

They walked outside and when they got into Josie's jeep, Otto said, "What the hell was that all about?"

"Guess who's shacking up with Hank?"

Otto frowned, then his eyes widened in realization. "Brenda?"

TWENTY-FOUR

Time was not on their side. Hank would contact Brenda as soon as Josie and Otto left. They drove back to the PD and put together a rough outline of their case to present to the prosecutor. It wasn't a requirement, but Josie had found spending the extra time often helped her ensure she had key details mapped out before making an arrest. Realistically, if the prosecutor wouldn't support her, the arrest wouldn't stick.

Josie and Otto walked across the street to the courthouse, where Tyler Holder, the forty-one-year-old county prosecutor, had his office. He had been at the job a little over a year, and so far, local law enforcement were pleased with his efforts. No prosecutor would make every cop happy; but at least Holder appeared motivated by justice rather than the political career ladder.

He wasn't in his office but Josie and Otto found him in the courtroom, where he sat at the prosecutor's table taking notes.

He stood and motioned for them to join him.

"They throw you out of your office?" Otto asked.

Holder smiled. He wore a distinguished gray suit, a white shirt, and a red paisley tie. Josie suspected the high-dollar clothes were leftovers from his days as a lawyer for the Houston Oilers—before his new wife convinced him to leave fame and fortune for love and a desert speck of a town sorely in need of a new prosecutor.

"I like the solemn atmosphere. Gets me grounded before the first day of a trial." He pitched his pen onto the table and turned his full attention to Josie and Otto. "What's on your mind?"

"Ferris Sinclair and Billy Nix."

"Ah. It all wrapped up a little too conveniently, didn't it? Billy kills Ferris, then commits suicide?" Holder said.

Josie smiled. "There's been a twist. Here's the short version. Billy Nix had been screwing around with Ferris Sinclair, a kid who was obsessed with him and the fame that went with Billy. Brenda found out, but wasn't able to stop things for fear that Ferris would go public with the affair and ruin Billy's chance at fame and fortune as an outlaw country singer."

"Outlaw?"

"Country outlaw singer. Johnny Cash, Willie Nelson, Steve Earle?"

Holder smirked and nodded. "Ah, outlaw. Like Willie Nelson getting busted for pot all over Texas."

"You get the idea. They're tough guys. You can't be a gay country outlaw singer. Your music wouldn't sell. Especially if your career hasn't taken off yet. So Brenda has been sitting by for the past six months watching her husband get led astray by this man who is not only ruining her marriage, but who is derailing her husband's career."

Otto put a finger up. "A career that Brenda has devoted her life to. She had a record deal close to signed before all this happened."

"To top it off, when Mitchell Cowan performed the autopsy, he discovered Ferris was HIV positive. We believe Billy just discovered this fact. The day before the fire, we found Internet searches on the Nixes' home computer that dealt with HIV/AIDS. When I informed Brenda, she appeared to know nothing about it."

"I think Brenda's a better actor than she is a singer," said Otto.

"Are you telling me Brenda Nix killed Ferris?" he asked.

Josie glanced at Otto. "We believe so." She sighed, dreading what was to come.

Holder narrowed his eyes at her. "You don't have anything that ties her to the dead body, do you?"

"We believe she left the Hell-Bent—"

Holder shook his head back and forth and cut his hands through the air to stop her. "'We believe' doesn't work. Do you have a gun, something more than an empty syringe?"

Josie hadn't realized he knew about the syringe. She had kept him up to date to this point, and she hadn't mentioned it. She was impressed. "We're not relying on the syringe. It doesn't help the case. We have the Zaner stun gun, registered to her, that was discharged the night of the murder. And we have eyewitnesses that placed her at the bar, but then lost sight of her during the time when we believe she drove home, stunned and murdered Ferris Sinclair."

"You know this won't work. I'm not sure why you're here. You have nothing that indicates to me with any certainty that she killed Ferris. I've no doubt she wanted him dead, but I need proof."

"If we don't bring her in now she will leave. Her house was destroyed from the fire. It's hard telling where she'll go."

"Josie. If you bring her in, you can't keep her. No charges would stick. I won't support this."

"I also found a bottle of Xanax in Hank Wild's medicine cabinet. Brenda's bottle," Josie said.

Holder considered her and pursed his lips. "I won't even ask what you were doing in Hank Wild's medicine cabinet. But again, so what? She was screwing Hank while her husband was screwing Ferris. It's a screwed-up world. But that doesn't put a murder weapon in her hand."

"Why not charge her and see if she breaks?" Josie said, feeling the heat in her face.

"There's nothing to charge her with!"

"Thanks for your time," Josie said, angry at his unwillingness to help. "We'll be back."

"You can't be that surprised," said Otto. They stopped on the sidewalk outside of the courthouse.

"She'll leave town." Josie checked her watch. Two hours had passed since they talked to Hank. "I want to talk to Patty Netham, Brenda's sister. I'm going over to the motel to ask Patty to take a walk with me. While I do that, can you go talk to John Lummin about the timeline? He was the one who sat and talked to Billy at the Hell-Bent when he couldn't find Brenda. Maybe John can connect us with someone who saw Brenda leave the bar."

Otto walked back to the PD to get his jeep while Josie walked a block over to Manny's. She knocked on the door for Room 5, but no one answered. The drapes were closed and she didn't hear any movement inside. She walked down to the office and found Manny inside the office washing his front window with spray cleaner and a wad of newspaper.

"Hey, Manny."

"Josie! Good to see you."

"I'm looking for Brenda and her sister."

"You just missed them. They left maybe a half hour ago. Packed up and moved out."

Josie felt the flush in her face. She was furious. They were going to let a murderer drive away to a new life.

"I need you to tell me exactly what was said. Every detail."

Manny lost his pleasant smile and looked worried. "Okay, let me think. She gave me the key and paid with a check. She seemed like she was in a hurry so I didn't chat much. You can tell when someone doesn't want to chat. I asked if she would need the room again. And she said, no, she and her sister needed to get away. She said—" Manny closed his eyes and put a hand over them as if trying to replay the conversation. "I think her exact words were, 'I just can't take all the sadness. I have to get away from here for a while.'" He opened his eyes again, searching Josie's face for some clue to her questioning.

"What kind of car was Patty driving?"

"A white one. A newer Honda Accord."

"You have a license-plate number?"

He screwed up his face like he'd made a mistake. "No. I didn't bother."

"Thanks, Manny. If you hear anything from Brenda or her sister, you call me immediately."

Josie jogged back to the department and found Otto on the phone. He hung up and said, "John told me he talked to Billy for almost half an hour. He said Billy kept looking around the room. He seemed irritated that he couldn't find Brenda."

"Did John see Brenda?"

"He saw them when they walked in, and that was it. He said Billy left their table to go find Brenda, and that was the last time John saw him."

"Brenda and her sister are gone. They packed up and left about a half hour ago. She told Manny she needed to leave the sadness. He doesn't know where she was headed." Josie stood up and leaned over the table, fed up with sitting and talking. "Let's go pick her up. I want a confession."

"Holder's going to be pissed."

"Not if we get a confession. If it doesn't work, we cut her loose. What can it hurt?"

"Well there's three basic ways out of town. They'd either take FM-170 toward Big Bend, or head to Presidio to catch 67 north to Fort Davis, or more likely, 67 all the way up to the I-10."

"We've lost a half an hour. You take 170 and I'll take 67. They could have made it to Presidio by now. Grab your car and I'll call you after I talk to Susan."

They ran to their jeeps and each headed south toward Presidio. River Road was the only paved road out of Artemis that led to a highway. Highway 67 was in Presidio, thirty minutes away. It was a two-hour drive to the interstate, so her odds of catching up to them were good. Josie called Deputy Susan Spears, since she was already familiar with the case. Susan was working traffic and took off immediately toward the highway.

Josie called Otto. "We finally caught a break. Susan's on duty. She's headed toward 67 now. I'll head that way too. If they went that way, she'll be able to overtake them pretty quick with lights and sirens. I'll be far enough behind that I'll catch them if they aren't that far out."

"Good enough. You want me to stay on 170?"

"I think so. It's so remote, she may have figured no one would expect her to take that route."

"Will do."

"I have Patty's number in my sent calls. I called her from the hotel, the day we discovered Billy's body," Josie said. "I'll try and get something out of her. Location, direction."

"You think that's a good idea? What if you call and it spooks Brenda?"

"Maybe that's a good thing. She might pull something stupid. Right now, I just want some indication of where they are," she said. Josie didn't have time to second-guess. "I need you to call Lou to get the license plate for Patty Netham. Have her put it out over the radio when she gets it."

Josie hung up and made it to Presidio in half the time it usually took. In Presidio, she weaved between traffic on the busy small-town streets, scanning the road for midsize white cars. She passed one white Accord, but the driver was male. Once she pulled onto Highway 67 and onto a straight shot she scrolled back through her calls and found the number with the Tennessee area code. She pressed send and after what seemed an eternity, Patty answered her phone.

"Hello?"

"Patty. This is an important phone call. This is Chief Gray, but I don't want you to acknowledge you're on the phone with me. I believe you could be in danger. I want you to smile and say you're visiting your sister. You'll be home in a few days."

There was hesitation, and then in a halted voice she said, "Yes, I'm visiting my sister. I'll be home in a day or two."

"Patty, we believe your sister killed Billy. I need you to pull over at the next exit with a gas station. As soon as you can get away from Brenda you call this number and tell me where you are. You hang on to the keys, tell Brenda you're sick, and that you need to walk around the parking lot until you feel better. Say something. Smile, say, yes, that's fine."

"Oh, yes, that's fine."

Josie could hear the tension in her voice and hoped Brenda wasn't paying attention. "Can you just tell me what road you're on? As if you're telling me what route you're taking home?"

"Oh, sure. We're taking Interstate 10 home, we're just outside Alpine."

Josie heard a voice in the background. "Who are you talking to?"

"Oh," Patty said, "just a friend."

"Who are you talking to?" Brenda repeated, her voice louder this time.

Josie said, "Tell her my name's Pam."

"Okay, talk more soon."

The phone went dead. Josie tried to call back and received voicemail. She called Brenda's number and received voicemail.

She called Susan. "I talked to Patty Netham. They're just outside of Alpine. I'm guessing forty miles from the interstate. I told her to pull off at the next rest stop. I think Brenda caught on that something was wrong."

"I'm just coming into Alpine. I'm running ninety-five, so I'll be on them any minute. How far out are you?"

"I'm fifteen minutes behind you. You have backup that way?"

"No. Call dispatch for me. I'll let you know as soon as I make contact."

"Be safe. Her sister could be in danger if Brenda has a weapon."

Josie recognized Lou Hagerty's voice as she dispatched the make, model, and license number of Patty Netham's car. Josie called dispatch to get every car available on 67 outside of Alpine searching for Netham's car.

Josie called Otto and filled him in. For the next thirty minutes she drove in silence, waiting to hear back from Susan. The hills and beige countryside blurred through her side windows as she whisked around the other cars.

The phone rang. "It's Susan. I'm behind a white Honda Accord, two females in the front seat. The plates match the number. I'm five miles from I-10."

"Okay. I'm two miles behind you. Pull her over before we hit the interstate. Wait for me. We'll approach together."

Josie's phone rang again.

"Josie, it's Lou."

"We've got Brenda. I'll call you in a few."

"Hang on. You better hear this. Yvonne Ferrario just returned your call. I told her you wanted to know if Brenda talked to her that day at the Hell-Bent. She said she and Brenda sat out back to talk because the smoke was bothering Yvonne. Yvonne said Brenda went back into the building when they were done, and Yvonne left at about six."

"Lou. I have to go."

"Hang on! When Yvonne pulled out of the Hell-Bent at six o'clock, she followed Hank Wild down Highway 67, headed toward Artemis."

"Son of a bitch." Josie took a second to process the news. The information changed everything. "You're the best. Call Marta and get her over to Hank Wild's house. Don't let him leave. Place him under arrest for withholding information if she has to."

Josie hung up and tried to figure out the new information in relation to Brenda and her obvious relationship with Hank. Brenda hadn't left the Hell-Bent to kill Ferris. Hank had. And he set Billy up to take the fall. That's how Hank "knew" all the details.

Josie saw the flashing lights up ahead on the highway and was relieved to see Patty Netham's car pulled off on the right side of the highway. As soon as Josie pulled up Susan got out of her car and they stood to the side of her police car. "I just got a bombshell. I don't have time to explain. Call Otto and tell him to get back to Artemis. Tell him to call Lou for details and to watch Hank Wild. Don't let Hank leave town."

Josie approached the passenger side of the white Accord and knocked on the window. Brenda rolled the window down looking terrified.

Patty bent her head so that she could see Josie outside. "What is going on?"

"Brenda, I need you to follow me back to my car. I need to speak with you."

Brenda looked paralyzed, as if she couldn't figure out the next step.

Josie repeated, "I need you to step out of the car."

Brenda glanced at her sister and then got out of the car without another word. She got into the passenger seat of Josie's jeep and Josie got in the driver's side and shut the door.

"Why didn't you tell us about your relationship with Hank Wild?"

"What?"

Josie stared at her.

"I don't know what that has to do with anything."

Josie raised her eyebrows. "This is the man who Billy called the night he walked around drunk on the streets of Artemis. Hank gave your husband a baggie filled with pills that killed him. Hank provided the resources for your husband to commit suicide. And you've been sleeping with both men, and you didn't think that was relevant to the investigation?"

She opened her mouth in shock. "I never slept with Hank. How dare you!"

"Your shoes are in his kitchen. Your pills are in his bathroom cabinet."

"No! You've misunderstood! I stayed with Hank just two times, just when things got bad over Ferris. Both times were after I confronted Billy about Ferris and he refused to admit anything. I had to confide in someone. It was killing me. But Hank's a friend. That's it. There's nothing between us except friendship!"

"Did you see Hank leave the Hell-Bent the day of the evacuation?"

Her face faltered. Josie wished a judge and a jury were privy to the question and response that cracked the iron resolve, the response that allowed the soft truth to finally be revealed. The momentary realization, one-half shock and one-half panic, in that order, was as reliable as any smoking gun; it just wasn't admissible in court.

"What time did you see him leave?" Josie asked.

She shook her head, her eyes wide and innocent. "I didn't see him leave."

"I'll help you then. He left at six o'clock and drove to your home where he killed Ferris Sinclair. He ended your—" The passenger-side door of the Accord parked in front of them opened. "What the hell," Josie said, and opened her door. She motioned for Susan to watch Brenda.

"I need you back in the car, Patty."

"I need to talk to my—"

"Back in the car. Now!" Josie pointed toward the car, her voice hard and loud.

Patty raised both hands in the air as if Josie were pointing a gun at her. She walked back to her car, and faced Josie once more before entering. Josie could see the agony in her expression. "I just want her to tell the truth. Tell her that's what she promised me."

Josie got back in the jeep and said nothing. Brenda had heard her sister's pleas. Josie didn't need to say a word.

Brenda folded her hands in her lap, sitting primly in her sensible khaki capri pants and blue polo shirt, her world completely destroyed: husband, home, and career all gone. She looked out the front window, her expression blank.

"Hank said he loved me. Do you know how long it's been since I've heard those words? I don't ever remember Billy saying them. He'd sign a note, 'Love Billy,' but he couldn't say it. He promised to love me in the marriage ceremony, but he never actually said the words. And, the irony is, I don't love Hank. I didn't want him to love me. He thought he was solving a problem, saving me by killing Ferris. Billy and I?" She looked at Josie, her expression earnest. "We didn't know.

Hank did this on his own. He called and told me this morning. He said you were asking questions about us. I just panicked. I couldn't take one more blow. I told Patty and begged her to leave with me. She wanted me to come to you, to tell you what Hank had done, but I just couldn't take one more drama."

Brenda paused and stared out the window. Josie waited for her to finish.

"The craziest part of all of this?"

Josie said nothing and Brenda turned to face her.

"All of this was over love."

TWENTY-FIVE

Hank Wild was arrested for first-degree murder later that afternoon. When Josie explained to him that Brenda had told the police everything, he stood up from his couch and said simply, "I'm ready." Josie handcuffed him, read him his rights, and drove him to the Arroyo County Jail, where he was processed. He confessed to suffocating Ferris Sinclair, and to planting the syringe under the couch to make it look as if Ferris died from an overdose. The prosecutor stated that Billy Nix's suicide would stand as the cause of death, and no charges would be filed in relation to his death.

Hank had offered nothing more in terms of why he had killed Ferris, but Josie thought the answer was clear. Billy had what Hank had wanted but couldn't have. Hank destroyed his own life in the process of getting it. Sadly, the same thing had happened to Ferris, Billy, and Brenda. Josie wondered how many people ruined their lives in search of something unattainable: love, a career, a place to call home. Josie wanted a tidy family in the suburbs, but was it what she needed? It had certainly proven elusive enough, and perhaps for good reason.

At the jail, Josie talked with the prosecutor, who said no charges would be filed against Brenda at that point. She and Patty were free to go.

Josie followed Brenda and her sister out into the parking lot where Patty's car was parked. Brenda pulled her sunglasses out of her purse and slipped them over her eyes. She turned to Josie and said that she and Patty were headed back to Nashville and that Billy's body would be transported and buried in her family's cemetery.

"I hope you're able to find peace, Brenda. You've been through a terrible ordeal," Josie said, wishing she had something more to offer than empty words.

"You know what hurts the most?" she said. "I was trying to save my marriage. When the fire came raging through the county, Billy and I talked about losing our home, losing our town, like everyone was doing at the time. When we left for Austin, Billy agreed to turn his phone off, to leave Ferris behind for the weekend. I wanted so much to make it work. I wanted us to get away from Ferris and from the gossips at the Hell-Bent who thrilled at the stories of Billy's undoing. As much as people wanted to see him succeed, they also loved the idea of him failing." Brenda's face clouded up and she looked briefly at her sister, who was standing quietly, watching her. "When Billy found out about Ferris's death, I could see in his eyes, he thought I had killed Ferris. As did you." She considered Josie for a moment as if she were still trying to make sense of it all. "How could I be so completely misunderstood, when what I wanted was so simple?"

——————

Josie got home from work at 5:45. She taped a note on the front of the door that said, "Use your code. I'll be ready in a minute." She took a quick shower, pulled her hair up in a ponytail, and dressed in jeans and a pale-yellow tank top. When she stepped from her bedroom at quarter after six she found Nick standing on her back porch laying a steak on the grill. In a pair of jeans and a Fender guitar T-shirt and loafers, he looked completely at ease. She opened the kitchen door and stepped outside into the early-evening heat.

"Sorry I'm late," she said.

He pointed a pair of tongs at her before picking up the other steak off a plate. "Forgiven. But we need to talk."

Josie stood beside him as he sprinkled seasoning on the steaks.

"Here's the deal. I know how to cook meat. But the sides? If you want vegetables? That's all you."

"That's what you wanted to talk about?"

"That's it."

She went inside, smiling, and found a can of baked beans and two potatoes to microwave. In half an hour they were eating at Josie's kitchen table as if they'd been fixing dinner together for years, discussing work, hanging out like old friends.

On the darkest edges of her thoughts, she acknowledged that this was way too easy. Whenever life flowed along too easily, it typically signaled looming disaster. Josie had confided this feeling to Otto one day and he'd told her, "Most people view their glass as either half full or half empty. You view yours as broken." He had hurt her feelings at the time, but she thought of his words often and tried to reframe her thinking. She reminded herself now—enjoy the moment.

———————

After they ate and washed the dishes, Nick suggested a drive. "I want to show you something. Grab your hiking boots."

They drove Nick's SUV, a black armored vehicle with chrome, black leather, and an onboard GPS tracking system that would rival anything the military could devise. He headed south on River Road. Just five minutes from her house he pulled off onto the side of the road and pointed toward the Rio Grande. "Do you scout this area on a regular basis?"

"You mean search for signs of crossing?" she said.

He nodded. "I'll show you."

They locked up the SUV and took off walking through the sandy desert scrub toward the water. The temperature was still in the upper nineties, but with sundown, the heat's edge had softened. Josie felt herself taking the role of student as she walked beside Nick, who obviously had a purpose for bringing her here. As chief of police, and a rather dominant partner in a relationship that had lasted several years, she did not find this a comfortable role to play.

Nick pointed toward the river. "You have one of the most influential cartels in Mexico right across the border from your home. You need to scout this area for signs on a regular basis."

"Are you serious? We barely have the manpower to take regular calls. Then we have something like the Ferris Sinclair murder and we put everything else on hold. Right now I have two burglary calls I've barely responded to. I don't have the time or manpower to prowl the river."

They hiked a quarter mile and then walked down a ten-foot rocky slope that dropped off and led to a sandy bank and the river below it. Nick pointed to the left and Josie saw two kayaks across the river on the Mexican side that had been hidden from view. The sight made her instantly furious.

"Five minutes from your house, Josie." He gestured behind them. "This place doesn't make sense as a crossing. The mountainous terrain in this area would add days of dangerous travel to an illegal's passage into Texas. Ten miles south of here they could cross with no detection, and a flat stretch would lead them north without the mountains. Drug smuggling makes even less sense. They would have checked out the area. They would have known a cop lived within a few miles of here."

She nodded.

"If you plan on staying here, you need to keep a constant vigil. They're watching you. Watch your back, or move elsewhere."

She was a cop. She didn't need a safety sermon. They stood for several minutes along the edge of the river, scanning the bank for prints, and she had to acknowledge Nick was right. Just a few short months after the terror subsided, she had let her guard down.

They walked along the bank in the direction of the kayaks across the river. On the U.S. side, they found an area along the bank where the Mexicans had obviously ported and climbed the ten-foot sand rise.

"I know this doesn't go down easy for you, Josie. Taking advice. But it's what I do. The Medranos are like a giant octopus with tentacles prying into every crack and crevice, looking to exploit, to make money, to increase their power. You are an impediment to them. An embarrassment. Not only have you effectively stopped their migration into West Texas," he looked over at her, "but you're a female. I'm not sure you understand the significance of that fact."

Josie picked up a handful of stones and skimmed them out across the water, watching them zip across the brown surface before sinking to the bottom. "I'm still alive. He must not want me dead too bad."

He turned his dark eyes on her. "It's not so easy as that. You're an anomaly to them. A curiosity. And I can't quite figure out how you've accomplished that. And that worries me."

Josie had never met the Bishop, the current leader of the Medrano cartel, but his brutal rule was notorious. They walked the bank for another two hundred feet and after finding nothing they hiked back to the kayaks.

Josie scanned the river for any sign of movement on either side. She bent down and pulled her Beretta from her ankle holster. She stood and took aim on the kayaks, then shot half a dozen holes in them, the gunshots loud in the still evening. The kayaks jerked with each bullet. She replaced her gun, secure in the knowledge that they were incapable of crossing the river for now. She hoped to send a clear message. *I too am watching.*

Driving back to Josie's they were both quiet. When they reached her house Nick parked and shut the engine off.

"Let's not talk shop any more tonight. Come inside?" she asked.

When they walked back into Josie's house they found Chester hadn't moved from his place on the rug. She found a bone in the pantry and slipped it between his paws.

Josie went to the stereo and put a Norah Jones CD on. She smiled at the rich mellow voice. "I wish I could dance, just so I could move to that music," she said.

Nick came up to her from behind and pulled her hair off her neck. He kissed the hollow behind her ear. "This is why I don't get involved with people I work for," he said.

Josie turned around and faced him, placing her hands around his waist and slipping them under his T-shirt to run her fingers along his smooth skin. She leaned forward and kissed him lightly and whispered, "Why don't you want to get involved with me?"

"If something happens to you?" He cradled her face in his hands, his own expression fierce. "I don't think I could deal with it."

She placed a finger on his lips. "This type of talk is strictly against your rules for romance. Didn't you tell me to quit thinking like a cop?"

His expression faltered, and she could feel his hands relax, the tension broken.

She smiled and reached her hands up around his neck. "Teach me another rule."